I was Sold to My Dead Brother's Best Friend

Jaqueline E. Pearson

DEDICATION

To Emily, who was patiently
waiting to go to the park while I finished. To the
Fans that supported me every step of the way. My
mother who worked on editing

CONTENTS

PROLOGUE

When I was eight, my older brother turned eighteen and went out to celebrate with his friends. I remember being so mad at him because he didn't invite me to go. In return, I destroyed a good luck charm he made me. I did not regret it at the time, but the next day, when he didn't come home, I blamed his disappearance on my action. Max was my brother and my best friend. We did everything together, except that night. He went missing and I felt as if I could have prevented it somehow if I had only been there, with him.

Flashback

Max, eighteen, black hair, light brown eyes, sweet smile. My big brother, who tickled the eight-year old me on the couch in the living room. He was wearing blue jeans and a metallic-shirt. His hair was a casual, attractive mess.

"Come on, don't be mad," Max said, giving me his best puppy dog eyes.

"No!" I said, avoiding looking at his pouting face.

"Annie, please, pretty please with a cherry on top?" I shook my head, still not looking at him.

"I said no!"

"P-p-p-please Annie!" I tried to hide the smile. "I saw that smile Annie," Max says, releasing me from his tickle attack. Max walked into the kitchen.

"I'm still mad at you! I only smiled because you quoted my favorite movie, you dork head!" I called after him.

"I got you to smile and say more than four words to me, so I win!" He came walking back in and sat next to me on the couch.

"No, you cheated! You used Roger Rabbit against me, and you know I always laugh at that!"

"Annie, I would take you with me if I could, but I can't, it's not safe and we're going to be out really late. And there won't be a way back when you get tired." I was still upset. I was not going to let him get off that easy.

"No way!" I crossed my arms to highlight how I felt. "I still want to go."

"I know, but how about I make you a special promise?" I was slightly intrigued.

"Tomorrow I will take you out, wherever you want to go and I will spend the entire day with you." He smiled his impossibly charming smile and I folded.

"Fine," I said. He hugged me and kissed my forehead.

"And on your eighteenth birthday, I promise you a present that will blow your mind and you will forget all about this day." With that, he stood and walked away.

That was the last time I ever saw my brother. My best friend just walked out of the house and never returned. When our parents awoke the next morning to find he had not come home, they started calling the friends he went out with. Everyone said he left early and went home. We called the police, and there had been a missing person search. But after months of nothing, the authorities finally closed the case and expressed their condolences to us. He just vanished without a trace, leaving me heartbroken. I never got to spend my day with him like he promised. He left me here, all alone.

TEN YEARS LATER

"Annie," I was suddenly brought back to the present, ten years later. This was my eighteenth birthday.

"What?" It was my best friend, Macy, Her hair was in a bun. and it looked like she had taken great care with her appearance.

"Joel is waiting. He said to be there at six. You only have three minutes! Come on, Annie! you have to go, and don't blame your lateness on me." She laughed, and I gathered my stuff up and headed out of her bedroom.

"I'm going, I'm going. We can't have him mad at me on my special day." Then we both laughed, and I gave her a hug..

"I'll meet up with you later at the bar, okay?" By the time the words had left her mouth, I was already down the stairs, waving goodbye to her parents and rushing out the door to my car.

In truth, I was now daydreaming about what Joel had planned for me today. He was always so secretive when it came to giving me gifts. Joel had been my boyfriend since freshman year, and I knew I loved him more than the way fish needed water. He had replaced the whole "my brother left me" feeling years ago with passion that I never knew I held inside of me. If I'm being honest, I was no longer a virgin anymore either, losing it to Joel after junior prom. It was wonderful. But I won't want to go into details.

My phone buzzed and I saw a text message from Joel:

Baby, you're late as usual, hurry up & get here. Please. Can't wait any longer.

This brought a smile to my lips. I couldn't wait to see him! And be greeted me with a kiss when I arrived at his house. He was waiting for me on the front porch. He wore a nice black button down shirt and dark blue jeans, his normal attire.

There he was, leaning against the railing with that sexy smirk on that wonderful face of his. His sandy blonde hair was kind of messy as if he just woke up and was way too cool for a comb. It made me want to run my fingers through it. I melted into his arms. He leaned down, pulling me into a close embrace.

"Finally, I've waited all day for my kiss." He mocked me, stealing another kiss, short and sweet.

"So what is the surprise that you are hiding from me?" I asked, succumbing to his charms and to the urge to run my fingers through his beautifully messy hair, making it look as though he got shocked by a light socket. His eyes brightened and he motioned with his head for me follow him.

"It's inside, so come along, my family is waiting." He grabbed me by the hand and pulled me to the front door.

"Is your family's here?" I was a little let down that I wasn't going to get my personal alone time with him, if you know what I mean.

"Yeah they wanted to be here for this."

"What for?" I asked as we walked in, his mother and father stood at the kitchen doorway. His little sister sat on the couch playing on her phone.

They were all dressed nice like him, which made me start to feel like I was a little under-dressed. He never told me to wear something dressy. We stopped in the center of the room as he spun around, hugged me firmly and pulled back.

"I love so you much Annie." I smiled at this.

"I love you too, Joel." He kissed me and then suddenly got down on one knee.

"Annie, I love you a lot and I have no idea what I'd do without you." Joel pulled out a little black box from his pocket and as he opened it I couldn't help but gasp.

"Annie, please, grant me my greatest wish and become my wife?" He was holding a simple but beautiful diamond ring, staring into my eyes, biting the corner of his lip, waiting for me to respond.

ODD SIGHT

I was not expecting this. Don't get me wrong, we never talked about it or anything, although we did mention that we were going to be together forever. All I could do was smile as tears of joy fell from my dark-green eyes. I was barely able to speak. I was just so happy and shocked. I repeatedly nodded yes. He picked me up and held me close.

"Thank you so much," he said, kissing me over and over again like there was no tomorrow. We finally broke apart when we heard his father clearing his throat loudly. His parents were smiling, as was Joel. His mother suddenly burst into tears and rushed to me.

"Oh darling, I knew you would say yes." She started to wipe my tears as we look to see Joel and his father shaking hands. He walked back over to me and picked me up once more, and I allowed myself to wrap my legs around him. He was beaming.

"I love you so much Annie." And I didn't doubt it.

"I love you too." I said, meaning it with all my

heart.

"Well, I think it's time you tell your parents Annie." We both look to Joel's parents as they held each other lovingly.

"They're right, I never asked for their permission. I was just so scared that they'd say no, or if they did say yes, they would spill the beans before I got to ask you." I kissed Joel after he finished the sentence.

"I'll head over there now. Why don't you get changed for later when we meet up with everyone,, and I'll prepare them for the great news." I said, and kissed him once more.`

"You are so wonderful, I am so lucky to have you!" All I wanted to do was go upstairs and let him have his way with me.

"Go. I'll see you in a few." he said, and I kissed him again. But we are interrupted by his parents, who obviously had seen enough.

"Okay, that's enough. You two would just stand there kissing each other the whole night if you could. Now get a move on." Joel's mother burst out laughing after saying this.

Joel walked me out to my car, kissing me the entire way until he finally pulled away. He said needed to leave, otherwise we would be caught by his parents doing unthinkable things in the back of the car.

We kissed one last time, and I jumped into the car. As I drove away, I dialed Macy's phone, to announce the news. Her response had been to burst into non-stop joyful screaming lasting the entire journey back to my house. Joel didn't tell her his intentions because he knew she could never keep a secret like this from me. When I finally arrived I was crying with joy again. Macy was now super excited that she is going to be my maid-of-honor. She could not wait to start planning my wedding, and even wanted to come over tonight to begin.

In my driveway sat a really nice, brand new black sports car. I made my head spin. My parents were not rich, but we weren't poor, either. We were just good and average according the current economy. But this car was obviously expensive, and way out of my parent's price range. Plus, they would never buy me a new car just for my birthday no matter how much money they had, would they?

I locked my car and started heading to the front door, imagining the possibilities of why this car was there. It was pretty dark by this time. I fumbled with the key as I tried to put it into the lock. I got them in, but sometimes the door sticks, and I don't know why. Tonight it happened and I had to push kind of hard before the door opened. I stumbled in, my phone and keys falling to the ground. I picked them up immediately. I stopped and admired the ring that encircled my finger, a smile crossing my face for my love of the piece of jewelry. I knew my parents were in the living room. I rushed to the doorway to tell them the news, excitement filling me.

"Mom, Da-" The pair of them sat on the couch, my mother crying into my father's shoulder as he held her close to him. My little brother, who turned two a few weeks ago, was playing with his toys near the couch. On the other side of the room, standing with a smile across his face, was a man who caused me to faint.

HALLUCINATING

I awoke to find my mother and father standing above me with worried expressions. My mother held a magazine, fanning me. They stepped away as I opened my eyes.

"Oh, honey, are you okay?" My father was helping me sit up as I was shaking my head.

"Honey, go get her some water," my mom said, while my father walked int the kitchen.

"I thought-I thought I s-saw." I was still shaking my head trying to clear the image from my mind.

"Just calm down and relax, you fainted and might have hit your head hard," she said fanning me again. It felt good on my now sweaty face.

"Mom, I think I might be hallucinating, I thought I saw...I thought I saw Max on the couch." It was hard to say his name, it still hurt that he was gone.

My father had gotten back with a nice cold glass of water and they were both standing as I sat on the ground. It felt nice as the refreshing water went down my dry throat while I took deep calming breaths and started to get up. They both reached for me to help me stand so I didn't fall again and held onto both my arms as I was standing there.

"I think you might want to sit down." She looked scared and glanced at my father.

"Mom, I'm fine, I might not have eaten enough or it might just be the excitement of today's events, or both."

"Honey please, come sit down, there's a lot of things that need to be said and I think you need to hear them as well." I was pulled to the couch while tensing up when they first moved, I was expecting to see my dead brother sitting there smiling at me again.

"Sit, we'll explain." My mom reassured as my father started moving to the stairway.

"Just breathe and remember to give him a chance to explain." She backed up to return sitting on the couch and looked down at her hands like she was scared.

"Let who explain?" She didn't respond.

"Mom, what is going on; explain, what there is to explain?" She just hung her head as I heard my father coming down the stairs and I looked at him. "Dad what is going on, what is mom talking about?" He lowered his eyes to the floor as the figure behind him caring my little brother moved aside and my mouth just fell open.

I sat there as my father walked and sat down with my mother and put his arm around her, holding her tight. The man walked over to where Benny's toys were in the corner and gently sat him down. He then came over and sat in the chair opposite of my parents. Or, more correctly, I should really say 'our parents'.

The brother I believed to be dead for ten long years was now sitting next to me, looking as if he didn't have a care in the world. He did not look at me but seemed to be studying the carpet. We all just sat in silence as I watched him, my parents watched me, and he watched the floor.

After what felt like eternity of just staring at him, he finally stood while pulling out a packet from his back pocket and handed it to me. He finally acknowledged my presence by making eye contact.

"This will explain why I'm here," he said hesitantly. I couldn't even move to take it from him; I just continued to stare at him. I was speechless.

He rolled his eyes like he had done when I was little and handed another packet of papers to my parents who took them silently. I watched him as he walked back and sat down again. He took a drink of the water that sat on the coffee table in front of him. He looked the same as the day he left. Max must be almost twenty-nine now but seemingly had not aged a day since his eighteenth birthday. He was wearing very nice, expensive shoes, a pair of dark dress pants and a black button down shirt. A mens Breitling Navitimer watch sat on his wrist. I'd seen pictures of them. Couldn't remember where just then.

"Well, like I was telling you before Annie came home, I have been sent here on behalf of my friend who is the Prince of this Country." I started laughing at this point. Everyone just looked at me like I had grown a second head. He spoke in a very sophisticated, adult-like manner   But he had gone insane.

"You idiot, we live in the United States of America, we don't have royalty, we get elected officials."   I began laughing because that was the only sane thing I could think to do, but nobody thought this was funny except for me.   I started wondering if I was asleep, and having a nightmare. Or perhaps I had suddenly gone insane

THE CONTRACT

They all just kept watching me blankly as I continued to crack up laughing. I felt like I had gone insane by this point and the men in white were going to come take me away to a padded room very soon. My brother sat down and looked at a really expensive looking phone. It was one I had never seen before.

"Max, is this for real?" I managed to hear my father say between giggles. His serious voice always scared me. This was certainly no exception

"Yes, he is willing to pay even more if it will help with yours and Benny's futures." Max was saying, looking over at him and smiling. "It will also compensate you for the distress of my disappearance." He again tried to hand me the package of papers. This time I was able to take it from him.

"As well as for Annie's." My parents just nodded their heads in seeming agreement.

"For me? What is that supposed to mean "for Annie's"?" I said in a mocking tone.

"Well Annie, if you will read the contract that the prince has drafted up it will explain everything." My parents were whispering quietly.

"I don't want to read any contract. I want you to tell me what that last statement meant." Shock was melting into anger. I tossed the paperwork onto the coffee table that sat in front of me. My brother shot me a disappointed look.

"Annie, the Prince is my boss as well as my best friend. He realized you were his mate fairly shortly after I left," he said, as if his leaving wasn't a big deal. He broke my little eight year old heart. All this time I and my parents had thought that he was dead, and he left of his own volition? His own free will?

"How could you say this to me, as if you don't even care? Do you even know how hurt I was when you didn't come home that day? And now you are saying you just left me like I was nothing to you, Mom and Dad were nothing to you." He looked at me and said nothing. He pulled out his phone and messed with it.

"Annie, this is not the time to speak about your anger toward me."

"Oh, I think it is a great time to speak about it." I stood up to make my point clear. I reached for my phone that was going off in my pocket.

It was a text from Joel. A giant grin stretched across my face, he was going to be here soon. I looked up from my phone to see they all were looking at me, with confused expressions. I put the phone away and turned to my parents. I had to tell them about what had happened at Joel's earlier. Max stood as if he was going to say something, but I cut him off by stepping closer to my parents.

"Mom, Dad, before I came home I was at Joel's house. I have something really important I have to tell you before he gets here." My father stood up fast.

"You better not be pregnant, I'll kill that pest." My father was a very tall, well-built man. He could be very intimidating.

"Dad, no! I'm not pregnant, geez! I thought you all had a little more faith in me."

"Sorry sweetie, that is usually how that conversation starts." He sat back down next to my mother.

"Like I was going to say, I was over there before I came home to our...company," I sent a glare in Max's direction who was messing with his phone again. "but Joel has asked me to marry him." I showed them the ring on my hand. "And I said yes."

"No!" My father's voice boomed throughout the house.

I was in shock. I stood there looking at both my parents, and I could feel the intense gaze of my brother. I was so confused. I didn't know why my father would react this way about me getting engaged to Joel. But he had no right to tell me what I could and couldn't do with my life! I was eighteen, an adult, and I could make my own decisions about my life. I felt my hands curl into fists. I think I wanted to hit my own father.

"I agree, father." I turned to look at my brother

that had come closer to us.

"What?" I shrieked.

"Annie, you heard your father, he said no." I looked back to him with an overwhelming amount of resentment and hurt.

"But-but-" I couldn't even think as my heart ached. I could feel the drops of tears running down my face.

"Annie, if you would stop interrupting and listen to your brother and the Prince's proposal you would agree with us about our decision to not let you marry Joel," my father said, giving me a very stern look.

"No," I replied as sternly as I could right back. "You can't tell me what to do, I'm an adult and I am going to marry Joel whether you like it or not." I pushed past my brother and started making my way to the stairs, but my father grabbed my arm and stopped me from leaving.

"Annie, you might be an adult, but under this roof you do as we say, do you understand?" Max said. My father and my mother standing together. They both gave me a look saying to do to as he said.

"No, let go of me. I'm leaving. I won't be under your roof for much longer. Joel will be here soon , and his parents love me." I tried to pull me arm free, but Max's grasp was like an iron clamp.

"Young lady, you are not going anywhere with Joel, your mother and I have decided to sign the contract." Not being able to marry Joel was the only thought that crossed my mind.

"Wait, what does that contract say? I thought I was only to get reimbursed for pain and suffering due to Max's disappearance!"

"Annie, the contract is for both you and-"

"What, I'm not the one that went missing?" I interrupted.

Max responded, "No you haven't, but you will tonight, technically, when the Prince comes for you." He looked at his fancy watch. "Which will be very soon."

"I'm not going anywhere with this Prince of yours," I sneered, slamming my foot down on his which made his grip loosen, more from shock than my inflicting any damage. I pulled away from him and ran up the stairs.

Pearson

I'LL CATCH YOU

I got too my room and slammed the door locking it so nobody could come in. I ran my hands through my hair, panicking about what to do. I was crying and I couldn't think straight. I just kept screaming profanities, so they could hear me. I grabbed my phone and dialed Joel's number, dropping my phone a few times before I got it right. He answered only after two rings and I felt my heart dropped the second I heard his sweet voice.

"Baby I'm going to be there in a couple of seconds," he sounded so happy, and I felt so guilty that my parents were ruining our special day.

"Joel..." was all I was able to get out before he interrupted.

"Annie what's wrong, please tell me!"

"My brother is..."

"Baby its okay, I'll be there soon."

"No, you don't understand he's here, in my living room!"

"What, Annie your dead brother?"

"No he's not dead, he's here now and there is this prince coming and he wants me to go with them..."

"Annie you're starting to scare me. You're not making any sense, baby." I was crying so hard trying to explain.

"Joel, my parents said I can't marry you and they want me to go with my brother and this guy they say is a prince!"

"What, I thought your parents liked me," there was hurt in his voice "they don't want you to marry me?"

"Joel I need to get out of here, I need to leave with you now. Do you think your parents will let me stay with you for a few days?" The phone was quiet for a few seconds and my heart started hurting even more.

"Yeah of course they will, they love you. I'll be there in a second. Get something ready and toss them out the window and when I get there I'll help you out, okay?" I smiled with relief at his words.

"Oh, thank you, I love you!" was all I could say.

"I love you too, now, get ready!"

I did as he said by packing a bag of clothing then filling my backpack with toiletries and other personal items. I tossed them out the window onto the lawn and went to grab my cell off the table when I heard Joel yell out my name. I walked over to the window and saw him standing below. I looked back at my room, and decided to climb out the window. Almost immediately I regretted this idea, but it was too late now and I really need to get away from my parents and my not so dead brother.

I was not the biggest fan of heights and I started to doubt Joel's ability to catch me if/when I fell, from my second level window. My arms were starting to burn, but I knew I did not have the strength to pull myself back up to the safe confines of my room.

"Annie, its okay, just let go I'll catch you, I promise!"

"I'm scared" I yelled in response. "On the count of three just let go. I'll catch you. I won't let you fall!"

"Okay." My voice sounded as if it were coming from someone else.

"1...2...3..." I let go and made the mistake of looking down to see Joel, who was laying face down on the ground. I couldn't wrap my mind around what I was seeing. I screamed. I heard Joel scream my name. Then I felt to arms catch me, in a bridal style. My thoughts were running fast. Did I imagine him on the ground? I had my eyes closed so tightly, I was afraid to open them. Joel must have caught me and I was being held. I heard a voice whispering into my ear, which I could barely hear it over my pounding heart.

"Its okay. I caught you, you're fine. You can open your eyes," and I slowly opened them in time to see Joel pushing himself off the ground, turning around to look at me.

"What the hell was..." I looked to see who was holding me fearing my brother had figured out what was going on.

But it was not my brother. It was a man I had never seen before. He must have been about the same age as I am. He was staring down at me, with a look of bemusement. The sun was not fully set and the sky was a mixture of light and dark blue, yellows, purples, and orange. His eyes against the dusk sky were the prettiest light and dark blue color I had ever seen. He had short, choppy, light brown hair and full lips that had a slight up curve to the corners. He was wearing similar clothing to my brother, and he looked good. After all, I'm a teenage girl with hormones. I still look now and then. Don't get me wrong, I loved Joel and he beats him hands down in comparison to my savior, but he was definitely nice eye candy.

HIS BLOOD

"You bastard! Why did you push me out of the way? You could have really hurt her!" I looked back at Joel who was visible angry.

"Boy, if I hadn't pushed you, she definitely would have gotten hurt." The stranger started to turn to walk away. I realized he had not set me down, and I began to struggle to get out of his hold.

"Let me go!" I yelled at him and he did as I asked without hesitation. I moved over to where Joel was standing and grabbed my bag up off the ground.

"Annie, let's get out of here. I already texted Macy to meet us at my house," I hear Joel saying. The strange man was watching me. He seemed amused and oddly curious.

"You're not going anywhere," my brother said as he came around the corner of the house flanked by my parents.

"Screw you, Max, you have no right to tell me what to do!" I grabbed Joel's hand and squeezed looking for reassurance.

"Annie, don't be difficult," my mother said, as we

walked toward Joel's car. Suddenly, I felt Joel's hand ripped away from mine as two hands clamped down on my shoulders.

"What the hell! Why do you keep pushing me?" Joel yelled. The stranger was standing between us.

"You will not touch her again." The stranger commanded Joel. How dare he? I realized it was my brother holding me.. He was watching Joel.

"What?" Joel cried, moving toward the stranger. He was a lot taller than Joel, who was at least a head taller than me.

"You heard me, boy," was the stranger's threatening response..

"Excuse me, I don't think so." I stated. They both looked at me. I managed to break free of my brothers grep, making my way to where Joel was waiting for me. The stranger stopped me.

"Stop your mine now, I order you to stay away from him as well." I cannot tell you how much this infuriated me. I thought my brain was going to explode.

"Who do you think you are? That is my fiance and I will not stay away from him, you're the one that need to back off, dude."

"Annie, do not speak to the Prince that way." My brother looked seriously annoyed when he said this. I looked back at the stranger standing next to me and holding onto my arm. This was the so called "prince"?

For some reason I was shocked and surprised he was not only a young man, but actually pretty hot. Of course, he was an asshole. I didn't understand how he was able to convince my brother and my parents that he was a Prince. There was no such thing as a Prince here in the United States. What was wrong with these people, falling for this ludicrous story. I yanked my arm away from him. Good-looking or not, his actions proved he was no Prince in my eyes, and he never would be. I moved closer to Joel again and was about to grab his hand when suddenly the "Prince" was in front of me so fast, holding me with both hands. My brother was now holding Joel in the air by his neck.

"If you don't listen to me, we will kill him and his blood will be on your hands" I heard Max saying.

"NO!" I screamed. "Let him go! You are hurting him!" I tried to move out of this strangers' grasp, but his grip was to strong. He bent down to whispered into my ear;

"Take off that pathetic ring and give it back to him. Send him away, before we have to kill him." He then let go and moved away from me. I looked at him with my tear blurred eyes. "The choice is yours. You must make it quickly." He stood waiting, watching me as I looked over to where my brother and Joel were.

Joel was struggling and trying to get free of my brother hand and was turning a deep red. His lips, his amazing lips were becoming paler by the second. My brother just stood there like there was nothing in his hands, although Joel weighed at least 170 lbs. How was he able to do that? It was unnatural for someone to be able to do that! I looked down at my hand, slowly sliding the ring off. The movement made me feel as if I was the one being choked and my chest was burning. My brother lowered Joel to the ground where he collapsed onto his back. I rushed over to him.

BEING DRAMATIC

"Joel… Joel are you okay?" He was just laying there, gasping for air. "Joel I'm so sorry, I love you don't forget that!" he raised his hand to my face as he struggled for get his breath back.

"I'll…. Never…stop…!" he coughed a few times. "I …love…you!" I then felt a steel hand on my shoulder pulling me away from him just as I was about to give Joel a kiss.

"No, I will not allow that." It was the Prince. I knew there would be a bruise if he did not relinquish his hold soon. "Max, take Joel to his home." My brother nodded, and literally began dragging Joel back to his car. "Mr and Mrs. Erickson, please, let us continue our conversation inside," This so called tyrant "Prince" was saying. All I could do was let the tears flow. I wanted to die, but even more, I wanted to kill them all!

They had destroyed my life in the span of about an hour, and they were all acting as if nothing had happened at all. We were somehow back in the living room and I was sitting on the couch. Next to me sat the "Prince". He had a smile on his face, as if he was somehow happy about something. He had his arm around me and held my hand with his other hand. I was in shock that nobody seemed to care. I loved Joel so much and I was forced to say goodbye to him to save his life! Did that just happen? My heart was just broken even more then when Max 'left'. This was all so wrong.

"Annie please stop crying, you are being way too dramatic. This is what we were trying to tell you before you stormed off." I could not believe the words coming from my mother.

"I'm being dramatic? You all just ruined my life, along with Joel's." I drooped my head to my hands and sobbed even harder. I felt the Prince start rubbing my back. I stood up and gave him my best death glare. "I hate you all And you," I said to the Prince, "You don't have any right to touch me!" My brother came walking in at that moment. I ignored him and I tried to walk back up to my room. I pulled out my phone and started calling Joel.

"Do not call upon him." The phone was suddenly out of my hand and in the Prince's. He crushed the phone between his thumb and his forefinger.

I backed away from him as my brother came up on my other side. He took my arm and guided me back to the couch. I was scared. I kept seeing my phone pulverized in his hand. That was definitely not normal, in any way, to be able to do that to a phone with only two fingers. Was I in the twilight zone or what? My parents both masked a worried expression with a big fake, happy smile. What was wrong with them, they could see this guy was not normal and neither was their perfect Max. But they were going along with them.

"Like I was trying to say, Annie, the Prince has offered our parents an overly generous amount for you." This freak was trying to buy me? I turned to my parents.

"You self righteous jerks, you are selling me to this crazy person?" I stood up and tried get past my brothers hands from me. "The very same crazy person that had made all of us believe that Max was dead?" My parent averted their eyes from me as I yelled at them. "Along those lines, this freak has convinced you that he is a prince. Hello, am I the only sane person here? There is no prince in this country!"

"Annie, will you please stop ranting and listen? If you would, you would see what we're doing is best for everyone?" My father was actually pleading. His face was that of a desperate man. It made me shudder.

"How is it best for me to be sold off, like I'm a car or something?"

"Annie, the Prince is going to provide for your moth and I so that Benny can live a really good life. We will not have to worry about money ever again." I shock my head.

"What is so wrong with the life we have now? I know we're not rich, but... but I never ever heard you complain before." I broke down again and sank to the ground.

"True, but wouldn't you like to see Benny go to

that elite private school and get a wonderful education? So he can have a chance at a wonderful future?" I looked over at Benny who seemed to be oblivious to everything going around him. He was coloring in his dinosaur book, and seemed very content. "The Prince can give the world to you. I'm begging you to listen. He wants you to marry him and become a Princess and eventually a Queen. You will be rich, cared for and protected for the rest of your life." I couldn't understand what they talking about. I didn't want this. Their words became a dull drone, just background noise.

The door bell rang, followed by very angry pounding. My brother stood and walked over to the door. As he opened the door, a blonde blur shoved past him making him stumble back, with wide eyes. Macy was standing close to the couch the Prince was sitting on. There was that amused look again as he looked at her. He was so smug! She was holding hand held tazer and a small can of pepper spray. She was ready to use them, too. This made me smile. In the real world, she was finally getting to use all her self-defense class training.

"Annie, lets go! I'm busting you out of this place. If any of the rest of you move I won't hesitate to attack." This made me giggle, cause I was finally going to get away. Thank heavens for my crazy best friend Macy.

WE NEED TO LEAVE

"Annie, let's go. Now, please." I stood up as Macy and moved toward her, but was always facing everyone in the room.

"Macy!" I heard Benny shout. He was getting up and walking in her direction. He had always adored her, which I found really cute.

"Hey my little man, I need you to do me a favor okay" His little face lit up as she spoke to him.

"Okay, for you Macy," His chubby cheeks went pink as he looked to me, then to our parents

"I'm really sorry, sweetie, I can't stay and play stay and play with you right now, and may have I have to say some bad words to these two bad guys here." He gave them a pouty look. "I need you to go upstairs so I do not scare you or upset you, can you do that for me?" he nodded his head and began to go up the stairs.

I was right next to Macy as everyone watched Benny climb the stairway, moping all the way. We all turned back to face one another as my brother moved toward us with a small half smirk on his face, blocking our closest pathway to the door. The Prince still just sat on the couch seemingly amused. I really wanted to punch him. As my parents just sat motionless with shock and confusion at Macy's behavior. They thought she was a sweet, quiet girl and they were wrong.

"Well, well, it's been a long time Macy." my brother looking at Macy very odd like, wait a second, I think he was just checking out my best friend, oh my god ewwwwwwwww.

"Back off buddy boy, I'm not interested in what you're selling, so unless you want to be tazered and peppered sprayed I suggest you move." Max just laughed as he took another step closer to her.

I'm sure you all know what happened next when, you piss Macy off with a tazer in her hand, and invade her space. Yep, that's right, she used in on Max. I shut my eyes and heard the electric clicking noise as she did it. I heard her gasp and I stopped, my eyelids flying open. My brother was still standing no longer looking amused. She stiffened, and hit him with another shot. She was pressing it into his stomach and null I could hear was the repetitive clicking noise Max didn't even flinch.

"Will you stop that?" he snatched the tazer out of her hand. "It tickles, and I'm not in the mood right now.." OMG!, he was checking her out for sure this time! Macy was frozen. I looked toward the door and started backing up and maneuvering us to get closer to it..

"I don't understand, you should be on the ground!" Macy stood staring at him and he at her as the Prince went over to stand beside him.

"Macy it doesn't matter now, let's get out of here," I pleaded. She finally broke eye contact with Max, and started backing up with me toward the door.

But my brother made one quick step and was somehow now right in front of her as she raised her hand and sprayed pepper spray right in his face. Finally, a reaction! The spray caused him to bring his hands up to his eyes. We were almost out the door when he caught up to us. The whites of his eyes were a black color, and he was visibly angry.

"Now that really pissed me off," he said clenching his teeth. We were out the front door still looking back at my brother. We froze as he spoke. We saw what was in his mouth. There were two very long, very white, very sharp looking teeth, canine teeth. Man, they were freaking fangs! I heard Macy gasp at the same time I did. She saw what I had. If I was crazy, then she was too. Or was this a dream, it had to be because this could not be real!

"Annie, we need to leave and we need to leave right now!" Macy said, as she made another step back and I followed as well. We were down the porch steps. Both Max and the prince were standing side by side at front of the door looking down at us. I was scared out of my mind. This was not my brother, and I do not even want to know what that thing is he has brought here. As we made another step back, toward the street, I heard Macy scream "RUN!!!!!!!" We both turned and made a mad dash for her truck.

I was Sold

GET TO THE LAKE

Her truck was parked on the street directly in front of my house. We got in and slammed our doors shut. Macy was visibly shaking when she was trying to get her keys in the ignition. We jumped and screamed at the sound of light knocking on the window. Max stood outside her window with a half-smile plastered across his face. She looked back at me and her eyes widened. She was looking past me, and I slowly turned to look, hiding my full face with my hair and peeking through. I was so scared to really see at what Macy was looking at. Although I had a theory, I just needed to see if I was right. Of course, the Prince was there, just standing outside my window and looking at me. There was no visible emotion on his face. I flinched as Max spoke.

"Macy, can you unlock the doors please?" Max was saying, giving her a great big smile. We both froze expecting to see those fangs again. But nothing more than normal human teeth were showing. "Macy, look at me. Please unlock the door for me." Macy sat there frozen in place. It didn't even look like she was breathing. I saw her hand move and start reaching for the button to unlock the doors.

"Macy!" I screamed, "What are you doing? Don't unlock the doors just start the truck and let's go!" I screamed as she jumped and turned to look at me with horror written all over her very pale face. "Oh my god!" Macy screamed, turning the key in the ignition. We peeled out of the spot leaving them standing there. "I can't believe I almost just did that!"

"Macy, its okay, we just need to get away from..." I paused I didn't know what they were, or really what to call those things. "Them." was all I could think of.

"I'm not crazy right? You saw what I saw, Right? Tell me you saw what was in your brother's mouth? Oh my god, this can't be happening! I'm not crazy. Annie please answer me!" Macy's pleaded, her voiced drenched with panic. Her breathing became audible, and was much quicker than normal.

"Macy," I didn't know what to say. I just sat there with my mouth open collecting flies.

"Annie, you saw right?" I just nodded my head, "Your brother is a vampire and I think his friend is one too!" The truck fell silent for a few moments.

"That's not my brother, my brother is dead." I said. Macy didn't respond. There was nothing to say.

We kept driving and I just sat there, looking out the window. I knew where we were going without even asking. We were on the road that took us to a dead-end in the middle of the forest surrounding the town lake. We found it a few years back when Macy first got her license, and we had gotten a little lost. But our discovery was the quickest way to the lake and it was free parking. We just had to walk through the forest. Someone had posted a wooden sign that said 'Easter Lake' with an arrow and we were dumb and crazy enough to follow it.

I sat in silence remembering all the fun we had that day. Laughing about how I was convinced that it was a trap, and movies would be made about our deaths. It was completely dark now and the moon was high in the sky and very bright. I could see a lot out here in the dark. I hadn't noticed before, especially on such a dark road, but there were lights following behind the truck. Two sets of car lights shined in the side-mirror, as I spun in my seat to make sure my eyes were not playing a trick on me.

"Macy!" I shouted in a panic.

"They're following us! I was so distracted I didn't even notice! Crap!" I felt the truck speed up

"Macy, we're coming to a dead-end, what are we going to do? We will be trapped like animals, we will be sitting ducks!"

"We need to get to the lake!" Macy inisted.

"Why so they can murder us and throw our bodies in the lake? Macy, I don't want to die on my birthday!"

"Annie, everyone is up here partying. Everyone is there right now. Let's hope those two won't cause a big commotion with half the town around us."

"Half the town's there, Macy?" I said, not sure that was going to work.

"Annie, now is not the time to start complaining!"

41

When we come to a stop, get out and run into the forest. They won't know where we're going. Call Joel and tell him what's happening and to meet us half way, and to bring people to help us." I shook my head

"I can't call him. The Prince, he broke my phone, he... he smashed it with two fingers..." I stuttered, recalling the memory in horror.

"I'll call him you just run and run like hell. I'll be right behind you."

We stayed on the road until it came to an end. Macy slammed on the brakes throwing the truck into park as we swung the doors open. I attempted to jump out in cool action movie style, but I failed and had an issue with getting tangled up in the seat belt. Macy was reaching for the phone in the center console as I looked back at the road and saw both cars had stopped. Two dark figures were walking toward us about 100 ft. away. It was hard to tell which figure was who because the lights on the cars were on.

All I could be see was their dark silhouettes. I glanced over to Macy, and she had noticed them as well. She screamed as the lights on the cars turned off.

"Annie run!" Macy screamed. She ran too, but in a slightly different direction. That move was dumb. Everyone knows you never split up, no matter what.

I ran as hard as I could, but became winded pretty quickly. I also kept stumbling, and ended up falling twice. The moon made it easier to see, but didn't help that much when the trees became denser and blocked a lot of light. My pace was slowing. I was so tired after everything I had been through. My ankle felt like it had broken glass in it from one of my falls.

I heard a noise that brought me to a stand still. It came from behind me and I spun to see if I could hear or see anything. I thought I heard Macy yell my name, but I wasn't sure until I heard a blood curdling scream that echoed all around. I called out to her, but there was only silence after that. I spun around and started running again when I slammed into a tree. I screamed, anticipating pain, but there was none. And I was still standing. I hadn't run into a tree, but was face to face with the emotionless, stone faced Prince. He was holding me up by my arms. I screamed and tried to struggle out of his grip, but to no avail.

"You need to stop running. I am m not going to hurt you." He pulled me closer.

"Let me go, you freak!" Was all I could say.

"I didn't want to do this. I was hoping to avoid this." I kicked at his shins, but it had no effect on him.

He opened his mouth, and I watched his canines grow out into the same fangs my brother had. He moved so quickly that I barely felt any pain as he sunk his teeth into me. I could feel my tears falling down my face as I was still struggling and trying to scream. My memory becomes a bit fuzzy after that. I remember feeling his hands tightly wrapping around my waist pulling me closer to him, as the other was softly on the back of my neck near where his fangs entered me and he was drinking my blood. The pain had gone and felt almost good. I felt my arms move on their own to bring him closer to me. I heard a growling noise coming from him. I looked up at the bright moon, and watched it until it started to fade and all went dark.

A LIVING HELL

I felt the warmth of the sun shining through my window and mentally criticized myself for not closing the blinds. It felt nice and warm but it was irritating at the same time because I like my sleep, and don't like waking up much at all. I was sleeping on my stomach and stretched my left arm out to reach for my night stand that held my phone. But it was not my bed. It was much larger then my twin mattress. I stretched out my arms like a snow angel. Confused, I pushed myself up and looked at the bed I was in.

I could not believe my eyes as I looked around. The pillows were ivory colored, trimmed with gold designs. The comforter and sheets were the same, and they were so soft. The bed itself was a King-sized, redwood canopy bed that had an ivory sheer tied to the post. There were three wide window doors that reached all the way up to the vaulted ceilings. Each door opened onto a balcony. The room had pale ivory walls with a golden chandelier. The redwood floors were covered with a luxurious white area carpet.

"Oh my god!" I gasped as I kept looking around, shocked to find myself in this beautifully elegant room.

I noticed there were double doors on both walls on each side of the bed. I got up and ran to the left door and saw what made my heart race. A room full of my clothing, shoes, jewelry. Well, some of them were mine, but not all, but I wanted them to be mine. This room was a closet-room, almost half the size of the bedroom I woke up in. There was a door to the right just off the middle of this room. I opened it and it was a magnificent bathroom, all white marble and gold trims. I saw my reflection in the mirror and noticed a bandage on my neck, and froze. What the hell had happened?

As I reached my hand to the bandage I removed it slowly, so I would not cause myself any pain. I saw my wound and screamed as all my memory came flooding back. My dead brother, and a "Prince" so to speak, who must have bit me, the douche bag. There was Joel, and my heart sank thinking about the last time I saw his face. And then there was Macy. I had know idea what had happened to her! I fell to my knees and started crying. Just then, someone knocked on one of the doors which probably led out of here. Thank God it was not the bathroom door. At least my privacy was being respected, at least for the moment.

"Who is it?" I asked in a shaky voice

"Annie, its Max and the Prince. Are you all right?" I wanted to throw the door open and murder them both!

"I am alright, no thanks to you!" I spat sarcastically, tears running down my face. "You bastards, I hate you both! I want to go home now!" I went out and sat on the bed, fully breaking down in anguish at the thought of all I had lost so quickly.

I heard them say something but I was crying too hard to actually hear their words. Words meant nothing from them. I was so hurt as Joel face flickered in my mind. That last look he gave me when I handed him back his ring. It was so pretty and it meant the world to me. I felt so cold and empty realizing my life was now over because of these selfish monsters. I became angrier and angrier as I thought about everyone I cared about. Benny would never be able to have his big sister while he grows up. I had no idea what happened to Macy. I prayed she was safe and helping Joel with the hurt he must be feeling.

I lost track of time crying. The intense sadness I felt kept criss-crossing back and forth to anger, then back to sadness. As I splashed some cold water on my face trying to calm myself. I saw my swollen eyes in the mirror, and I didn't recognize myself. I had lost every shred of happiness. All I saw was hurt and anger in my eyes. And Emptiness. I decided then and there that t I would die before I gave into these freaks. I was going to make their life hell until they let me go.

I walked back into the bedroom looking around for some type of plan or really anything that could even help me. I notice an iPod sitting in an i Home

It was hooked up to a sound system placed all around the room. A light went off in my brain. I searched for a song that portrayed lots of anger and would cause a ton of noise pollution. I smiled as I turned up the volume to maximum and turned up the base up too. I wanted to ensure I would at least blow out the windows. I made my way into the closet and found a drawer that held all types of undergarments. I swear, a male had to pick this crap out cause it was ridiculously sultry. I am secretly glad because it was going to work perfectly with my plan.

I stripped and put on a black lace bra, that was all lace and should not even be considered a bra, it was tiny and made my boobies look bigger then normal. I matched it with a pair of boy shorts that where the same lace as the bra. I grabbed a pair of black very high heels I knew I was never going to be able to walk in. The kind of shoes that were just for fun, I thought, as I sat them in the bathroom. I went back to the desk with the I pod I had chosen the song "Bleak Stuff" by Limp Bizkit, because it seemed like the perfect song that held all the anger I was feeling. I smiled and pressed play. My hands flew to my ears to protect them from the sound of how loud it was.

My first thought was to turn it down, but if I did they would know I did and I was not going to back down now. I ran over to the first set of doors and opened them, so the music had some where to go. After I had opened all of the balcony door, some of the pressure was relieved on my ears. Very quickly, someone was banging on the door. I smiled and walked into the bathroom ignoring who ever it was on the other side.   I closed the bathroom door because if it was my brother he would not intrude on me in here.

If it wasn't, hopefully the shut door would stop anyone else from intruding. I heard the sound of the door hitting the floor over the music. I ignored it and went back to putting on lip-gloss in my slutty outfit, as the door to my bathroom disappeared as the prince stood there with both hands gripping the door frame. He was baring his teeth.

Pearson

GET OUT!

I screamed as anyone else in my situation would have. I grabbed for the closest thing I could get my hands on to protect myself. I threw one shoe at him, but he just back-handed it away, causing it to break a vase next to him. Glass was shattering as I launched the second shoe at him. Suddenly, the music stopped and the room was silent. I briefly wondered who turned it off, then the thought was gone.

"Get out of here you perverted freak!" I screamed as he caught my second shoe and tossed it behind him and started walking toward me.

"No," he replied very aloof. "It's my house and you're my guest. Your little antics suggest you really just want my attention" he was smirking as I was backing away from him.

"Get out I'm practically naked and I don't want any attention from you and I sure as hell don't want to be your guest." I grabbed a big fluffy towel that was hanging on the wall and wrapped it around to cover myself from his lingering eyes.

He kept walking forwarded, as his smirk grew bigger as his shock his head. I could hear a small chuckle leave his mouth, as my back hit the wall that was furthest from the exit or the closet. I mentally slapped myself for not planning a better plan, beside piss them off and run. Did not think this thought and plan for what I should do, once I piss them off that they confronted me. He was now pressed up against me with his hands against wall beside my head. He was so much taller than me, I barley came up to his chin. I gasped at his actions and how intimidated I felt.

"Oh Annie, you don't have to lie, I'm the only one here," the prince said sarcastically. I heard someone clear their throat. I wanted to see who it was but I was too sacred looking into the Prince's eyes
.   "Well I guess your brother is here too," I heard Max chuckling, as the prince broke eye contact to share the joke. I felt like I was just smacked or something, and I was filled with anger.

"I was just reminding you that your parents want to meet her with in the next hour," Max said, leaning against the door frame, picking at his fingernails, "So I would recommend you both not be messing around or doing something you can't stop when they get here," Max was smirking at the prince, and he laughed. He started shaking his head slightly as Max ignored me all together.

"Thank you Max, now leave!" Before I knew it the princes was now looking down at me as I felt one of his hands cup my cheek and gently rub his thumb over my cheek bone.

Some how my anger started to dwindled the more I looked into his eyes. They held like a hypnotic power, but I was not sure because all thoughts started to dwindle as I felt soft fabric slowly slide down my body. Goose bumps formed and cover inch of my body as I felt the prince's arm wrap around my waist and pull me closer to him.

My mind was screaming for him stop as I felt my entire body heat up every place his body touched mine. This was wrong, he was controlling my body I thought, but he is not able to control my mind. He moved his face closer to me and I thought he was going to kiss me, and my as my mind screamed at me to run. But he didn't. He rested his head on my shoulder as he pulled me into him closer. I felt a little pain because he was squeezing me a little too tight. I heard him sigh, then he loosened his grip on me. The room seemed to spin.

"Oh Annie," I stiffened as I felt him brush his lips on my clavicle.

"I've waited so long to have you." He inhaled audibly. Anger filled me. "And now, I finally have you all to myself." He was now staring at my body with darkened, lustful eyes, as his fangs slowly grew longer. "You are so beautiful, and in that outfit..." he bit his bottom lip. "I love this on you, and I can't wait to take it off you."

That was what finally snapped me out of my dizzy, confused state. Forcefully I shoved him away as best I could. He only took a few steps back, as what I just did registered to him. I moved away from him as fast as I could because I was not going to let him use his magic on me again. He grabbed my wrist and spun me around as I tried to walk away from him. He looked angry now, the smirk disappearing off his face. Light bulbs went off in my head. I thought up the perfect plan and it was going to be wonderful as long as he didn't angry enough to bite me again. I could win this battle.

"What do you think you're doing Annie," he said, as I tried to pull my wrist away from him.

"What does it look like?" I gave him a look of duh, but he was not understanding.

"I was not done speaking, and I never said you could walk away from me." He approached mes as I backed away from him.

"Well first, I never gave you permission to touch me or invade my personal space." I said, as smart ass like as I could manage. He looked angry and I kept a board too cool for you look on my face, but I was scared he would hurt me again, because, let's face it he already did. "Second, I don't really feel comfortable with some one that is not my fiancé touching me. You know him, you almost had my brother kill him, his name is Joel." The prince had let me go at the mention of Joel and was once again gripping onto the bathroom door frame again. I could hear the sound of the frame cracking, I took this opportunity to turn away from him and walk over to the bed swaying my hips in an overly dramatic way. "Well I don't feel, comfortable with you seeing me in the surprise outfit that was meant for him, when I leave here soon." with that I was at the side of the bed, so I turned and did a jump and flopped on the bed.

It was the most comfortable bed that I had ever

laid on and I was sad to not have this when I went home. All at once I felt a pressure all over my body, so I opened my eyes to the prince pinning my arms down beside my head. As I looked him in the eyes, I screamed and tried to fight him and get away. His eyes were known longer pretty blue but were solid black and had white curvy line that looked like veins all over the endless black. I was truly scared and regretted trying to carry out this plan because he was going to kill me and there was nobody going to stop him.

Pearson

LISTEN REAL GOOD

He lowered his head closer to mine as I tried to pull away from him and keep moving. My arms were yanked above my head and I felt one hand grasp both of my wrists, as pain shout down my arms. His second hand appeared around my neck, as his thumb and index finger gripped my jaw. It hurt and I was unable to move. If I struggled at all his grip tightened. I held my eyes closed. I didn't want to look into those eyes that were all veined blackness.

"Annie, open your eyes!" he commanded angrily. I knew he was talking through clenched teeth. "NOW ANNIE!" I could not stop myself, my eyes flew open, and wanted to shut them immediately for fear of how close his face was to mine. "Listen, and listen well." His voice was really creepy and I was trying to shrink back into the bed but his grasp prevented me, "You will not mention that boy's name, in my presence, ever again. You are mine now, not his, only mine! You speak his name again, I will drag him here, drain him of all his blood, then snap his neck, all while I make you watch." A scream escaped my mouth as I started to sob harder. I knew he meant what he said, that he would hurt Joel, and I could not allow that to happen.

I noticed the grip on my wrist and neck loosened, as he moved his face away from me, I heard him sigh. I noticed through my blurry vision that his eyes were back to normal as his face was completely devoid of emotion. He was still holding me down but is was not as dominant as before, it felt gentle and caring which caused my anger to flair. But I held it in check, because I had already endangered Joel's life once today, and once was too many times in my book. He let go but then lifted me up so that I was sitting in his lap. I continued crying softly, as I could not control that. He picked me up, walked over to the bathroom, sitting me down on the counter. He then wrapped a towel around me.

"Here, wash you face and calm down." He turned the water on as he walked away into the closet.

He came back in shortly. I had finally stopped crying, but was shaking uncontrollably. I was frightened of him. He stopped in front of me and placed some clothing down beside me. He lifted a shirt to my head. I froze at his touch, He was dressing me, like I was a child. He put on a black tank top and moved the towel lower so that it was only covering my legs as he handed me a pair of black shorts.

"I'll let you finish dressing yourself." He walked out of the bathroom. I sat there for a few moments just not able to move until I heard a knock on the bedroom door. I quickly jumped down and pulled the shorts on along with the shoes that were sat on the counter and made my way to the bedroom.

"Where is she I want to meet her!" stopped just in side the door, I heard a young girl voice. It sounded really happy and hyper.

"Mom, she in the bathroom getting dressed" I heard a girl giggling.

"Didn't Max tell you that we were coming and not to be playing around?" she laughed even more, and I became angry grew toward this person for even assuming that I would be 'playing around' with the Prince.

"Mom it's not like she... its not what you were hoping for, and your going to have to give her time," I heard the Prince speaking in a lower voice to someone outside my door. He was talking so low it was hard for me to hear.

"Luke, what do you mean, its not what I was expecting? Is she not your mate?" Luke? The Prince's name is Luke? I wondered why I cared.

"No she is, I feel the pull and I already know I love..." I decided I was not going to listen to this crap anymore, so I decided to confront them.

There was a girl standing next to Prince Luke. She was a little shorter than me. She had dark blue eyes and long wavy ashy blonde hair. She had a confused look on her face. They saw me, and Luke moved away from her toward me. I instantly took a step away from him. But he was fast and wrapped his arm around my waist pulling me over to the now smiling girl. She met us half away and almost tackled me in the process of giving me a hug. I looked over to the sound of a chuckle as Luke had let me go. He was amused.

"Oh, it so nice to finally meet you!" she squealed as she let me go, "I'm Queen Krista, Luke's Mom." She waved her hand in his direction. "I'm so happy you're here. I finally have the daughter I've always wanted." At this, she pulled me into another tight hug. "Oh Luke, she so beautiful, but we all knew she would be." She grinned up at him as I took a step away from her. She turned back to look at me with the confusion written all over her face. "Sweetheart, what is wrong?"

"You can't be his mother, you look younger than me, what are you, 15?" I cried. She just smiled this great big smile.

"Do you really think I look 15?" She glanced over at Luke. "There no need to flatter me to win me over. I already adore you!" She took another step closer as I retreated back one. "Luke, why is she doing that?" she kept her eyes on me turning her head toward Luke. He was looking down at the floor.

"She not feeling the pull mother. She does not want to be here. She is angry that she is." Queen Krista looked stunned as she turned her full attention toward Luke.

"What? Luke, have you not explained anything to her?"

"I have tried. She has refused to listen. She thinks she in love with some human boy."

"I am in love with this human boy, he is my fiancé!" I interjected.

"What did I tell you?" He said menacingly to me.

"You said you would kill him if I mentioned his name again, which I didn't!" Luke was suddenly in my face baring his ugly teeth at me. I heard door behind us hit the wall with a loud bang.

"Silence to both of you!" A booming voice commanded.

Pearson

APOLOGIZE

"Your bickering is beyond irritating!" A tall, striking man strode into the room. He looked a lot like Luke, except he had light blue eyes.

"I'm sorry father," I felt Luke's elbow nudge me. I glared at him. Luke whispered into my ear to "Apologize." I tried, to no avail, to shake him off.

"Honey!" His mother squealed as he picked her up and spun her around. "I want you to meet Luke's mate!" They were staring into each others eyes like they had been apart for years. It was so weird.

They turned to face us, but still held on to each other, like their life depended on it. They looked really happy that they were in each others arms. I could feel the love there, in spite of my overwhelming anger. That's when the tears started to fall down my cheek again. The thought of never having this again, never being with Joel again, was breaking my heart. I was having a hard time breathing. I felt someone's hands holding me up as my body gave out. I knew they were talking, but I could not hear or speak. There was a lump in my throat and my ears felt really hot and on fire. I could see a little better, and things were not so blurry, but my chest was aching. I started to be able to hear what they were saying again, but it didn't help. I looked around the room as Luke sat next to me holding my hand, and his parents sat on the couch a few feet away.

"Annie are you okay? I pulled my hand away from his, as he looked away from me and pursed his lips together tightly. "You collapsed." Underneath his breath he hissed at me: "Please try to behave in front of my parents!"

"Luke what's going on?" His father's voice was demanding. It frightened me. I tried to be as still as possible, wishing and willing him to stop looking at me.

"It's nothing father. I think she just needs time to deal with and comprehend all this information."

"Do not lie to me. I am your father as well as the King. Please tell me what is going on. Why would she be acting this way?" He came closer, still gazing at me. I wanted to disappear.

"Jace, dear, she does not want to be here," Queen Krista was now next to him, trying to soothe him.

"Luke, I told you to find your mate, not pick some girl who you're attracted to!" He looked very disappointed. Luke averted his gaze. He looked ashamed.

"She is my mate, I feel the pull, I've known for 10 years." He answered him quietly, to my complete shock. He knew me for 10 years? Was he some type of stalker, too?.

"Why does she not feel the pull then?" Jace

waited for a response, but all Luke did was shrug his shoulders

"Honey, I believe that has something to do with the human fiancé,. She is in love with him and not Luke." She understood. Maybe she was my way out of this hell.

"Fix this now Luke, the ball is a week away and I will not have you embarrassing us or yourselves."

"Yes father," he finally looked up as he answered him.

"Honey let's go, so they can work things out. Plus, we have a couple of free hours I think we should" she paused and looked at both of us then looked back at Jace. "go play...." she laughed, "in our room." He smiled, picked her like she was a bride, sweeping her out of the room in an instant, the door closing quickly behind them.

Luke sat on the edge of my bed in silence, studying the carpet. He pulled out his phone and started tapping on it. He finally stood up after a little bit, and walked toward the door. He stopped, turned and looked at me, almost sad-like.

"Are you not coming?"

"Well that depends, am I going home?" I replied, sarcastically. Where did he think I should be going?

"No, it is dinnertime, and you have not eaten in a couple of days. I assumed you most be hungry."

"I'm not going anywhere with you, a vampire who wants to eat me. Especially for dinner." I mocked him. "I'm only leaving this room to go home." Luke turned left.

"Fine starve, see if I care." And he was gone.

As if right on demand my stomach growled at me, hating the decision I made. I loved food, but I was not going to give in to them and they might send me home for health reasons. I laid on the bed and stared up at the ceiling, watching as the light from the sun changed. My mind started to play tricks on me and I was imagining smell of delicious food. I started to really regretted not going with Luke, I was just that hungry. A knock came a few minutes later, cutting off my daydream about biting into a giant hamburger... I sat there for a few seconds, unsure about what to do.

"Who is it?" I asked, when the knock was repeated.

"Mary Bell, I'm your personal servant, Lady Annie." I walked over to the door and tried to open it, but it was locked.

"I can't open it, I don't have a key."

"I know my Lady. I was simply asking for permission to come in."

"Oh. Sure come in, everyone else does..." the door opened and a girl who looked a few years older than me came in carrying a tray covered with a silver lid.

"I brought you some dinner, as Prince Luke requested." She was so nice, and she was just doing her job I guess. I was also to tired to be rude to her. But I knew I had to stand my ground

"I am sorry, but I'm not eating anything from that douche bag Luke." I turned to walk away. "For all I know, he's drugged it." She looked horrified

"I can assure you, my lady, he did no such thing.

I prepared this meal and this food never left my sight." Mary Bell set it down and gave me a disapproving look.   "Besides, he only wanted you to have a peanut butter sandwich and water. I prepared a wonderful meal for you instead." She watched me.

"Okay, I'll eat it, but only because you defied him." She smiled her approval.

"I heard you were really difficult, but I don't believe you are. I think you are just confused and upset." I had to laugh.

"You have no idea. I just want to go home," I confided.

"But you can't," she frowned. "Now eat before you pass out from lack of food." She walked away and closed to the door, leaving me alone again with no way out. Well at least I had food.   Hopefully, it will help me think of a way out of this vampire prison.

Pearson

WHAT HAPPENED TO MACY

That night I dreamed I was at the lake laying in the sun, listening to people laughing. I felt someone poking me. It was Macy. She was looking at me with an irritated look. I tried to speak, but nothing came out. She shook her head, looking very disappointed. She stood up, brushed the sand off and took off running toward the lake. As I watched, I noticed there was nobody around, all the people were gone and it was just me alone on the beach as Macy ran into the water. She stopped, turned and waved for me to follow her in, but the sky had turned dark as the wind picked up. Thunder was echoing all around me. I turned away from the lake and ran in the opposite direction into the forest. That's when I heard the scream again. I had heard that scream once before.

I jolted up in the bed I had been sleeping in, the room looked the same as when I fell asleep, and the sun was already up. I looked at the clock and it said eight am. I groaned and flopped back on the bed, as the dream lingered in my mind. I had to have the answer about what had happened to Macy the night I was brought here. I jumped up and took a shower. I felt so dirty. I finally got dressed in a pair of dark blue jeans and a large shirt that hung off one shoulder. I walked to the door, but it was locked, of course. I should have figured that so I walked over to the night stand and started searching through the songs in the iPod. I guess this will get their attention. It worked last time. I wanted answers and I wanted my answers now.

I found a song by Kmfdm called Mini Mini Mini. Note: I have no idea what the song is saying I just really like the music. It seemed to portray the feelings I was having right now. I turned up the volume to high and before I pushed play, I opened the balcony doors for extra effect. The music started playing and it was almost too loud for me, so I decided to go hang out on the balcony. I noticed I was never going to be an escape via the balcony. This room was on the third floor, way to high to jump from. I could see a large pool and a basketball court, which had a large canopy over the top from here. I heard the music be turned off. I decided to ignore whoever had come in and pretended to be really interested in the grounds.

"Well, looks like someone is awake and in need of my attention." Luke said, in a voice sounding like he was amused. Which of course, made me angry.

"Don't you know it is rude to walk into someone's room without permission? Ever heard of knocking?" I turned to look at him briefly, to see where he was and if my theory was correct.

"It is my house, I do not have to knock if I do not

want to. You are my guest, which means you have no rights unless I give them to you." I wasn't looking at him, but I could tell he was not coming closer to me.

"Once again, I don't want to be your guest, so you can let me go home now, right?" I was mocking him again. I was leaning against the railing, looking back into the room.

"Annie, do you have short-term memory problem?"

"What? No, I do not."

"Then you already know the answer to that question, and I'm not in the mood to play games with you today." I noticed he looked tired, and his hair was not perfectly styled as usual. He was actually very unkempt looking, I noted.

"Then why not let me go so you don't have to play this game today."

"Annie why don't you come inside, my mother will be here soon." I smiled inwardly because this was the moment I was waiting for.

"Why don't you make me?" His face became stone. He looked at me.

"Annie, come inside, now!" He was angry. I smiled a big smile as he stood at the edge of the light which showing through the window.

"Why? I really enjoy it out here. Its nice and warm in the sun." I smiled. "Why don't you come out here and join me?" I said in a sweet innocent voice. I noticed his hands ball into fists.

"As you very well know, by the smirk on your face, I cannot go out and into the sun."

"So the big bad Vampire Prince..." I mocked, making air quotations, "can't come out into the sun? Isn't that a shame." I realized this was the first time I laughed for real since I became a prisoner.

"No I cannot. I was born a vampire, and never had human blood in my veins, which would enable me to go into direct sunlight. I can see you are pretty happy about that. Now, will you stop acting like a child, and come back inside?"

"Why, so you can attack me and invade my personal space some more?" I crossed my arms, and put my best smug face. "Nope, don't think I will."

I started to turn around to walk further away, when I felt a cold hand wrap around the back of my neck as I was pushed back into the room.

"Oh, I forgot to mention, your brother can go into the sun." I turned my head and saw Max looking at me all disappointed like. They were treating me like small child. I felt almost guilty until I remembered everything they had done to me. "You see, Annie, your brother was born a human, meaning he has still human blood in his veins and can still handle the sun." He looked so smug. "Eventually, the blood will fade and his length in the sun will be restricted." Max closed the balcony doors and walked back over to where Luke was standing.

"I have a question," I said.

"You're not going home, Annie."

"That wasn't my question, you asshole!"

"That usually is your question. And do not call me names, either, unless you want a repeat of yesterday." I flipped him off.

"What happened to Macy that night in the woods?" I demanded. "I heard her scream, and I want to know what you did to her. Did you kill her or just hurt her for helping me try to get away from you?" Max said something to Luke, but it was so low that it was not audible to me. Stupid vampires!

"Annie, Macy is fine. She was not hurt." I didn't believe him.

"If she was fine then, why did she scream? People usually don't scream like that unless something is really wrong."

"She is fine. I didn't hurt her anymore then Luke hurt you. Just leave it alone Annie." Max spoke up sounding little ticked off.

"So you did hurt her, how bad?"

"She is not hurt, Annie!" He ran his hand through his hair. "She is perfectly fine and happy."

"You're lying!" I yelled at him, standing up. "If she was fine, then she would not be happy with what you all did to me. She would be out there trying to find me and bring me back."

I was so angry I stormed past them and tried the door again, but it was still locked as I screamed in frustration. I didn't want to be in the same room as them, so I stormed into the bathroom and locked the door. I started pacing in the bathroom. They must think I was pretty stupid to actually believe their crap. I would rather the news be bad then to be lied to. That is just something I cannot stand. I heard a knock at the bathroom door and my anger flared once more. Why couldn't they just leave me alone?

"Annie, its Krista, are you in there?" I rolled my

eyes, and thought about how Luke was a stupid mama/s boy. "Annie, we have a meeting to attend, with Victor. He is the royal dress maker and we need to get you fitted." I stopped mid pace and opened the door to see Krista standing there alone, no Luke or Max in site. "Who are you looking for sweetie?" She looked behind her at the empty room.

"Oh nothing I just thought... it's not important."

"Okay then," her face brightened as she smiled at me. "We have to go or we'll be late, and the first rule you need to know, we must never be late." She grabbed my hand and dragged me out to the main door. Finally, I thought, I was getting out of my prison cell. I was finally going to be able to make an first attempt to run, and get back to Joel and Macy!

NOT HERE TO TAKE YOU HOME

As Krista dragged me into the hall, I was shocked at the sheer beauty that surrounded me. Everything was so wonderfully styled and perfect looking. Small chandeliers hung evenly spaced and were so shiny and pretty. I really like shiny things. I've been told I have the attention span of a cat around shiny objects. Large arched windows were in-between the four doors I counted that include mine, as Krista came to a stop at a grand staircase and pointed to a set of double doors across from the hallway we came out of.

"That is Jace's and my bedroom, and it will be yours when I pass my crown to you." My attention focused on her as anger filled my broken heart. "Oh don't give me that look, I know you do not want it, I just have to say it for listening ears." I noticed two men behind me that were dressed in black. Their hair was military, so short hair they almost looked bald. They were very tall and ridiculously muscle bound.

"Who are they?" I blurted out as I looked back at Krista.

"Those are... uhhhh..." she looked around biting on her lip "Oh they are bodyguards, yep bodyguards." She smiled at me like she had just won the lottery or something.

"Bodyguards, for what?" I asked, as her smile fell off her face.

"Uhhhh...." She grabbed my hand and started dragging me down the stairway. "For protection, that's what they do, silly." She was walking fast and I almost had to run.

"I'm pretty sure you're not telling me the truth." She stopped at that statement and turned fast as the grip on my wrist became tight.

"Are you calling me a liar? I'm the Queen, how dare you?" I was pretty scared of Luke, but the way she looked at me at that moment made me shaky, and I would really rather have Luke here and mad than her.

"I ... I ahhhh... I'm...s- so-sorry," I choked out as she glared at me, making me want to hide behind the guards.

She just turned and continued walking down a hallway that looked the same as the one before. She didn't talk the rest of the way through the many halls until we stopped in front of a double-wide door. She glanced toward me as we walked in. I heard a someone squeal as I grudgingly stepped into the room. The room was all pale, light and glamorous. There was a platform with three-way mirror next to an open doorway with a curtain hanging from it. A A young, effeminate looking man came bouncing out of another inside door with a big smile on his face.

Krista met him half way and they hugged each other. The man turned to look at me. A big smile spread across his face, as he started bouncing over to me. Of course, I instantly took a step back.

"Honey, I'm not going to hurt you!" he stopped a few feet away and looked shocked. Krista was next to him.

"I am afraid I frightened her on the way down, she's usually a little spit fire." He looked at her and grinned.

"Oh darling," he said darling very drawn out, I believe due to his very thick southern accent. "I know. Personally, I think anybody that's been here for the last 24 hours, knows about that." They both started laughing as their attention turned back to me.

"Annie, this Victor. He is the royal dress maker." He stretched his hand out and I hesitantly gave over my hand to shake his.

"Hello, it is very lovely to meet you, finally!" He looked at Krista. "After all, it's been a decade," Victor said. "Ten years since I heard you were coming. I'm so excited to finally put a beautiful face to such an interesting tempered person." They both started laughing again, as if what he said was funny. .

"I don't understand" They both just confused the crap out of me. Finally, Krista spoke up.

"Well, Annie, vampires have very good hearing and we try to not listen to you and Luke..." She paused, seemingly weighing her words. "Well the arguments you two have are turning into a form of entertainment for everyone on the estate." I was so mortified.

"What!" I gasped..

"Annie, it is not what you think. I explained it all wrong." She said, apparently regretting her choice of words. "It is more like a game." She smiled, as Victor was somehow behind here like a scared child seeking protection.

"That's any better!" I was seething.

"Yeah, it really just sounds bad anyway I try to simplify it." She pressed her lips into a fine line, and I noticed she looked like Luke when she did that.

"Why don't you explain it to me in detail, then?" I really wanted to know.

"Well, you might not like it, but we have a little pool going," she stated calmly.

"A pool? What is this pool for?"

"Well," she said dragged the word out. "Its kind of, a, well, several different pools," I nodded for her to continue. She started to look contrite, like a child that had been caught with her hand in the cookie jar. "Well, the first pool is to see how long you will go before you crack and finally will be with Luke. The second is for who wins the arguments on a daily basis, like you won today. I got three grand out of it. And the third pool we kind of gamble on all of it." She was smiling at me trying to keep me calm and reassure me this was all not malicious, but I wasn't having any of it.

"Does Luke know about this?"

"Oh, no! He would be very angry, and make us stop it. Really, its only for us girls in the castle."

"So you all know he basically almost killed me yesterday, and you all did nothing to stop him?" I was shaking my head in disbelief.

"Annie, Luke's head over heals about you, he would never truly hurt you." At this, I turned toward the door we had entered and I started walking out of the room very angry and on the verge of tears.

I couldn't bear to be in their company anymore. I stepped out the room and was about to walk down the hall to where I could see more stairs heading down. A few steps out the door I felt two set of hands around me as they lifted me up and brought me back to the doorway where Krista was standing. She looked almost disappointed and slightly amused at the same time.

"That is the other thing they are here for," she said, wrinkling her nose.

"What, for being rude and invading my personal space?" I spat at her.

"No, to prevent you from trying to escape." She no longer amused. "It is the only way you can be allowed out of your room."

"What!" I screamed.

"Luke has ordered you must have two body guards and a vampire from the castle with you whenever you are outside your room."

"That's not fair, I don't want to be followed around! He has no right!"

"I would hate it, too. But he does have the right, he is the Prince. You are not very well-behaved and we can't have you trying to escape."

"Can I go back to my room?" I pleaded, very distraught. My only real plan of escape was just lost. I started walking up the staircase. I got more ticked off as I noticed others in the hall moving out of my I didn't really care. I just wanted to go home and forget about this whole messy nightmare.

Next, I hear Luke laughing as he walked out of a door close to me smiling his big, bright smile. I wanted to slap him! He turned, glancing in my direction. His face fell instantly when he saw me. A person carrying a briefcase stepped into the hallway behind him and my heart jumped for joy as I ran toward them. It was Joel's dad. I think his name was David, although I never called him that. He told me a long time ago just to call him 'Pops'.

I ran straight to him and hugged him so tight, I was afraid he would disappear. I didn't want to let go of him. I'm not sure when I started crying, but there were tears running down my face, as he gently patted me on the back to calm me down. When I was finally was able to relax my hold and try to speak to speak to him.

"Pops you came for me!" I said weakly. He was smiling sheepishly. It faded at my words. He looked over to Luke.

"Annie," he said in a low voice. "I'm not here to take you home." confusion and dread washed over me.

"I don't understand! If you're not here for me, then what are you doing here with these monsters?" Luke just looked down, avoiding both of our gazes.

"Annie, I work here, I'm the royal family's accountant." I was horrified.

"WHAT!" I screamed at him.

"Annie calm down, my family has been in their

service for a several of generations now." I started crying again. I turned away from him. "If I had known that you were the Prince's mate, I would have never let your relationship with my son happen. Please understand..."

I really wish I had something to throw at him. "How can you say that? You said I was a part of your family less than a week ago!" I sobbed.

"I know, and I am truly sorry. But the truth is, you will be much happier with Prince Luke. It was meant to be. And Joel will find someone else." He tried to move closer to me, but I backed away.

"How dare you say that, Joel is your son!" I couldn't believe he was saying Joel would find someone else.

"I know, and we are helping him heal and move on." Was he for real? Was I ever going to wake up?

"He would be perfectly happy, if it was not for this jackass who kidnapped me away from him and brought me here with the help of my dead brother." I paused. "But I guess he's not so dead. But you already knew that, didn't you?"

He sighed. "Yes, we knew even before that he was coming here." I looked at him.

"We?" What was he saying?

"We as in my parents, wife," he paused and rubbed forehead. "My children." He was lying.

"Joel?" I couldn't even speak right as so many questions ran through my mind.

"Yes, we were aware of the truth about your brother, but it was best that you didn't know. We were not allowed to share that information with you."

I walked off after he said that. I just wanted to get away from them and the crowd of bystanders who were watching. I heard someone calling after me, but I didn't look back. I just wanted to get to out of this place and cry my eyes out. David had to be lying to me, there no way Joel would ever keep a secret like that from me. They must be trying to trick me. I felt so tired and confused as my legs started to burn from all the stairs I had to climb. But it felt better than the pain my head. I finally got to the top and just wanted and almost collapsed from being overwhelmed by all of the emotional trauma. Once I entered my room, I slammed the door shut behind me. But the bang I expected never came. I turned to see Luke standing in the doorway.

"Get out!" I screamed.

"I just want to make sure you were okay," He came closer to me.

"Get away from me!" Luke stopped, sighing.

"Annie, I know you're really upset, but everything that has happened is for your own good.."

"Leave me alone" I pleaded. I don't understand why you aren't listening to me!"

"I understand just fine, and I am listening."

"Then get out, I hate you and you have made my life a nightmare, I can't stand it when you're around!" He froze and his mouth hung open.

"You... you don't mean that." He looked so sad.

"Yes I do, I hate you, you ruined my life, and I will always hate you!" I could tell he knew I was telling the truth. His face turned to the familiar emotionless mask, and he turned away from me, walked to the door, and opened it. He turned his head slightly and spoke very quietly. "I'll have dinner brought up for you because I'm sure you do not want to eat with me." And with that he was gone. I realized it was only early afternoon, meaning this day was still not even close to being over.

Pearson

TELL ME WHY

Only a couple of hours went by, but it seemed like days. I watched as the sun slowly set. I had cried so much I could not cry anymore. I was devastated beyond what I could ever imagine. I was still not even sure if I should really trust even what Joel's father had said. For all I know he had been paid off by Luke just like my parents were. Mary Bell had brought food for me but I couldn't make myself eat any. After a while I heard my door open, and light flooded into my room that was pretty dark from the dusk settling in. The lights hurt my eyes, so I pulled the comforter over my head, the way I thought vampires are portrayed to behave when exposed to sunlight. The light to the room clicked on. Someone sat on the edge of the bed.

"Annie, I know you're awake, so please you remove the cover from your head," Max said in a quiet voice. I didn't respond to him, willing him to disappear. "You know I can make you if I really wanted to." I still didn't respond as I heard him sigh, and felt the bed move again: okay, but don't say I didn't warn you."

I heard something be put down on the night table by the head of the bed, then the room fell silent. I knew he was still in the room. Did he really thinking I was that dumb to fall for that? I really just wanted to scream at him, but then he would win and that was not going to happen. When I felt cold air by my feet at the end of the bed I knew what was going to happen. The blanket was ripped away from me as I instantly went into the fetal position hiding from the light.

"Annie, come on, get up." He sounded amused.

"No go away." I growled at I tried to hide my head in the mountain of pillows.

"Will you get up if I told you I had a present for you?" I froze, he was using my curiosity against me. After a long period of silence, he almost won.

"What?" I snapped.

I heard him chuckle then felt the bed move he was right next to me as fear of what he would do to me set in. Suddenly, I felt his fingers on my stomach and uncontrollable laughter erupted from my mouth. He was tickling me and there was nothing I could do. I was extremely ticklish and Max remembered this from when we were younger.

"If you come out I'll show you, but there are stipulations that come with the your accepting this present."

"Nope, not going to happen, go away."

I heard his sigh heavily. "I have other ways of making you agree Annie, so come out and have your present, please."

"Max just go away, I'm pretty depressed and you

are not making it any better."

"Please, Annie! Don't you realize what a big mistake you are making? I didn't kill anybody. I swear it! The whole things a setup. A scam, a frame job. Ow! Annie, I could never hurt anybody! Ow My whole purpose in life is to make... people... laugh!" I froze as he spoke the lines from long ago, as if time had stood still and we were still little kids.

I pushed him with all my might away from me as he just sat down on the bed and looked at me with confusion look plastered all over his face. I got up, just wanting him to go away, as he slowly stood up on the other side of the bed. He was watching me, a look of surprise on his face, as I gave him my best death glare. When he spoke again, it was as if he was addressing a dangerous animal or something.

"Annie, do you want your present now, or do you just want to talk first?"

"Why, why did you leave like that? You lied right to my face, Max, why did you do it?" I couldn't even. I was just so exhausted I couldn't get even express myself the way I wanted to since he reappeared.

"Annie, sit down with me and let me explain everything you want to know." He gestured over to the chairs sitting across from each other separated by a coffee table. "I'll also give you your present as well." I walked over to the chairs and slowly sat down, trying not to get to close to him.

"Give me my present, then. Tell me why you did all this to me. And why mom and dad did, too."

He sat down a plate with a big stack of snicker

doodles, and a glass of milk next to them. I immediately had to turn on my highest resistance button. I have a weird love for snicker doodles. I mean they're a lot to love unless you are allergic to cinnamon and that just sucks for you. But even the name, "snicker doodles", makes me smile. But I needed to control myself because I was not going to let him win me over that easily.

"I brought your favorite, to help keep you in a good mood, while I will explain everything that happened." I am pretty sure I gave him my most dramatic eye roll.

"How, do you know I even like snicker doodles anymore?" Max laughed. Loudly.

"Because I know you do, Annie. Your heart rate elevated when you saw them. Plus way you're eying them like a fat kid on a diet. I know you want them. Mary Bell made them. There is nothing wrong with them so eat them, and let me tell my story, please." He gave me the puppy dog eyes and pouted his lips a little. I snatched about four cookies off the plate along with the milk. He smiled at me like he always used to, and I could feel tears stinging my eyes. But I held them back. I could not show how weak I was.

"So explain." I said flatly.

Flash back according to Max:

It was about a month before my 18th birthday, and I was feeling uneasy about the entire thing. Our parents wanted me to go off to college at the end of summer, but I had no idea what I was going to do when I got there if I went. I was a pretty good student and I'm sure I would do fine in college, but it was just I had no idea what I wanted to do with my life.

I was at a park with a few of my friends, just hanging out, messing around, when my friend Alex showed up with guy I didn't recognize. He was with my best friend Jeff's girl, and I knew this was situation could turn into some type of altercation.

"Hey guys, this is Luke. He is new around here. I met him in line at the store." She smiled her "Be nice to him" smile.

Of course, Alex and Jeff got in an argument shortly after that leaving me and Luke on our own. I talked to him for a long time. He seemed really cool. He knew a lot about the music I was in to. You could say we clicked, and we became friends. It was a strange type of friendship. It was like there was a weird pull between us, this urge to hang out with him. I even wondered if I was homosexual and Luke was bringing it out in me.

After about two weeks, of this idea running thought my head, he finally asked what was bothering me. I explained to him how I was feeling, and that I had ever been interested in guys before. He explained that I was most likely not gay but the pull was probably because I was so close to his soul-mate. I was even more confused. It got worse when me told me he was a natural born vampire. I didn't believe him, of course, until he showed me his fangs.

Luke explained to me what soul-mates were and The bond was working through me to get his attention and bring his soul-mate and him together. We arranged for him to come over for a family night dinner, but since you were sick, mom didn't want anybody over. About a week out from my birthday, he asked if I would like to become like he was. A vampire. I was intrigued by this, and I said I would think about it.

As the week passed, but he had some business to attend to and was not around too much, so I was unable to reschedule the dinner with our family. My birthday was here and I was still unsure about what I would choose to do. You were mad at for not inviting you to go out with me. It was so strange you wanted to go out with me so badly. Usually when you wanted to go, if I said no, you were okay with it. But not this night. I almost caved and let you come to meet Luke, but I somehow knew it was not a good idea.

I chose to enter into Luke's world that night, and become a vampire. It was not as easy as I thought it was. I missed my family and friends. It was not what I had expected at all. After a month being in the amazing places Luke and I now lived in, he said we could go back and check on my family and get some personal things. Once we got there, I noticed the house I knew was gone. It seemed so quiet and still. We got to my room and Luke saw a picture of you. He seemed mesmerized as he picked it up.

"That's Annie, my little sister." Luke looked at me, and just handed me the picture and walked out the room.

After I had a bag filled with some pictures and some of my favorite things, I walked out of my room for the last time. I noticed your bedroom door was open. It had been closed when we we first came in so I walked over quietly and saw Luke sitting on the ground by your bed. You were sleeping peacefully. His back was to me and I asked him what he was doing.

"Your sister is my soul-mate" he said, with an voice filled with emotion.

"Luke she's eight, you can't be in a relationship with her." He seemed amused by that.

"It not like that right now. I just feel like a brother to her right now." I felt little ashamed for what had crossed my mind. "When she is older I would be her friend, and our relationship would grow into something more purposeful."

"She is my sister and I will protect her."

"I know. You must know, I will never, ever hurt her, all I want to do is love and protect her, too."

"Okay, but we got to go before someone wakes up." I stated truthfully. Luke sighed.

"Maybe we should stay and have you not be a missing person anymore."

"Luke, there would be too many questions," I said, after careful consideration. I don't want to put you and your family at risk."

"But I want to be around her." He looked so sad.

"I do too, but I've already hurt her and my mom and dad enough. I don't want to hurt them more."

"Your right, it is best to stay away." Luke decided, recognizing the truth in what I said.

As I finished telling Annie what happened, she was crying again. I had ripped open the would I had inflicted by my leaving 10 years ago. I walked over to her and hugged her. She hugged me back.

"I'm so sorry Annie; I never wanted to hurt you."

"But you did. And you have hurt me even worse when you forced me to leave my home and to leave Joel like this," she said, barely able to speak.

"I know you loved Joel, but I promise, if you give Luke a chance, you will understand why we did what we had to do." Annie pushed me away.

"He is your mate and when you accept this, you'll see." I tried to explain. "I know how it feels. I have felt the bond with my mate. It's so wonderful, I can't even describe it to you." She looked at me confused.

"You have a mate?" I froze. Crap, she was not supposed to know about that yet.

DANCE LESSONS

"You have a mate?" I demanded. Max looked petrified of me. Really?

"I'm so sorry Annie; I never meant to hurt you." He tried hugging me again, and I wanted to hug back so much. But no, I pushed him away.

"I know you think you love Joel," he continued. "But Luke truly is your mate and when you accept that, you will not feel the hurt anymore."

"You have a mate?" I repeated. He looked away, like he was all guilty. He stood up and walked away from me.

"Annie..." he paused "I do have a mate." He said, almost in defeat.

"When were you going to tell me?" He ran his hand through his hair. "Were you ever going to tell me?"

"I was going to tell you when the time was right, but there has not been a good time. This really isn't a good time."

"It is for me. I'm here now and waiting, so spill." Max shook his head.

"Trust me, now is not the time to talk about my

mate with you." he walked to the door.

"Max, stop! I'm not done talking to you!" I yelled. "You owe me that much. Please talk to me after everything you have done." He looked back at me, his eyes filled with remorse. I was surprised.

"You're angry, Annie. There is no point talking to you. You won't understand right now." He opened the door..

"No, you don't get to just run away again!" I felt so lost and empty, like when I was a child. "You have ruined my life twice now and all you have to say is that you're not going to talk to me?" I pleaded. and he wouldn't even look me in the eyes. "You have no idea what it was like after you left to go play vampire. Mom wouldn't even talk to me or anybody in the beginning. She said I reminded her too much of you." I started to cry. "She destroyed every picture that you were in, including all of my baby photos because she didn't want the reminder that her perfect son, her golden child was gone and probably dead."

"Annie I'm sorry, I didn't mean for any of that to happen." He came back and tried to wrap me in a familiar bear hug. Again, I could only push him away.

"Of course you didn't mean for any of that to happen. You were self-centered. You only cared about yourself and what you wanted. I turned away, pulling the comforter of the ground.

"I'm so sorry Annie." He was giving up. I heard the door open and close. I turned the light off he had turned on. I wanted to be in the dark.

I decided all I wanted to do was sleep. Today had been an awful continuation of the horror that had become my life. I was tired of dealing with these stupid vampires. They were all emotionally unstable and so self-centered. They all needed to go to anger management. They need to stay out of other people lives. At the same time, I had to consider the probability that I had lost my mind. How could vampires be real? How was my brother still alive, and a vampire? I was not sure when I fell asleep, I just remember waking up into another day of the nightmare, still filled with anger and mourning for my lost life I was missing so much.

I took a long hot shower, trying to wash away the pain. When I finally got dressed, I made my way over to the i Home and searched for a song to tick off my bastard of a brother and his best buddy the cry baby mama's boy Prince Luke. I laughed to myself at the thought of why they have not taken this away from me yet. I thought vampires were supposed to be smart? Not so smart! I guess the movies got that one wrong because these vampires are seriously dumb.

The song I selected was Still Counting by Volbeat, mainly because I the words described these two douche bags perfectly. I hit play and lay on my bed and waited to see who would show up to start yelling at me first. As I lay there, very comfortable on my bed, nobody came barging in to turn it off. I propped myself up off the bed as I realized they weren't coming if they hadn't by this time. Maybe they figured out they are never going to win this war with me.

The song finished and another started to play, but I shut it off and walked over to the door and tried to open it. Still locked, of course. Briefly, I considered what would happen to me if there was a fire. I would be trapped. I walked out onto the balcony annoyed that they never even showed up. But I was also relieved that they were not bothering me, either alone.

I heard a knock at the door. I yelled to whoever it was to come in. It was just Mary Bell and she had a tray of food in her hands. I went over to her. It smelled really good and it hard to hate people when the food was just so yummy.

"I brought your breakfast and your itinerary for the day."

I had a mouth full of pancakes as she handed me a paper. I wiped my hands and read the following:

Eight: breakfast
Nine to twelve: dance lesson
Twelve: Lunch
Two: Final dress fitting
Six: dinner

Right, I thought sarcastically. I saw Mary Bell go in and come out of my closet carrying a pair of heels. She sat them down next to me. I stared at her. She looked at me. I could tell she did not approve of my attitude.

"The shoes are for your lesson," she said. "You need to learn to dance in them. You need to start practicing. It is a bit difficult."

"I don't want dance lessons. Why do I need to take them?

"For the Ball, Annie. You were being fitted for a ball gown, so of course you know about it." She said the word "Ball" kind of slow as if she didn't think I understood.

"It might have been mentioned, ones or twice," she sighed.

"The Prince will be here a little before nine to take you to your lesson."

"Oh yippee, just what I have always wanted. I get to be personally escorted everywhere by an asshole.

I heard her chuckle slightly as she walked out the door. I ate what I could of the breakfast she brought me. I ate slowly so I would be late and irritate Luke when he came to get me. I so wanted to wipe that ever present smirk off of his face. The door opened, and I knew it was him because he never knocked. My privacy meant nothing to him.

"We have dances lessons. We need to get to." he announced, rather coldly.

"Well, I'm not done eating so you will have to wait." I said, taking another bite and ignoring him.

I felt his hand wrap around my arm pulling me up from where I sat. I stumbled to get my bearings. He wasted no time ushering me out the door. I was astonished to see two guards standing there, all stoney faced. I yanked my arm away from his grasp and turned back toward the bedroom door, but he held on tight.

"We have to go, and I'm not in the mood for your

little hissy fits."

"I need to get my shoes, Mary said I needed to wear them." He reluctantly released me. "You could have just said that." I walked back into the room, grabbed the shoes and walked back to the door where they stood waiting and watching me.

"Never asked." I said this and felt superior. I walked out into the hall and past them, ignoring them as much as possible.

He quickly caught up to me and walked slightly ahead of me, which ticked me off. Although I had no idea where I was going for these dumb dance lessons I didn't want didn't need, I was forced by my mother to take dance classes after Max had left. I was already a pro at stupid ballroom dancing. These vampires were just so dumb!

I gasped as we reached a gorgeous ballroom. It looked like a page right out of Beauty and the Beast, only even more elaborate, if possible. I heard a chuckle come from behind me. Luke was such an asshole! What did he think was funny? My reaction?

"Annie this is Josh, he will be teaching you to dance, so you can be ready for the ball." Right.

"It's a pleasure to meet you." Josh offered me his hand. I took it. After all, it was not his fault I was forced to come here. "So, let's start. Luke, hold onto her and Annie, place one arm like so..." Luke took a step closer to me, but I was not going to have him touching me.

"I'm not dancing with him. I don't need dance lessons, I already know how to ballroom dance." I stated this as arrogantly as possible, just to make sure Prince Luke looked like the fool he was. Luke scowled and Josh just looked confused.

"Fine! I don't have time for this anyway," Luke growled. Josh, please make sure she is telling the truth, and knows how to dance, then have the guards take her back to room." And then he was gone.

With that, Josh just grabbed onto me with very shocked expression.

We started to dance for a few seconds, and he sighed audibly. I looked at him. He widened the gap between us. Normally the dancers bodies would be touching or almost touching. It looked like we were touching as we spun around a few times. We almost appeared to be dancing in a classical style due to the space between us. The look on his face when he bothered to look at me revealed he was angry with me. Finally, my curiosity got the best of me.

"What's with the face, am I dancing incorrectly?" His eyes met mine. They were cold

"No you're dancing is fine," he said, then looked away.

"Then what's up with the way you are acting, then?" We stopped dancing and he let go of me a bit roughly.

"Why did you behave that way toward the Prince? It was unseemly and uncalled for."

"Because he is a rude, argumentative jerk that has no respect for other people's feelings." Josh looked at me like I had just grown another head.

"Wow, you have been here for what, four days? You know nothing about him," he said, shaking his head again. "I have never, in my entire life heard somebody say that about him."

"Well obviously you don't know him very well because he has ruined my life and doesn't even care." I started to walk away toward the door.

"Excuse me, I was around before he was even born. I think I know him very well," he said, stepping in front of me. "Maybe if you stopped thinking the world revolved around you, you would have noticed his face after you so rudely and arrogantly refused to dance with your mate."

"His face? I'm pretty sure you could see his anger toward me. I laughed. "I'm sure I'll punished for that later." I crossed my arms and glared at him.

"Wow, I heard you were a bit of a brat, but I was hoping they were mistaken."

"Oh yeah, is that what do you think I am?" I said as sarcastically as I could.

"I think you're a bitch and nothing more." I didn't respond because he walked out of the room. At the doors, he turned and started for the stairs. He stopped, then turned back to me. "Oh, and for your information, his face was that of a man who would have traded the world just to be able to dance with you. But honestly, I don't think you are good enough to have the Prince for your mate. He deserves so much better than a spoiled little bitch."

With that, he left me in the empty ballroom, somehow feeling like I was the one in the wrong. In a way, he was right about my behavior, but he was also wrong about why I was behaving this way. I saw the guards move in close. They never even looked at me although I know they must have heard everything. They accompanied me back to my room. I closed the door quickly. I just wanted to be left alone.

Pearson

THE BALL

I was kind of guilty about my behavior in front of Josh. Of course he didn't understand, how could he? I was being held against my will. I was forced me to come here. His precious "Prince" had ruined my life. Of course I am acting a little bitter in light of everything that had transpired over the past few days. I was suffering loss, depression and shock.

Mary Bell appeared in front of me and motioned for me to follow. Once again I ventured out of my room, the guards following.

We stopped when we reached an amazing dining room, with a table that could easily seat about 20 people. At the head stood Luke and his father, King Jace. Queen Krista Krista came in at the same time as me through a different door. Mary slightly pushed me forward and I went to the opposite side as Krista did. The lunch was awkward. Krista talked a lot and everyone else just responded when spoken too. Luke did not speak to me, which was nice for a change. Still, I felt bad at the thought that I might have actually hurt his feelings. I went to the fitting with Krista after we finished. The dress was very beautiful and it fit like a glove although Josh never actually took any measurements from me.

I went back to my room and went to bed, exhausted from the day's events. I felt as if I were sinking into a depression and I just didn't have the strength to climb out of it. I forgot about the dinner I was to attend that night, but nobody woke me up so I assumed it was not that big of a deal. I was awakened in the morning, surrounded by a group of people and it freaked me out

"Annie, we have to get you ready for the ball, so get up and take a shower." Mary Bell insisted. I unwillingly got up and jumped in the shower.

Once I got out and put a towel around me, the bathroom door burst open and I was surrounded by people dressing, brushing and generally fixing me up. This seemed to go on for hours. My hair was pulled and twisted in every direction, as my face was poked and prodded with make-up and creams. Two of them were doing my hands and feet, as one hand fed me. This kept getting me in trouble with the the make-up people about having to redo my lips. It was entertaining for a while, but I was getting really tired of sitting in this chair for so long. Not to mention, I was not allowed to look at what they were doing to me. For all I knew, they were making me into a clown. I really hate clowns, they're just so creepy. Eventually they made me stand as they slipped on the dress and they all just stood there looking at me with big goofy grins. I knew it, they had made me look like a clown.

"What?" I said, more than a little annoyed. "Do I

look that bad? I swear if I look like an evil clown, heads will roll!" They all laughed and moved out of the way of the mirror.

"Annie, you look like a true Princess!" Mary Bell said. I was speechless at what I saw. I could not believe it was me. I looked pretty damn good!

"Mary! Of course she looks like a Princess, she is a Princess!" Some of the crowd were laughing as I just sat their unable to look away from what they had done to me.

My hair was up, but had lots curls hanging all around my face framing it perfectly. My make-up was flawless, yet it looked very natural. The dress was a beautiful light blue color that brought out the blue in my eyes and almost made them look like they were sparkling. They were right. I looked like a Princess, but I certainly didn't feel like I one. I know every little girl wants to be one and I am sure I did once upon a time, but then I grew up and it wasn't what I wanted.

I was brought out of my thoughts by the sound of the giggling but it was cut short by a knock on the door, which seemed to echo throughout the room. Mary Bell took my hand and pulled me to the door. My stomach did a flip-flop as realized I was going to a ball in my honor. I really just didn't want this kind of attention.

When Mary Bell opened the door, Luke stood with his back to us. He slowly turned around, and I know my mouth almost fell to the ground. He wore a suit that looked right out of Cinderella. He was Prince Charming. His usually messy hair was combed and styled very neatly, all slicked back and I just wanted to mess it up. Somehow, it looked wrong on him. He held out his hand to me. I glanced at Mary Bell, who nodded to me and I placed my hand in his. I felt this fire rush through me, then I was filled with anger at him for making me feel like this. For keeping me a prisoner here. He guided me to the stairway and we started descending down the stairs toward the sound of soft music and people talking

"Annie I need you to do me this small favor," he said, not looking at me, but was looking straight ahead.

"What?" I answered, after a few moments of silence.

"Can you please just pretend that you are actually happy and you want to be here?" He asked quietly, still looking away, as we came to a stop in front of a huge curtain.

"Why? I don't really like lying to people." He sighed, letting go of my hand. The fire sensation went away.

"Annie, please, I just cannot deal with it tonight," his voice cracked and I felt the guilt again. "I need you to just play along for just tonight, please?" I did not respond verbally, but nodded my head. Suddenly, I heard a trumpet. Our names were announced by an unseen voice and the curtains parted revealing us to a large crowd in a massive Ballroom. We were standing at the top of the most elegant staircase I had ever seen.

"Smile as we descend. I will lead you to the

center of the floor. We dance, then everyone will introduce themselves to you," he murmured to me. I was overwhelmed.

We walked down slowly as everyone watched. I felt like bolting right back up the stairs and hiding in my room. We finally made into the bottom. Of course, we were in the center attention in the room and Luke and I started to spin around in an elegant style. He was a great dance. I looked at Luke, but he was not really looking at me. Once the tune ended, everyone applauded us, and people surrounded us, all talking at once. I smiled and responded perfectly to people, but I just wanted to escape. I felt like a puppet. As if he could read my mind, Luke whispered in my ear:

"We will be able to leave soon, after we talk to the oldest of our kind." He ushered us up to an older looking lady who sat alone and seemed very melancholy.

"My lady, this is my mate, Annie," I smiled at her and she looked up at us, smiling back.

"I give this union my blessing," she said, as if her mind was somewhere else. She looked away. Luke and I proceeded to the stairs, to make our exit, I hoped.

"What is with that lady, she seems so sad," I blurted out, curiosity getting the better of me, as we started up the stairs

"Because she is." He replied in a flat tone.

"Why?" I looked at him. He refused to look at me and just shook his head.

"She lost her mate a long time ago. She is the

only vampire to ever survive losing a mate."

I decided not to press the conversation anymore because he looked so deep in thought. Besides, I was exhausted from the preparations for this Ball. We got to my door as Luke stopped and I turned to look at him, but he just looked off down the hall, avoiding eye contact with me once again.

"Thanks for not acting normal tonight." he said simply.

"It wasn't that bad beside these damn heels. Everyone was really nice." I said, at the same time, wondering why I was being so nice. Was I giving up?

"I'm glad you enjoyed yourself." With that, he pushed open my door and walked away. Leaving me with the Guards, of course.

I went inside, closed the door, and jumped into the shower. I let my hair down, and scrubbed my face clean. I put on some comfy jammiest, lay down and drifted off to sleep. I dreamed of the Ball as I danced around the room in Joel's arms. He looked so happy and I felt happy, too. It felt right, but he suddenly stopped and looked sad as he let me go. I tried to stop him, but he just shook his head, kissed my forehead, and was gone. It felt so real it shocked me from my sleep. I could still feel Joel's lips on my forehead. It was very late and all was silent and still. I fell back to sleep, but it wasn't peaceful.

WHAT ARE YOU DOING

After a night a restless sleep, all you want to do is sleep in late and be lazy all day. Will that's at least what I want to do, but that would be too much to ask in the ridicules vampire mansion. I was rudely awakened by the sound of male laughter and a booming noise. It all seemed to fade away. Finally, when it was perfectly silent again the laughter came back and the booming noises it was a basketball hitting moment. I opened my eyes and notices all my windows open, I cursed whoever opened them up. I got up to yell at whomever was outside and close them so I could go back to sleep.

I look outside to a lot of boys around my age, or at least looked my age for all I know they could be older the 7th great grandfather. I was really starting to think vampire is basically just pedophiles that never die. They were all standing on the basketball court as they divided into teams. I got angry, they're all off having fun playing their game and I'm locked in a room bored in a really awesome bed. I stood there glaring at them though it was kind of hard because there was a big canopy over the court. It was see thru, but cast a shade over the entire court. Then, my mind caught up in my thoughts, born vampires could not go into direct sunlight.

I got really angry that I am stuck in this stupid room, maybe I wanted to play some basketball, and they never asked me. I would not have played, but it would be nice to get outside and fresh air maybe chances to escape when they weren't paying attention. I was standing there imagining an escape plan while outside and I was kind of failing at because I didn't really know where I was, but something sparkly caught my eye. It was a pool on the other side of the court. Now that would be something I could enjoy. I walked over to my door and banged on it and yelled out.

"I want to leave this room" I yelled out, I knew there was guards out there and at least they could call for someone.

I walked away from the door and went into the closet and went to the section that I had seen a few days ago. I grabbed and wrapped my hand around a little yellow bikini, it didn't have poke dots which would have made it even better. I chose the yellow because it complimented my skin tone really well, and I felt made my eyes pop a little. I heard the door open and Mary called out to me as I was changing into the swimsuit and slipping my feet into another pair of heels.

"Annie?" she sounded confused

"I'm in the bathroom changing"

"I know where you are, I wanted to ask if what I

heard was correct?" I walked out with a magazine in one hand and a big pair of sun-glasses in the other

"That depended on what you heard?" she looked at me with a smirk on her face

"You are requesting to leave your room, am I correct" she said as I walked over to the night stand and grabbed my iPod

"Yes, scenes those rude boys out there woke me" I pointed to the boys that were playing their silly game

"Annie you know you can't leave the room unless escorted at all times" I rolled my eye

"I know that," I said a little overly sarcastically "that's why I have you and the guards" I gave her a duh look

"Annie I'm not allowed to escort you, I work in the places, I'm not high-ranking to do that" okay small set back

"Well I want to go swimming and lay out" I pointed to the sound of laughter that floated in from outside "And I see my brother and Luke along with Josh out there and they're all high-ranking are they not" she looked at me biting her lip and was watching me crisply

"Yes they are and what is your point?"

"The pool next to them and I'll have the guards" I gave her a small innocent smile

"Annie I still do not have authority to take you out of the room" she looked down at the ground "if I was to break the rules and you ran or got hurt they would kill me, and I really like my life and don't want to die" I sighed and puppy dog eyes her

"It's not fair I want to go swimming and I promise

not to run" evil grin in my mind I would run at any chance

"Annie I can't I'm sorry" she said as she started to walk away

"Could you ask Krista, or someone who is high-ranking, to just escorted me to the backyard, then they're free"

"Annie people are really busy and" I cut her off

"Please Mary, it can't hurt to just ask, maybe Krista would help find someone to take me out" she shakes her head

"Let me go talk to the queen and I'll see what she thinks of the idea, but you need to understand if she says no, then that is the last word, understand?" I shook my head in agreement "I would not get your hopes up, your behavior was not good over the last few days, but the only thing that could get you a pass outside is how well you did at the ball which was remarkable by the way.

With that she walked out and I lay on my bed listening to the sound of a basketball hitting the cement and by shouting and laughter. I was getting nervous that both torment plans was not going to work and I would not beagle to get the feel of the land to a future attempt to escape this hell. Okay it really wasn't hell and I am being a little on the dramatic side, but Luke is a demon and that I will not change on. I laid looking up at the coffer-Ed ceiling.

After a long period, of me just looking at the ceiling and counting how many squares were in the room. I counted 52 squares in the room that were overly decorative and served no purpose except for me to lay here and count them. That's how bored I was, just sitting in this room waiting to see if I am allowed out. I heard the door open and did my super awesome ninja roll off the bed so I was Standing for whom ever walked in. It was Mary and she didn't look very happy as she walked back into the room.

"Annie, the queen said you can go out to the pool and I'm allowed to go with you this time, but..." she looked at me very intently "if you try to escape or anything in that nature it is my head on the line."

"Mary I'm not trying to escape I just want to go outside, I need to get out of this room and do something of my choice" she watches me suspiciously

"Annie, so help if you're lying to me after I put myself on the line" she looked very serious

"I will not run, you're my only friend here so I would rather not piss you off" she sighed and nodded her head

"Okay then let's go, I'll show you the way"

I started jumping up and down because I was so happy, I had not been outside besides on a balance in what feels like forever. I followed Mary down many stairs, and got a few stares from other people walking in the hall or in other rooms or offices. When we finally got to the back doors Mary looked little sad and angry at the same time.

"Lady Annie, you forgot a towel in the room" she looked back to the stairway

"No I didn't, I'm not really in the mood to swim, I just want to lay out and soak up some sun" she looked at me subspecies

"Very well, I will be here when you come back inside" she started to walk away

"You're not coming out with me?"

"No I have other jobs to tend to"

I walked out the door and headed down the steps which was hard to do with these stupid heal. I mean heals are great for two reasons only, first making your legs look good, second there so pretty and we have to collect as many as possible to match every outfit. I have a small addiction to shoes, but heals are the horrible invention to my feet they hurt and I tend to fall a lot in them. So walking down a stone stairway to get to the basketball court then the pool was a little nerve racking.

I finally got close to the basketball court where all the boys wired playing and they all slowly at some point stopped to watch me walk by to get to the pool. I just kept thinking to myself not to fall at this moment. I was trying to distract and put Luke through a bit of torture, but falling flat on my face would not help. I made it to the pool with a no problem though, so I was internally pleased. I heard a few cat calls and witless thought in my direction that always end in a growling noise of what sounded like someone getting punched.

After I sat down in my chair, my plan started to fail as the boys went back to playing their game. Their game was ridiculed trying to watch because they moved too fast to even keep track of. Once second they were passing at one end the next some were dunking at the opiate end. It needed taped and played in slow motion for me to understand what was going on. I gave up and was basically ignored, while they were playing. So I decide to give them a little show, and no striping or anything like that I'm not a whore I have a boyfriend remember.

I grabbed the bottle of lotion that I had brought out with me and popped in my ear buds to listen to music. I decide to put the lotion on in an overly dramas way that I know would at least get a couple of their attention. At first I decide not to glance over to make it look like I did not even care that they were there. I heard the basketball more often bounces than it had been before as I rubbed the block into my legs making them shiny, then they really are. I glanced under my eyelashes and almost cracked up laughing at Luke and Max looked madder than a hornet, as the other just oiled me. I win as a small smirk came to my face.

"What do you think you're doing?" I had not even heard his approach

"What does it look like" I didn't even look at him and continued rubbing the lotion into my skin

"It looks like you're trying to get everyone's attention" I knew he was smirking and I just wanted to chuck the bottle at him, but I didn't I just scoffed at him

"As if, I don't want to get a sun burn" a few of the guys jumped into the pool as the other slowly came walking over.

"You under a canopy Annie, you're not going to get that sunburn" dame I forgot that part, but I got a rebuttal for him

"I can still burn, just as you can burn on a cloudy day" I smirked back at him and he just seemed to debate what I said.

"Who said you could come outside anyway, I don't remember giving you permission" I wanted to punch him so bad

"Your mother said it was fine, scenes you were playing, so could I" some of the guys were watching us and smirked in laugh as we continued our glare down.

He broke first and I had won again in one day it a great feeling and you should all try it. But then he took off his shirt and I froze, dame these vampires in their sexy body. Dame my teenage girl hormones, he did that on purpose because I bested him. He had muscles everywhere and they were glistening with sweat, gross, but so hot at the same time

"Your right I don't want to burn, he grabbed the lotion out of my frozen hands and starts rubbing it in, I'll say it again dame vampire "I don't want a tan line from the shirt even is better don't you think?" as I glared at his yummy body and smirked back at the gloating Luke

"Yeah, I normally tan naked, so I don't get tan lines, Joel thinks it's the hottest thing" I smirked at him "but you pervert would like that too much" All of a sudden I was lifted off of the bench I lay on and saw Luke caring me closer to the pool.

"What are you doing put me down!" I screamed and tried to get out of his grasped

"I will, I just think you need a cool off" I heard others laugh as I was falling into the ice-cold pool.

I resurfaced freezing and beyond words pissed off, as Max and Luke laugh there buts off outside the pool, the other guys laugh as well I even saw my guard chuckling. Oh, mark my words they were going to pay for this.

Pearson

A PARTY

This was the coldest pool I had ever been in, plus Luke tossed me in with the stupid high heels still on. I was humiliated. When I finally got to an area I could stand and try to climb out, some guy blocked my path, still laughing at me. He was taller than me in my heels, but still slightly shorter than Luke. He had a perfect muscular body like Luke. He had blond hair with gray eyes that looked almost a freaky white at first glance.

"Hi Annie, my name is Bobby," he said, taking my my hand and kissing the back of it. I heard a low light growl from behind me. I was getting used to growling.

"Hello Bobby, it's nice to meet you," I smiled, a big flirty smile, because I knew Luke was watching.

"I do apologize for my immature friends here," he stepped a little closer to me and I had the feeling that I really needed to step away from him, but didn't want to show how uncomfortable I was.

"It's okay" I managed to squeak out. He was only a foot in front of me. I felt almost scared.

"Bobby! Leave her alone!" I heard Luke say in a

very loud, deep voice. Bobby automatically shrank away from me, a sheepish grin on his face.

"Oh relax, Luke, I was just playing." Hearing his words I wanted to run far away, but didn't want to show my fear so I started walking again calmly.

"Hey Annie, are you coming to the party tonight?" I froze as I looked over to where Bobby was sitting on the edge of the pool, having an intense stare down with Luke.

"She is not going!" Luke said, before I could even think about responding.

"I was unaware of any party, but I would like to go." I smiled my most flirtatious smile at Bobby. At this, he finally broke eye contact with Luke and gave me a wink.

"Good, your presence would make the party that much more fun," Bobby said, kind of gloating. He turned back to face Luke. "I know a lot of the other guys and their mates are dying to meet you. Undoubtedly, you will be the life of the party." I was about to respond when Luke interrupted me.

"She is not going, Bobby." I climbed out of the pool.

Luke! I was so angry with him.

"You're not going to the party Annie." He was obviously infuriated, too. I flipped him off.

"I am going, and there nothing you can about it."

"Oh, I think there is."

"Then I'll just ask your mother for permission." I heard all they guys crack up laughing at this. He just stood there in silence as I grabbed my stuff and headed toward the mansion.

I didn't get any type of come back after I threatened him with his mother. I finally knew how to get an upper hand. Luke was a mama's boy, and whatever she said would make him yield. As I walked into the back door Mary and Krista stood there talking, but stopped when they saw me and just gawked at me like I was a headless chicken. Mary turned and grabbed a towel out of a cupboard and came over and took my stuff as I wrapped a towel around myself.

"Annie, I thought you said you were not going swimming and were just going to lay out."

"I was not intending to go in the water, but Luke had other ideas," I said, as Krista came closer to me.

"What did my son do?"

"He threw me into the pool because I was distracting his friends." They were trying to hide their amusement. "He got mad when I said I was going to his stupid party."

"He's going to the party. Luke lied to me," his mother complained. Now it was my turn to hold in my laughter because I'm pretty sure I just got him in trouble. "Annie, don't worry, you will be going with him to that 'party' of his." She took off, and Mary and I went back to my room.

I decided that I was going to take a nice, hot bubble bath to waste time before the party although I was not really sure what time it actually started. It didn't really bother me that much because I would arrive when I wanted to, anyway. I sat on edge of the tub as I drew my bath. What are vampire parties like, I thought. They couldn't be much different then the human version. I mean, the ball was just like I expected of any regular ball. Maybe there was a good reason for Luke not wanting me to go, but if it was dangerous, then why was Max silent the entire time? I would hope that if I would be in some sort of danger, Max would step in and try to protect me. I decided to push all thoughts of the party out of my mind. I just wanted to relax and warm up. That pool was really cold and it didn't help when I walked into a cold mansion. I was freezing!

After soaking about an hour, I got out and began to rummage through my closet to figure out what I was going to wear. I couldn't decide because I was not sure what type of party this was. I slipped on some pajama bottoms and a tank to wear in my room inside because it was almost noon, and I figured I had a lot of time to kill being bored in my room. I saw that a tray of food with a note next it. I opened the note,

Annie,

Since you informed my mother of the party I was attending tonight, I am now required to take you along with me. We will be leaving at eight so be ready on time. Please do not dress in anything vulgar or I will make you change. I suggest you eat and possibly take a nap so you're refreshed to stay up little later than you usually do.

Luke

Right, I thought. If I wanted to wear something

vulgar, I will. He's not my father. What does he take me for, I've been here a week and have dressed as I normally do, except the first day with my failed seduction attempt. But only he saw me and I heard no complaints from him. I ate my food, still more than a little annoyed. After awhile I got bored and sleepy, so I decided I would take a nap, but not because he told me to. I just had nothing else to do.

Mary woke me around 6, and she helped me pick out a suitable dress, and did my hair and make-up. I told her I could do it myself, but said it was her job, blah blah blah, I stopped listening as she listed her reasons for her doing it.

A few minutes before eight, a knock came at the door and Mary went to open it. I looked in the mirror to check myself out one more time. When I finally walked out Luke was leaning against a chair. He looked me over, which ticked me off. Even though I caught myself checking him out, too. He was wearing a dark blue button down with his sleeves rolled up to his elbows, with a few of the top buttons undone showing his undershirt. He wore normal jeans which were a dark denim and old man shoes. I giggled to myself with the thought of him showing up at a party wearing dress shoes.

"Seems Mary did a good job dressing you for tonight." Whatever, I thought, walking to the door. He spun me around. First, I have some ground rules. You will obey them or I will have you sent home like a child, understand?"

"Ground rules, really? I feel more like a child the longer I'm here." Luke sighed and continued talking.

"First, stay where I can see you at all times." I

"What if I have to use the restroom? Are you coming in there with me?"

"You will tell me and I or Max will escort you there, understand?" I nodded in agreement, just to get him to stop talking.

"Second, there will be lots of other men there, some with mates, some without. It would be wise if you didn't flirt with them."

"Then what's the point of going to a party if I can't have fun?" I couldn't believe how fearless I was becoming.

"Our parties are different then the human parties. Human parties are basically only a few steps away from full-blown orgies," he said, his grasp tightening slightly on my arm. "Our parties are a gathering of friends. The men gamble and the women socialize and do whatever you do when girlfriends get together."

"I still want to flirt. I liked it that Bobby was nice, almost a gentleman. He actually talked to me." I was actually lying. Bobby really kind creeped me out.

"You will not flirt with other men, it's highly unlikely they will flirt back. If there mates see you, they will take it as a threat and they will attack you." His voice sent a shiver down my spine. There will be no flirtation, understand, they will not care that you're a Princess." He said letting go of my arm and backing away from me. "It's time to go, Max is waiting downstairs for us."

We walked down in silence. I was still irritated

that I may not be able achieve any type of revenge at this party. I was really wanting to flirt my ass off there, but was not happy at the thought I could really get hurt by someone's crazy mate who would view me as a threat. Ha! A threat to a vampire. Right. We reached Max, who was standing outside next to a short limo. It seated four people in the back and two in the driver's area. He was chatting with the Chauffeur.

"About time, we're going to be late." the driver opened the door and we all got in.

"Max, where is your mate? Isn't she coming to the party?" Luke sat next to me looking confused.

"You told her about..." Max cut him off really fast.

"It slipped out about me having a mate when I talked to her one-night." They looked at each other for a long minute.

"So what's the big deal with me knowing about your mate, Max? She is my future sister-in-law, after all. Why wouldn't I want to know all about her?" Max shook his head.

"Annie it's just not the best time for us to discuss this. She is back at the palace and cannot see you because she was recently turned into a vampire." I scoffed at him. "What does that have to do with anything? Oh wait I know, both of you just think you know what's best for me." They both looked away from me.

"Annie, that's not it, she could really hurt you. She is not in control of herself yet. It is best if you and any other humans aren't around her for now.

Max seemed sincere, but I still felt like they were hiding something from me.

We were silent for the rest of the duration of our trip, each of us engrossed in our own thoughts. We drove for what felt like hours, but it was probably like maybe, 30 minutes. It was just tough being in such a close proximity with people I really could not stand. The house we stopped at was bigger than my parents house, but much smaller than the mansion I was being held prisoner in. However, I'm not really sure if prisoner is correct because the fact is, technically I believe I was sold to them. Ir occurred to me that technically I was a slave. I was sold as property.

Everyone was climbing out of the car. I was lost in my thoughts as I slowly followed them up to the front door. I almost ran right into Luke's back as he stopped unexpectedly and moved to wrap his arm around me. He basically ignored the dirty look and my slight struggle to get away from him by holding me tighter. I gave up as we walked into the house and I was distracted by the people greeting us. We arrived in a room where there was a bar along one side that was mostly surrounded by girls. On the other side of the room there were tables where guys were playing cards. Luke pulled me over to the bar where some of the girls were chatting. They stopped when they saw us approach.

"Ladies, I would like you to meet my mate, Princess Annie." All of their faces lit up as they checked me out. " Annie, this is Josh's mate, Susan." She was a pretty brunette, who smiled at me. "This is Bobby's mate, Mickey." I mentally sighed, glad to know he was taken. "And this is Leah, whose father is part of the royal court." Leah also smiled at me, but something about it didn't quite reach her eyes.

"It's so nice to meet you all," I smiled at them as I became part of the group.

"Excuse me, I have some gambling to do with your mates." They all laughed as Luke walked away. I started to feel a little unsure of myself.

"Annie it's so nice to finally meet you, we have heard so much about you," Susan was saying. Mickey was nodding her agreement. Leah just stood there looking bored and unamused.

"Well I hope they're all good things," I said nervously.

"Well, we have heard some pretty entertaining things!" Mickey said.

"I think it is really wonderful that you are Luke's mate, and I have bugged Josh to introduce me, but he was being so difficult about it." She looked over to where he sat. He noticed and winked at her.

"I want to buy you a drink, I think you earned one, from what I heard happened today." She looked decidedly amused.

"I am sorry I don't like tea, it tastes like I'm eating a flower, sorry." They gave me a strange look.

"How would you know what a flower tastes like?" Mickey asked, looking doubtful.

"When I was little, Max dared me to eat a flower for a dollar and I did. It was so gross, and now I can't drink tea because it reminds me of it." They burst into laughter as I was about to give the drink back to the bartender.

"It's not tea Annie, it's a Long Island Iced Tea" Susan giggling. "It is a mixture of rum, vodka, tequila, and coke. No tea, I promise."

"Oh I'm not old enough to drink." I hear the Leah girl scoff and walk off as the other girls rolled their at her action.

"Annie, you can drink here, the human laws do not apply to you anymore," Susan said. I took a sip. It was not as bad as I originally expected.

"You like?" Mickey asked, and I nodded my head.

"It's good, I had a sip of a beer once and it was so gross, I decided I was going to stay away from all alcohol, but I like this drink."

"Wait a minute, you have never been drunk before?" Mickey asked, surprised. I shook my head no, "Oh we're going to get you wasted Princess," all of a sudden Bobby was behind her resting his chin on her shoulder.

"Baby do you think that is wise to get the Princess drunk?" He winked at me and I felt kind of scared of him again. Plus, I liked Mickey and I didn't want to ruin a new friendship.

"Yes I do, now go play with your friends, and we shall play as well." Mickey pushed him away and he acted kind of sheepish and moved away all tucking his tail and all, which which made me giggle as I watched him.

"Your mate is kind of intimidating," I said taking another drink, it was starting to taste eve better.

"Oh he is a big old teddy bear, but he acts all tough because he's Luke's personal guard." She stated this like it was not a big deal.

We hung out talking for a long time, and after a few more Long Islands and even a few shots, I was past tipsy, I must say. I was trying to get up and find the restroom because I was about to pee my pants . When I was able to stumble out of the room and figure out which direction the restroom was, I went in and splashed a little water on my face to try to sober myself up. I was so drunk it only made me feel cold. When I walked out I bumped into someone who was standing right in front of the door. This made me angry. Who stands directly in front of a door that someone may come out of. It was Leah. She was almost the same height as Joel. Her hair was black and she had dark green eyes, which were very pretty and made me a little jealous. She looked more than a little annoyed that I had bumped into her, but it was her own fault for standing there.

"You humans are so pathetic." Wait what did she just say? She continued, "Thinking you can just do as you please, but you can't."

"W-what? I was shocked at what she was saying.

"You don't belong here, understand?" she said putting her hands on her hips. "I never invited you to my party, I only invited Luke."

"I'm sorry, I was unaware that I was not invited." I slurred most of this so it probably sounded as if I was mocking her, which I was a little bit. She was being a bitch to me, right?

"I am only going to say this once, Luke is mine. I'm the one deserves to be his Princess, not you." I tried to step around her, but she persisted. "Listen girly," I said. "I don't want Luke, or to be a Princess, so as soon as you figure out how I can get out of here, tell me first, so you can have him." I stumbled around her and leaned up against the wall to support myself.

"Wait, you don't want Luke, why?" She stood next to me looking down at me with narrowed, disbelieving eyes.

"I have a fiancé, and I love him very much. I just want to get away from this nightmare and back to him as soon as I can."

"Luke said you were his mate, is he lying then?" She was still blocking my path.

"I don't know and I don't care, all I know is that you're starting to piss me off and I don't want to be with Luke." I tried to step around her again. "My goodness, I don't understand why it is such a hard concept for you people to understand." I said loudly as I walked away from her back to the bar.

"What's going on, Annie" Mickey said, as I sat down next to her.

"That girl Leah really pissed me off just now." both Susan and Mickey snickered. Susan downed another shot.

"Oh ignore that sour puss, she's just mad because Luke didn't pick her." Mickey laughed.

He really can't stand her. She throws herself at him. I understand why, though."

"She practically told me I was to stay away from him and that he was her's." I laughed. They j joined in.

"She is obsessed with him, basically." Mickey

took a drink "See, a long, long, long time I mean so long ago it would blow your mind," she giggled. "Her family was the royal family and they were not good at it to say the least. They were horrible and imprisoned a lot of vampires or enslaved them if they didn't *'agree'* with their *'laws'*. Mickey and Susan laughed uncontrollably.

"That does not seem like something to be laughing about," I observed. Then, I hiccuped, which made them laugh some more.

"It is because Luke's family came in and slaughtered the lot of them except for the children. They're not blamed for what their parents had done..." Susan said. Mickey piped in:

"Since then, their family keeps trying to regain power by marrying a prince, but you can't marry the prince unless you are their mates." She said this, cracking up again.

"She was so mad when she found out that you were coming tonight. I just wanted to smack her," Susan said. "I don't know what was she thinking. If she invited Luke, did she honestly think that he was not going to bring his new mate?"

"I only found out about the party a few hours ago. Luke didn't really seem to want me to come. Actually, Bobby's the one who invited me." They burst into laughter again. They were so drunk they laughed every time I spoke.

"Annie, they mind tricked you," Mickey said. I stopped laughing.

"What?" I was afraid of the answer.

"Would you have agreed to come tonight, if Luke

had asked you?" I was silent for a moment.

"I don't know, probably not, he ticks me off," I said. Susan laughed.

"Oh, we know all about it, Annie," Susan replied.

"That's why Bobby asked you and Luke pretended to not want you to come, because he knew that would make you want to go. Mind games, they mind tricked you." I realized it was true.

"That sneaky little bastard." I said as I downed the rest of my drink and they continued laughing. I started plotting my revenge.

REVENGE

I sat there glaring down at the elaborately designed bar counter as the girls continued their chattering and merriment. . I felt my heart beat faster and faster at the thought that Luke concocted such an elaborate scheme to get me to come to this party. I just didn't understand why he couldn't just ask me. I might have even have said yes out of pure boredom. The bartender hands me another drink as I spun my chair to face the other side of the room. Both girls followed my action. I looked over to where all the boys were sitting playing cards. I assumed they were playing poker, but I wasn't really sure. I saw Leah sitting very close to Luke, in an overly obvious attempt to flirt with him. I made a mental note to tell her a lot of guys don't like that kind of overt flirtation by desperate chicks, like she was definitely coming off as.

"She cannot see that he has no interest in her whatsoever," Mickey sighed. "She is making herself look trashy. Everyone knows Annie is Luke's mate."

"I know, she is just lucky Annie has not been changed yet or we'd have a real cat fight on our hands." I mentally became very excited, because Susan basically just gave me what I thought was a brilliant idea.

"What are you grinning about, Annie?" Mickey was giving me a quizzical look.

"What I like to call stage one of my revenge."

With that I jumped off the bar stool and walked over to where the boys were very enthralled with their little game. Leah sat batting her eyelashes at whatever he was saying, but he looked kind of bored and tired. I came closer as Luke stopped what he was saying and turned his attention to me. I could see Leah giving me a death glare from the corner of my eye. He was sitting in a comfy looking swivel chair and moved so he was facing me as I walked by the head of the table where Max sat. I ruffled his hair as I passed and I heard a small growl as he was trying to fixed his hair. I stood beside of a slightly altered looking Luke, as he took another sip of the beer in his hand.

"Are you having a good time?" He said this with a touch of sarcasm. I noticed his eyes drifting from my face to look my body up and down.

"Yep," I said, with an emphasis on the P. "I made some new friends." I motioned to Mickey and Susan, who were now sitting in Josh and Bobby's laps.

"I'm glad you're enjoying yourself." He sat his beer on the table, as I put on this super dumb act of being innocent, making my lips look all pouty.

"Soooo..." I was trying to make it sound like I was more drunk than I was. "What-cha playing?"

looking back at him with big, puppy dog eyes.

"Five card draw." He sat up in his chair and leaned closer to where I stood.

"Sounds fun." I said, as cute and innocently as possible. I glanced at Susan, who was in an intense make-out session with Josh. Mickey sat giggling as Bobby whispered something in her ear.

"It is entertaining, really, do you want to play?" I looked down at the table and shook my head no.

"I don't know how," I said and started to I move away.

"Stop." I glanced back at him as he motioned me to back. "Please, come sit, I will teach you." I moved closer to him, and he pulled me onto his lap. I mimicked a giggle I heard Mickey do earlier.

"Wow, I feel like not sitting here anymore and watching my little sister get hit on." Max got up and left the table amid raucous laughter. Everyone seemed to be in on some joke. As he walked away, Leah followed.

"I second that," she sneered.

Luke attempted to teach me how to play. I have no idea what he said because the only card game I know how to play is go fish. I played along, and made sure to whisper in his ear questions that I thought sounded convincing. As the hour or so passed, Luke became started touching me more intimately, which made me want to throw up, but I had to convince him to trust me for my revenge to work. I finally excused myself from the game as both Mickey and Susan were back at the bar talking to Max. Luke said we would be leaving soon, once they finished the game. I grabbed another drink and started drinking it as quickly as I could, to get through what I was planning. I sat next to Susan as she hands me another shot. Max shoots me a disapproving look.

"You know, you're not exactly drinking age yet." I downed the shot fast, and looked back at Max as the girls laughed.

"Oops, maybe you should have mentioned that around the first drink." I said. Max rolled his eyes at me.

"You will regret this in the morning, I'm sure." Bobby came up and Mickey through herself into his arms as he stood there laughing.

"I tried to stop them earlier and failed." Both Luke and Josh came walking up. "Annie, how much have you drank tonight?" I shrugged my shoulders.

"I don't know." I smiled up at him innocently. "The same as them." I pointed to Mickey and Susan, as they hung their heads in shame, but in truth it was only about four drinks and maybe two or three shots over the past 6 hours.

"Well I think it's time we get you home and to bed, you won't be too happy in the morning." I groaned and looked sadly up at Luke.

"But I don't want to go, I want to stay and play with my new friends." I tried to give him the puppy dog eyes again, but this time it didn't work.

"I think their mates want to take them home to have some personal play time." I glanced around the room, and they were all laughing. I noticed Josh and Bobby were both holding Susan and Mickey like it was the end of the world.

"I personally think Luke wants to have some personal play time with Annie!" Mickey said, as everyone cracked up laughing. I could feel myself blushing. I knew I was getting red not only from embarrassment, but from anger that anyone would actually think I would want to have 'playtime' with Luke!

"You do realize I'm standing right here. She is my sister." Max glowered. "Can I get a ride from one of you, I'm not riding back and being subjected to this kind of behavior in close quarters and all." More laughing as Luke offered me his hand and I placed mine in his. We walked out of the house to the car.

I got into the car first. I was feeling really uncomfortable. I was getting afraid to try to carry out my "plan." What would I do if he doesn't respond well or he figured out what I doing. My stomach started to feel queazy and I was almost sure I was going to be sick from the alcohol, fear and/or the stress.... That would really put a damper on my plans. Suddenly, his fingers slowly intertwined with mine. It gave me the courage to actually go forward with my plan. I looked up him. He was staring straight at me. I fluttered my eyelashes a second and new I was still blushing. I looked away as he embraced me. I felt his other hand cup my face so I was looking directly at him. His thumb stroked my face lightly, he leaned in and slowly started to nibble slightly on my lips.

In was a fast movement he pressed his lips to

mine, then backed off immediately as if he was afraid of my reaction. He should be. I normally would have murdered him for even thinking I would want him to kiss me, but now I needed him to kiss me. This going to be the best revenge possible. His lips pressed against mine gently as I controlled my urge to push him away.

I just kept telling myself, "It will be over soon, and Joel will forgive me," over and over. After a few moments, I felt his arm wrap around my waist and pull me on his lap so I was now straddling him. I felt his hands roam around, but not everywhere mostly on my sides. I decided to show him that I was willing to move along with basic kissing to something little more. Inwardly, I wanted to kill him. He may wish I did, my revenge will be so sweet. I moved my hands to the collar of his shirt and started to unbutton the shirt, but he grabbed my hands and prevented me. I froze, fearful he realized it was a trick.

"Annie we cannot do this," he sighed. "It is inappropriate to be intimate more than this." Luke motioned something to the driver. Inwardly, I was seething with uncontrollable anger.

"Oh, I guess I just got so carried away," I covered, and moved to get off of him, but he stopped me.

"I didn't say you had to get off me, in fact I very much enjoy this arrangement," he grinned. I kind of wiggled around some more. He groaned, gripping my hips tightly. "You are making it very difficult for me to control myself," he said, looking almost regretful. "Good," I thought.

"You wouldn't dare, don't forget the driver," I said innocently.

"Is that a challenge little girl?" I guess he was a little drunker than I thought..

"Maybe..." I decided to wiggle just a tad bit more since he had loosened his grip.

"You asked for it!" He kissed me on the lips much harder than I expected. I guess I must have done something he liked...

He eventually started to kiss my jaw line and nibbled on my ear lobes, which in other circumstances, would have worked. The only thing he was doing for me was building my rage. I was feeling so disgusted at this moment. Unfortunately that all changed when I felt a sharp poke while he kissed my neck. Before I could stop him, he bit me.

It hurt for a few seconds then started to feel really good and I didn't want him to stop, as all of my thoughts focused on how great it felt. I felt him remove his fangs causing me to involuntarily whimper. The wound started to sting as blood trickled down my neck. I was able to think clearly after a few moments. I was now overwhelmed with the rage, but still had to pretend I was liking what he did to me. The car came to a stop right after this, and the door opened. He pulled me out of the limo then back into his arms. We started walking up the stairs back into the mansion, my prison.

"Luke!" I heard Max's voice behind us. He was definitely ticked off.

"What?" Luke stopped, sounding annoyed.

"She's intoxicated, even if she gives you permission you cannot change her." Luke turned back and started climbing the stairs again.

"I know, Max. I'm just going to have some fun," he said with a determined look on his face. "Just let us be for awhile."

"She'll be ticked off again in the morning." LIKE, I wasn't NOW? Max was really getting on my nerves.

"Don't you think I know that, I will take what I can get at this point. She wants me now, so just leave me be and let me have these few moments." Luke sounded sad, almost desperate. He seemed to be pleading with Max. Max turned and walked away from us. The vamps are not going to make me feel bad about what I was about to do...NO WAY.

I did not want him. He deserved what he was about to get. I kept repeating this to myself. I was suddenly in my bedroom, laying on my bed, looking up at Luke, who was pulling his shirt off, tossing it away. His lips were on mine again before a I had a chance to process the fact I might be in over my head.

After a few seconds, he sinks his fangs back into my aching neck. Again, I was flooded with pure desire and want for him to never stop! I only regained my focus when as he removed his fangs, kissing other places on my body...I screamed as his hands wandered over my body in anger and frustration...He probably thought I liked it.

I was losing focus again as I felt the zipper in my dress opening. I was losing myself. Then, I was somehow lying on my bed just in my bra and panties. Reality hit me, this had to stop! He pressed his body closer to mine as he began to kiss me again. I knew it was time to crush him totally at this point, because I felt his overly happy mini friend pressing into against me.

"Luke!" I placed my hands on his shoulders and pushed him away as hard as I could.

"What's wrong?" He looked pretty freaked out.

"Well lots of things, but not all of them are important at the moment!" I said, sliding my legs out from under him. I stood up, and almost ran into the bathroom.

"Annie stop! Wait!" He grabbed my shoulder, spinning me around so fast I lost my footing. He caught me, and pressed me up against the wall. "Answer me Annie, what's wrong? Was I moving too fast for you? We can go slower if you want." He was pleading with me. Really?

"I just remembered what I was doing was totally wrong. I was about to cheat on my fiancé, and I don't think he would forgive me if I did this with my kidnapper." I was grinning like a buffoon as his face was the picture perfect of shock and horror. He quickly recovered his cold, emotionless mask I was getting use to seeing. "Can you let me go, I need to get ready for bed, and I suggest you do the same, in your own room." I tried to move, but his grip on my shoulder tightened and forced me harder against the wall. The whites of his eyes went black but the color was still there. Now, I felt fear.

"What is wrong with you? Why am I cursed with

such a horrible person as a mate?" Luke spat this last part at me, and I knew I had crossed a line. "I don't even understand how Joel could even love you of his own free will. I have no choice and will never stop loving you, but..." I don't know what came over me, but it was instant. My hand made contact with the side of his face. Hard.

He looked away for a few seconds, but as he slowly looked back at me his eyes went compactly black. His grip tightened and I crumpled from the pain. I couldn't move. He was pressing his entire body against me.

"All I wanted was for you to love me," he hissed, menacingly.

He moved fast as his fangs sank into my neck and it was not the same as before, it hurt a lot longer than before. I guess he was no longer being gentle with me. Everything started to blur as the pleasure came back and I was completely helpless. He was going to kill me and nobody was going to stop him. I should have never tried to take revenge by seducing him and then attempting to leave him high and dry. Everything was going dark as my body felt like dead weight. I thought I heard a scream, but darkness surrounded me as I went into a cold, very quiet, sleep.

WAKING NIGHTMARE

Beep

Beep

Beep

My head was pounding, and the most irritating sound in the world was happening right by my head.

Beep

I growled as my hand went flying to turn off the alarm clock. I was going to murder whoever put that thing in my room.

Beep

My hand came in contact with a metal railing as my eyes shot open in shock of hitting a railing that should not have been there. **beep** the instant I opened my eyes; I squished them shut as fast as I could. All my windows must have been opened because the light was so bright.

Beep

I moaned as I tried to open my eyes again, but failed.

Beep

"I'm never drinking again," I thought. My entire body was just aching. My head felt as if it had been split open by a metal pipe. I was going to vomit.

"Annie!" I felt a soft hand grab my wrist with two fingers. "Annie, are you awake dear?" I gasped as I tried to roll over, but was unable to. My wrists and ankles felt as if they were being held down. "Annie. If you can hear me, try not to make fast movements." I opened my eyes to see a very freaked out looking Mary, but had to shut them again because of the bright lights above me.

"Mary, it's too bright!" I managed to choke out. A second later, I heard the sound of blinds be closed above my head.

I opened my eyes slowly to see that I was in a small room with light blue walls. There were two doors and a television mounted high up on the wall.

Beep

I turned my head to see a monitoring device that was making that retched beeping noise.

Beep

Beep

It was my heart rate! and I jumped up in a panic. I looked back at Mary who was pressing a button on the bed very fast.

Beep

Beep

Beep

The sound was repeating faster and I felt like I was out of breath. I really hated the fact I was obviously in the hospital. Doctor offices were fine, but not hospitals. Just the thought the possibility that someone could have died in this room freaked me out.

Beep
Beep
Beep
Beep

I tried to get up, but Mary gently held me down as I struggled weakly.

"Annie, please, you need to calm down!" She looked at the door directly in front of me. "I need some help in here!" She hit the button again.

"Mary what's going on?" I kept struggling. One of the doors swung open and a man came running in.

"How long has she been awake?" I heard him say. I blinked my eyes open and shut long enough to see the doctor's face. It was John. He took a flashlight out and shined it into my eyes.

"About a minute. I came in to check her vitals. She was crying out and saying it was too bright so I closed the windows."

"Annie my name is Dr. Aaron Johnson. Do you know where you are?" I was confused, and glanced at Mary who was still looking frantic. "Annie, can you hear me? If you can hear me please answer the question."

"I... I...a ... in a hospital," I choked out, my mouth was so dry.

"Good," he smiled at me. "Do you remember how you got here?" I couldn't answer him.

"Josh, didn't Luke tell you what he did?" I was really tired and I didn't feel like being asked questions. "Mary can you please get me a glass of water, I'm so thirsty..." they both looked at each other, then down at me.

"Annie, my name is Aaron Johnson. I have been your doctor for the last eight months." I could not understand what he was saying.

"What? I don't understand. I just met you a few days ago." I looked to Mary. "Tell him! Tell him what happened. Has he has lost his mind?" I felt a hand on my shoulder. Mary looked at me like I was the one going crazy.

"Annie" I looked over at Josh. "This is your nurse Mary-Beth, my name is Aaron Johnson, we have taken care of you for the last eight months." I shook my head at them. I didn't understand why he was lying to me. "Annie, you were in a car accident on your way home, eight months ago." He looked at me as tears started to fall down my face.

"No, that's not what happened" I tried to move, but it was pointless. "My birthday was eight days ago.

"Annie, please, try and listen. You broke your collarbone and it punctured your lung. Your head also received a very hard blow which caused your brain to swell." Josh was saying this all very calmly.

"You're lying, why are you lying to me, you know what happened. I want to speak to Luke now!" I screamed at them as I tried to struggle against the restraints that were on both my wrists and ankles.

"Annie, we have already called your parents and told them you are awake now, they should be here soon."

"No, I don't want to speak to my parents, they're horrible people. They sold me off to Luke and Max.

I want to speak to Luke. That bastard is going to pay for putting me in the hospital!"

"Mary-Beth, can you get me an IV Push of Thorazine to calm her down please?" Josh said as she stepped out of the room. "Annie, I'm not sure who Luke is, but we will find him for you." Mary came back in.

"We're going to give you a sedative to calm you down, okay?" She said, in a soothing voice that wasn't working.

"No you will not! I want you to get Luke or Max in here now!" I screamed at him as he pushed a needle into my IV bag. "Josh! I was with you last night, why are you acting like this? I met Susan, your wife, you taught me how to dance and called me a bitch." A cold substance slowly started flowing into my veins and I tried to rip out the IV in my arm, but the restraints prevented me.

"Annie, my name is Aaron. I do not have a wife. Annie, please just try to relax medication take effect. When you wake up, your family will be here and we can talk more when you are more coherent." I was feeling tired, my body felt cold as I tried to fight the medication seeping into my veins. And then there was darkness.

The next thing I remember is my eyes opening, and feeling so dizzy and disoriented. I felt hands on my body. I was trying to focus on people's faces in the room. There was my mother; she was standing crying her eyes out. My father stood behind her with a big smile on his face. Benny sat on the chair trying to see around them. I was speechless.

"Oh Annie, I am so glad you are awake, it has been so long!" My mother said as tears poured down her face and she tried to hug me awkwardly. It seemed I was still being restrained to the bed.

"Mu... Mom..." I tried to say, but my throat was beyond dry.

"What is it Annie, are you in pain, does anything hurt? Doctor!!" she yelped toward the open door.

"Mom... I need a drink..." Her faced turned from worried to surprise and started frantically waving her hands around as she went in search of water. My dad stayed beside me with a smile on his face.

"How do you feel, kid?" I shrugged at him.

"My head hurts, and these doctors are lying to me." He looked sad.

"Annie, they're not lying to you." He replied quietly.

"Yes they are. We all know you and mom accepted the money that Max brought with him and sold me off to Luke."

"Annie baby, Max has been gone for over ten years now." He looked so sad. My father was not a man who allowed anyone to see how he was feeling.

"Dad, it happened! I know it happened! It was only a few days ago on my birthday!"

"Annie your birthday was eight months ago. You had a terrible car accident on your way home from Joel's house, sweetie." My mother came back in with a water bottle followed by Josh/Aaron.

"It is good to see you awake again, Annie. I just hope we are able to talk calmly, without the use sedation this time," He smiled and I glared back at him. They were all lying to me. I just had to trick them into admitting it.

"Doctor what is wrong with her? Why is she saying all these incredible, impossible things?"

"We believe Annie is suffering, PTSD, post traumatic stress disorder," he sighed, glanced down at me. "Annie went through a very traumatic event, and sustained a very serious head injury."

"We know all about the disorder. The question is, Doctor, is it going to go away? I mean, is she going to remember what has happened, and eventually get back to being normal?" My father sounded serious.

"Yes, sometimes this disorder is short lived. Sometimes people go back to 'normal' a short time after they appear. Other times, it takes a bit longer. But,, due to her youth and relative good health, I am confident Annie will pull through this with flying colors, and be back to her old self very soon." He smiled down at me.

I stopped listening as I noticed Ben sitting patiently in his chair. He was holding a large paper in his hands and smiling at me. He stood up and laid it on my legs as my parents walked out of the room leaving me alone with him. I knew Ben was so sweet and innocent. He would not lie to me and would agree with me that they all were lying. He climbed up and sat on the edge of the bed, grinning up at me with his cute little dimples. He reminded me so much of Max!

"Annie, I have missed you so much, I drew you a picture to make you feel better!" Ben showed me a picture of me lying in the bed looking like I was sleeping, and him, looking looking very said holding my hand.

"Benny, it's the most wonderful picture ever," I managed to say He stood there glowing at my words and hugged me, causing me a bit of physical pain.

"I'm glad you woke up. Macy has not been around since you went to sleep," he pouted. "But you are awake and now and Macy can come back!"

"Where did Macy go away, Ben?" I said, trying to figure out some kind of timeline.

"Daddy said she had to go away. He said she won't be back for a long time."

"Did that bad old Max takes her away?" he looked at me, confused.

"Max our older brother? I thought Mommy said he was dead?" he looked shocked. "Did Macy die!" he whimpered, and looked so sad! I didn't mean to make him upset!

"No, Macy is not dead, but where did daddy say she went?"

"He said she had to go to big kid school in another state. He said he saved a lot of money by you not going..." I completely forgot about college starting a few months after my birthday.

"Oh yeah, I forgot, silly me." Ben smiled, jumping off the bed as a woman came into the room followed by my parents.

It was Mickey, and I smiled. She had become a new friend to me a few hours before. Before Luke attacked me. She didn't look like the same fun and wild girl that I had met earlier. A girl who was tough enough to handle Bobby. She looked older and so professional, it just wasn't her. My dad took Benny's hand and walked out of the room leaving me alone with Mickey and my mom.

"Annie, this is Vanessa. She is a therapist here in the hospital." I felt my smile fade. "We think that it might be good for you to talk to her and she might be able to help you get your memory back." I heard my mother say timidly. I nodded my head at her, and she turned and followed Dad and Benny out of the room.

"Hello Annie, my name is Vanessa, how you are feeling today?" She was writing on a note pad as she spoke.

"I don't know, I wake up and everyone is telling me I've been in a coma for months, but I wasn't. My parents sold me into an arranged marriage to my brother's friend Luke, who is a vampire prince..." Tears started to fall down my cheek. "I was there for a week as I tried to leave and come back home. I have just gotten engaged to Joel on the day I was sold!" I was crying at the thought of Joel. "Oh my god Joel, I want to speak to him, can I please speak to him, Mickey?" She continued writing, looking very serious.

"Annie, we need to talk first. Then you may see your friends and family. Why are you calling me Mickey?"

"Because that's your name. You are Bobby's mate. Bobby is Luke's bodyguard. I met you last night at a poker party We drank and laughed for hours with Susan. Please, please say you remember!"

"Annie, you suffered a sever head injury, causing your brain to swell. You have been in a coma for many months. I believe during your time in the coma, you may have heard the voices of everyone around you and your mind created a dream world to help you survive." I was shaking my head no.

"That's not what happened! " I said, my face wet with tears.

"Annie, would you like to hear what actually took place? I feel it might help you remember if you learned the details" I stared up at the ceiling as my tears continued to fall, but managed to nod my head.

"Well Annie, on your birthday, apparently you left your friend Macy's house and headed over to your then boyfriend Joel's house." I interrupted her.

"What do you mean, by your "then" boyfriend?" My heart was sinking

"Annie, am I correct so far?" I nodded. "Well once you arrived at his house, the official statement from Joel and his family is..." she faltered, and I nodded for her to go on. "He broke the news to you that he would be attending NYU's summer program and he would be going there full-time starting in fall."

"No, he was attending the University of Seattle with me and Macy, you are wrong!" I shouted .

"Annie, Joel was wait-listed. He was approved by sheer luck. He is there as we speak, attending classes. When he left, he was not sure you would wake up..."

"No! He asked me to marry him! I said yes! He did not break up with me!" It seemed the room was spinning...

"Annie, please calm down, or else the doctor will have to sedate you again. I would really like to finish what we began here today." I didn't respond, but she keep speaking "After he broke the news to you, based on what his family witnessed, you became very upset and there was a bit of swearing and name calling. You then rushed out of the house, got in your car and drove off."

"That's not what happened," I replied, in shock.

"Based on witnesses' accounts, about 2 blocks from Joel's house, you ran a stop sign, and you were t-boned on the driver side, causing your it to flip over one and a half times. The other driver obtained minor lacerations, but no hospitalization was necessary." At least they weren't going to lie and say I hurt someone, too. "This young man was an EMT in training. He assisted you by helping you get out of the car." I watched her as she continued to read notes in a file, thinking that she was talking about someone else. "He reported that you were conscious at first and screaming for a 'Max'." Here, she paused and glanced over at me. "He said you were asking for Max to help you and then you passed out as emergency vehicles arrived. He saved your life by treating your head wound so you didn't bleed to death before help arrived."

I could not accept this. Max was still dead? Luke did not exist. This made me cry even harder for some strange reason. I couldn't be with Joel, Macy was off at school, and I've been in a coma. All I could think of was why did this happen to me? What did I do for me to have all of this bad stuff happen to me?   Mickey, or I guess Vanessa, held my hand while I sobbed until I passed out.

THE STORE

I met with the therapist once a day at first, to help me come to terms with the events that had taken place in my life. There is no way I believed them. I know what happened and I was not making it up. I didn't know what was really going on, but I was positive I was going to go to sleep soon and wake up to the reality I remembered. This had to be some sick, awful joke.

It had been three week's since I woke up in this hospital, and it was driving me crazy to sit and pretend that I had accepted everyone's version of what had happened to me. I had gotten a call from Macy almost on a daily basis. This was one plus. She told me about school and stuff. I missed my best friend beyond words and it was wonderful to know she was okay. For a short time, I was sure Max had killed her. I was glad to be wrong about that! She was the only person I believed because she would not lie to me. I still couldn't accept what they said. My mother came in with a big smile on her face as I was packing my bags, getting ready to leave this place and head home.

"Oh Annie, I'm glad your looking so well!" I was suspicious.

"Why, wouldn't I be?" I said, sarcastically. "Would the hospital release me if I looked bad?"

"Now, you have a young handsome visitor that I ran into at the market today before I came here," she laughed. My heart started racing as she always called Joel handsome. Could he have come for a visit? I glanced in the mirror behind me to to make sure I looked decent.

"Where is he?" I asked, so hopeful!

"He will be up in a few minutes. He decided to stop by after I told him you had woken up a few weeks ago," she said, re-arranging the stuff I had already put into my bag.

"Why didn't anybody tell him sooner?" she looked at me, confused.

"We didn't think you would be interested in meeting him. I mean, you really don't even know him, Annie." I stopped as my heart sank.

"What? Mom, who are you talking about?"

As if on cue, I heard footsteps as I saw my mother's face light up the way Ben's does when Macy comes over. I turned to see the mysterious person who had my mother acting like a school girl with a crush. I froze as he stood there in the doorway with a smile plastered on his face, as he took another step into the room. My mother took a step toward him, but I started backing away from them.

"Annie, I would like for you to meet Lucas. He was the other driver who was involved in your accident. He helped to save your life.

"Hey, it's so nice..." I cut him off as I was on the verge of going blind with rage. I could barely catch my breath.

"Are you kidding me? Do you honestly think that I am that stupid, Luke?" I screamed at him as my mother looked horrified. Luke stood there with a stupid look plastered on his face.

"Annie, what is wrong with you, this boy saved your life, don't be so rude to him! I raised you better than this!" Mom hissed the words at me.

"No, he did not save me, he's the one who put me in here!" I screamed at her. "He is a freaking vampire that tried to drink me dry and now he is trying to make me think I'm crazy for some reason." I took a breath as he backed away. My mother looked beyond mad.

"Annie, I thought we had moved past these crazy ideas you had when you came out of the coma. They weren't real! Your mind couldn't handle the truth, so it made up a different version of events to help deal you with it all."

"No, I know what happened, and I don't know why you are all lying to me. For this "thing" that took Max away from us." I screamed this, tears falling again. I don't think I really stopped crying at for 5 minutes the past 3 weeks.

"Annie, stop acting this way, we are not lying to you!" She said, in a strangely calm voice. "We understand that you believe what happened was real, but you need to understand, what you are saying is not even possible."

"No way. I'm not going to play along with

whatever he is up to," I said, pointing at him. He was standing at the door, looking pretty awkward.

"I'm sorry," he stuttered. "I didn't mean to cause any problems," he said, looking around nervously. "I think I should go, before I cause her to be more upset." He left the room very quickly. I could finally breathe again.

"Annie, what is wrong with you? That boy did nothing to deserve to be treated that way." Mom looked so disappointed. "If he hadn't helped you at the scene of the accident, you wouldn't even be here. He also didn't have to wait at the hospital until we showed up to tell us what happened. You should be grateful, not spiteful. You owe him an apology." I had no words for how I was feeling.

I watched her walk out the room. A cold day in hell when I was going to apologize to that monster! I sat on the edge of the bed as my dad came into the room.

"I saw Lucas leaving, seems like a nice kid. You ready to get outta here?" He was way too chipper.

"Yeah, I can't wait to get out of here and sleep in my own bed again." Dad grabbed my bag and draped his arm over my shoulder, giving me a half h hug.

"So what did you think of Lucas?" He said, as we walked down the hall.

"His name is Luke and I am not playing along with whatever this is, okay?" He looked at me pretending to be confused, but didn't press the subject. Mom was waiting in the car. It was a very quiet trip home.

One week later...

I just sat on the couch, bored out of my mind, watching TV with Benny, who wasn't even really watching it. But I did not dare change his channel or he would throw a fit. My mother was running around the kitchen as she was always cooking since I came home. I was bored and lonely, and starting to think it was the only thing I could look forward to, besides my daily gossip call from Macy. She had a new boyfriend. I hardly went out of the house unless I was forced to go see 'Vanessa', my therapist, every day for an hour. Such fun, like hitting my head against a brick wall.

"Annie, can you run to the store and get me a few things?" Mom asked.

"Sure, I'm taking your car since mine is gone." I tried to say it sarcastically, but she didn't seem to realize or care. Didn't even seem nervous about me driving...

"Okay, then here are the keys, money and the list of things I need. Please be quick about it and do be careful," Okay, maybe she was nervous. "I don't think I could handle going through that again." Or being pretty darn fake.

I decided I was going to go wearing my lazy outfit, which was basically a pair of basketball shorts, a spaghetti strap top that had a built-in bra for really lazy days when I don't even feel like wearing a bra. I pulled my hair into a messy high pony and slipped on some sandals as I grabbed the list and stuff, through on some sunglasses and headed outside. I got in the car, and that's when I noticed something. I was not afraid to drive. I remember the first time I was in an accident, I was scared to drive the next time. But there was nothing. Just my life of pure boredom. Oh boy, I get to go to the store!

Five minutes later, I was there. The list was quite long. I got a cart and started going up and down the aisles checking items off the list as I put them in the cart. I was in the last aisle getting hygiene products for everyone in the house it seemed, when out of the corner of my eye I see Luke just standing there with a soda in his hand, smiling at me.

"Hey Annie, how are you?"

"I'm fine, you?" I said not fine.

"I'm okay, just came here with my girl to get some things for camping this weekend," he said. Why did that make my heart feel so empty?

"That sounds fun," I said looking away from him. The word 'my girl' kept echoing over and over in my head.

"Its always lots of fun. Hey, do you want to come? There will be a lot of people there." Was he insane?

"No thank you." I said, looking for the hair dye my mother wanted.

"Oh yeah, I forgot you think I am a ..." he made finger fangs at me. "Well, you know what I mean. I just thought you could use some fun. Macy told me you seemed very sad lately." I glared at him.

"You talked to Macy?"

"Oh yeah, right after your accident, she was pretty

mad at me for a while. But we kept talking and became friends before she left for school. I chat with her sometimes on Facebook." Right, did he really think I was stupid to believe this game he was playing?

"Oh, she never mentioned being friends with you or even knowing you," I said as nonchalantly as I could manage. He was about to say something when a very irritated voice came from behind me. I knew that voice anywhere.

"Lukie, there you are!," said a girl I was familiar with from high school. This was not a person I liked much, either. You know the type, dumb, air head cheerleader. I was the rocker chick, we had nothing in common. "Oh hey Anna, I heard you died. Guess I heard wrong," she gave her cat swallowed the canary grin. I was going to kick her ass.

"The name is Annie, Alex-ass, and no, I didn't die, I was in a coma."

"Oh that sucks for you. Hey Lukie, why don't we get out of here before we end up in a coma from boredom,"

Luke gave me a sympathetic look as she started to pull him away. I heard her not so quiet voice say "She is such a slut." I started to laugh at that as I saw them both turn around and look at me. Wow, to my right was the contraception isle.

"Hey Lucas," I grabbed an extra-small size box of condoms and tossed it to him. "I recommend you use protection, you never know where that cum-dumpster's been." I took off walking in the opposite direction. I felt very satisfied with myself. For the first time in a very long time almost felt like my old self.

Just then, my phone gave me a *'pinged'* with a Facebook notification. I had a message, no, a I had a friend request from Lucas, attached with a message that stated 'you owe me'. I debated whether I really wanted to accept him as my friend, so I decided I would ignore it for a few hours. I wasn't that excited to have him as my friend in any capacity.

I got home, and my mother helped me unload the groceries, talking about all the kinds of things I couldn't care less about. I told her about running into Luke at the store, and she seemed disappointed at my reaction. My dad overheard us and laughed his head off. I went to my room. I had had enough of family time.

As I sat looking at the computer monitor, I just glared at the friend request. I was still debating about accepting.

Family dinner, then I went back upstairs and decided to accept his request because curiosity won out. I really wanted to see what was on his Page. I went straight to the message he sent me.

{*You owe me for that little stunt in the store; do you have any idea how long I had to listen to her bitch about you?*} Ha, I thought. Just the effect I was going for.

I answered him:

{*I'm so sorry, I didn't realize my actions would upset anyone. Please accept my apologies for your pain and suffering*}. I hoped he would appreciate my words, which were dripping with sarcasm. I got up, intending to go veg out downstairs in front of the TV, but almost immediately there was a notification ping. I sat back down.

{*Why do I have the feeling that you don't mean any of that?*} I decide I was not going to reply right away. He could wait, like, ten minutes, after I get done stalking other people's albums. I decide to reply, finally:

{Because I don't.} Instant reply:

{*We should go out and get coffee or some thing to eat sometime.*} Was he asking me out while he was on a camping trip with his girlfriend?

{*I don't think 'your girlfriend' Alex'ass would like that very much..*}

{*As friends, please just meet me for coffee.*} How could I not be skeptical of him, I'm sure he was up to something.

{*Why?*} I asked.

{*Cause I think you need a friend, and you seem like somebody I could be friends with.*}

{*I don't know...*}

{*Please get coffee with me or I'll have to ask your mother to ask you.*} I looked at the computer in shock.

{*You aren't that desperate, are you?*}

{*I will, but you could just avoid that and get a cup of coffee with me in a public place, so I don't try to suck your blood. That is a joke, I don't drink blood.*}

{*Fine.*}

{*Great, I'll see you on Monday at three at the*

coffee stop.}

I lay down on my bed and stared up at the ceiling. Was I actually meeting up with Luke of my own free will? I smacked my forehead, could I be any stupider? I was walking right into his trap. Whatever this was, he was not going to win! I was just going to have to prepare for Monday, two whole days away. Then, the realization that he was on a trip alone with Alexis, the schools biggest bitch in the world, made my heart feel so empty. I hated feeling this. And it confused me.

I started searching Facebook for Joel. I needed to talk to him. But I couldn't find him on my friend list. I looked for old messages to tried to send him one, but they were all gone. I cried as I realized he had not only not contacted me, he had even unfriended me. I couldn't find him anywhere, he must have blocked me!

The next day I went to his old house and saw the For Sale sign in front of it. The house was empty with no trace of Joel or his family. At that moment I hated Luke more than I had ever hated anyone. knew he was behind this. I was going to get him to admit he was Luke, I knew it! I would wait till Monday to try a seduction plan again. This time he can't bite me! I heard an evil laugh escape me.

BLACK OUT

My meeting at the coffeehouse was today, as I was slightly nervous because it was a sunny day. He would have to walk in direct sun to get inside, so when he doesn't show up, I will know why and then I will have caught him at his own game. I arrived early to get a good seat with a view by the window to see if he would actually show up. Five minutes passed three and he still has not shown up. I should be happy, right? I picked up the newspaper and searched for my favorite comic, 'Get Frizzy'. I just loved that mental cat. As I giggled to myself, someone sat down in front of me. I looked up and saw Lucas sitting down with an ice tea in his hands.

"Hey sorry I'm late, I was doing laundry and lost track of time." Damn, I thought to myself. I did not get to see him come in.

"Its fine, I've only been here for a few minutes," I sighed.

"Good. So, how was your weekend?" He was so Nonchalant..

"Boring. Yours?" I thought about how I stalked Joel's old house, and wondered how Luke would feel about that.

"It was okay. I had to listen to Alexis complain the entire time. She is not really the outdoorsy type." As he said this, I notice him checking out the bimbos flirting with the coffee boy behind the counter.

"You know, it's rude to check other girls out when you are with another girl." He raised an eyebrow at me, which I had never seen Luke do, but something that Joel always did.

"I'm sorry, I did not think you were the jealous type," he said, looking amused.

"I am not really jealous. I just think it's rude, plus you have a girlfriend. How do you think she would feel if she saw how you doing that?"

"She would not be happy, but you are not interested in me any way, so I highly doubt she would care too much. As for the chicks over there, I don't know, she may care." I laughed, but then there was just nothing else to say. Awkward.

"So, there is this party tonight at the lake, do you want to go?"

"Let's see, with Alexis and all her bitchy friends? I think I'll pass."

He laughed. "It is not just her friends. I have my own friends. You should get out the house and socialize."

"I don't think so, I really do not need you to take pity on me, for the accident, or whatever. I agreed to coffee with you. But I think that is as far our relationship is going to go."

"Annie, I do not pity you. I like you, and your crazy sense of humor. I would like is to be friends."

He smiled, kind of sad. "You are one tough, stubborn little girl. Macy warned me about that."

Joel always called me his stubborn girl. We always argued about silly things for no reason. It felt as if my memories were being listened to. The last argument Joel and I had came flooding back. As I felt a hand be placed on top of mine, the familiar burning sensation angered me and I yanked my hand away from his. He had a concerned look on his face as he withdrew his hand back to his side of the table.

"Are you okay, you looked, like you were about to cry." He was right. I could feel brimming in my eyes.

"I'm fine," I lied. "I just remembered something." He looked at his hands.

"Do you want to talk about it?" I shook my head no, not wanting to meeting his gaze.

"If you need someone to talk to, I am been told I am a pretty good listener."

"No thanks, I just need some time. I don't really know you. I really can't trust you, or anybody, especially right now.

"I get it Annie, no need to explain," he said, standing and stretching. "I have to get home and finish cleaning up my house before my mom comes home. But I will pick you up at eight o'clock tonight, then?" What? I thought.

"Mama's boy," I mumbled. He heard me and laughed as he started walking away.

"Hey, I never agreed to go, " I yelled after him. "You don't even know where I live." He turned around, walking backward as he spoke.

"Too late, I decided for you. Your parents invited my family over for dinner when you were..." he paused. "I know where you live." And he was gone.

I grumbled to myself because he left as soon as the sun was behind a large cloud. The parking lot was very shaded, anyway. I left shortly after that. I got home to an overly curious mother, waiting by the door and ask a million nosy questions. After I had finally settled her down, she was running around like kids in a candy store for some reason.

We ate dinner as mom tells the entire story about my meeting Lucas in the coffeehouse which was beyond boring. I went upstairs and dressed in some jeans and a simple tank top with my swim suit underneath so in case I get bored, I could go for a swim. I heard the doorbell ring and I made my way down the stairs as I heard my mother speaking

"Oh it's so wonderful to see you again, Lucas. I knew you two would hit it off." She gushed over him. I was beyond mortified. My dad sat quietly on the couch, watching TV, ignoring them.

"MOTHER!" I whined at her. Lucas might get the impression I told her I was into him. I certainly I was not.

"Oh there you are, Annie. Lucas is here to pick you up for your date," she beamed.

I started walking toward them, my head down. I am positive my face looked like a sunburned albino.

"Mom! It's not a date! He is just picking me up and taking me to his girlfriend's beach party." I said this, way too loud. The neighbors could probably hear me.

We somehow left, and after a very awkward drive, we pulled up to the beach entrance. I was disoriented. He had not taken me to the secret hangout in the woods. I kind of sighed in relief that Macy did not tell him about our hidden passages. I sort of started getting deja vu from that night in the woods.... You could say I was still not 100% sold on the idea of the accident. It does sound more possible than vampires kidnapping me, I admitted to myself. The only thing is, how do I know all these people that I had never seen before? Like the doctor, the nurse, the therapist. Lucas I can understand, I was still somewhat conscious when he pulled me out of my car and I must have seen him. Another thing still troubling me is the fact I still had no memory of the accident.

We both got out of the car very quickly and started walking toward the beach. I felt an elbow bump my arm. I looked up and Lucas was smiling.

"Hey try to have some fun, will ya?" He said. We were walking toward Alexis, who was standing around, talking to a few guys.

I walked a different direction. I saw a few people I knew from school. Somehow, I still felt out of place at this party. Everyone kept asking me about the accident, and what being in a coma was like. I wasn't sure what to tell them, not sure I knew the answers myself. So, I lied. Said it was like being asleep and I could not remember the accident. I didn't, so I wasn't really lying.

After a couple of hours, I was getting bored. People were leaving. Those that stayed were couples, mostly. I hate feeling like a third wheel. Sunset came and went. It was night at last.

I went closer to the water's edge drawing pictures in the sand with a stick. I heard someone coming closer, sand crunching. Someone standing beside me. I looked up to see a pretty ticked off looking Alexis. My being here seemed to be the reason, which made me glad I came. If her eyes were weapons, I would be dead, of course.

What are you doing here? I certainly didn't invite you," she hissed. I went back to my sand doodling.

"Ah, your boyfriend invited me actually." I looked back up at her with my most innocent look. "I was not really given a choice in the matter. He insisted, really." I just wanted her to go away.

"Yeah, well he told me he feels sorry for putting you in a coma. He feels like he has to be nice to you." I shrugged.

"Thanks for stating the obvious there Sherlock," I said, taking off my flip flops and wading into the water. It was cold and warm at the same time. Odd.

"Well, guess what? Lucas is my boyfriend. You don't have a chance. You can leave anytime now."

"He is all yours, Alexis," I said, almost laughing at this irony, if I wasn't so sad about losing Joel. I looked at the moon. What a beautiful, full moon.

"Yeah. I heard all about how Joel broke up with you and left to go off to school. You obviously are desperate." I sucked in my breath. What she said actually really hurt.

"Okay, thanks once again for telling me what I already know, are we done here?" I looked out at the water.

"Lucas is definitely the hottest guy around and I am not going to let you sink your dirty claws into him like you did Joel, so back off." She stomped off.

I did not want to be there anymore, feeling sorry for myself, actually. And hating that I let Alexis get the best of me. I started stripping off my clothing and waded into the dark water slowly until it was up to my shoulders. I turned and started to float on my back. Floating is something I love to do... I also really enjoyed listening to the waves, the sounds of the night as I looked up into the night sky. There were not many stars because the moon was so bright it was outshining everything else.

I was finally at peace, able to be alone for the first time in weeks. It was a wonderful thing. Until it was broken by a giant splash in the water close to where I was. I instantly tried to see what was happening. I noticed a few people in the water looking like they were swimming toward me. The rest of the crowd on the beach were looking at me with a strange expressions on their faces. The two guys coming toward me stopped, as I made my over to them. It was Lucas and a boy named Grant who, I had talked to earlier in the evening.

"Annie, what is wrong with you?" I looked at everyone, feeling dazed.

"Nothing is wrong with me I was just swimming." I looked at Luke with my best "duh" look. Grant had already turned around and was making his way back to the beach.

"Yeah, well next time tell someone you're going

out in the dark to swim. And when people call to you, respond, so they don't think you are floating face down in the water dead!" Actually, I did not stop and think about what it might have looked like from the shore.

"I'm sorry I did not hear anyone. I only heard you in the water splashing...." I was embarrassed. Again. I got out of the water and Grant was waiting with a towel for me to dry off with.

"Annie, I have been drinking tonight so I cannot drive my car..." Lucas was saying.

I heard a squealing noise..."Oh Lukie, such an amazing thing you just did! Trying to save poor Annie again," she kissed him on the cheek. I looked away grabbing, my clothes off the ground.

"Alex, it is no big deal. You should get home before your parents file a missing persons' report." I heard her make more obnoxious whining sounds. Decidedly NOT pretty. Somehow, Lucas was walking over to me, tossing his key in the air .

"You ready to go, Annie?" I nodded, and we started to walk to his truck.

"Wait, I do not know where you live, or how to get home from there" I took the keys and was sitting in the driver seat.

"I didn't consider that," he said, rubbing his forehead.

"Well I guess I am taking you to mine, then." He looked at me all confused like.

"Why?"

"Well, first, my parents will murder you if I do not come home. Second, I think your mother will be okay if you stay the night in a living room of friends' house because you had a little to much to drink, then trying to drive home drunk?" He nodded.

"To your house it is, then."

The next morning I was being poked and it was really annoying to be woke up by someone poking at you. I groaned and rolled over to see my entire family standing around me my staring down at me. Let me just say it is creepy.

"Annie, there is a half naked boy on our couch downstairs, mind explaining?" I think it was my mother demanding answers. I groaned, I was so, so tired.

"He was too drunk to drive, so it was either I stay at his house or he stayed here." I rolled over again, trying to bury my head deeper into the pillows. Dad was laughing again.

"Well I think Annie made the right decision coming home." I heard him say.

"Fine, wake him and feed him, then send him on his way. You understand we have to go to work. Benny starting his summer camp today and we will be gone most of the day," Mom said. Why did she seem to have a mischievous tone? I expected her to wink at me next. I closed my eyes tightly. I did not want to see that!

I went back to sleep for a few hours. I glanced at the alarm clock and was shocked awake. It was almost noon. I ached all over as I dragged myself out of bed. I needed to get something to eat. I wondered if Lucas was still downstairs. God, I really hoped not. Hopefully, he took off while I was still asleep. Somehow, both answers were not what I wanted. I was such a mental case! As I came down the stairs, I could see Lucas was still there, on our family couch without a shirt on. My eyes were like, glued to his torso. Damn, his body was just like how I remembered. Just like it was at the pool that day. It was yummy by anyone's standards. I am not sure how long I was gawking at him, but it was enough for him to feel my presence and open his eyes. He smiled at me.

"Looks like someone was enjoying the view," he said, amused. I am pretty sure I disappeared like a ghost I ran so fast into the kitchen to hide from him. Unfortunately for me, he got up and followed me. "It's okay Annie, I do not mind being mentally raped, by you you at least," he laugh again.

"I was not doing any such thing. I would shrivel up and die first.," I said, trying to make myself busy enough not to have time to look at him.

"Just keep telling yourself that," I glanced at him. He was leaning against the kitchen door frame, still topless. I felt myself blushing.

"Will you go put a shirt on, I need to feed you, then send you on your way."

"Really, that's not what your mother says." I froze, looking him in the eyes. I willed myself not to look at his body!

"What are you talking about, my mother gave me those directions this morning." He held up a piece of paper. He was smiling and I took it from him as quickly as I could.

Dearest Lucas,

I washed your shoes and shorts, to make sure they were clean for you when you get up and go home. Please feel free to stay in my home and make sure Annie makes you as comfortable as possible. There are condoms in the upstairs bathroom under the sink, if you don't have any. Be safe and have fun, I hope you will stay for dinner tonight.

I was trying to burn a hole in the note my mother left him with my eyes. I was also considering how to strangle her to death next time I saw her. I would not really kill my mother. Not really, but it is a good way of expressing how furious and mortified I was. She basically told him it was okay for him to have the sex with me, while he has a girlfriend. OH, and wants him to stay for dinner afterward. I heard chuckling from behind me, as I could not even force myself to look at him. I was so embarrassed, yet also I was feeling unreasonably nervous. All of a sudden, I his arms warp around me I start to pull away, but he stopped me.

"Lucas you have a girlfriend, don't do this!"

"Nope, no girlfriend. Alexis broke up with me this morning. She found out I stayed the night here."

"What! Great! I am never going to hear the end of this!" I tried getting free, but he held onto me, turning me around so I was facing him.

"Yeah sorry about that. The good news is, I am free to date a very hot chick that I have so much more in common with." He leaned his head down close so our lips were close and my body was molded to him. I wanted him but my mind was screaming to stop!

"Luke...I" I pulled away. He looked disappointed as he let me go.

"You still think I am a vampire?" I was taken aback. "You called me Luke. You only did that one other time, in the hospital right after you just woke up. You told people I was a vampire."

"I didn't mean to." I was not sure how to respond. "I know you are not a vampire. It was a mistake. My brain misfiring, or something." I looked away.

"It's okay, I just made me crazy to think that you didn't like me because you think I am a vampire," He said, a little melancholy

"It's not the vampire thing. It's that I am not sure of anything anymore."

"Do you like me Annie, even as a friend?" I bit my lip, thinking I knew I did not like Luke. But I was unsure about how I felt for Lucas.

"I don't know. I feel something for you, but not sure what it is. I need more time."

"All relationships have to start somewhere. We can try being friends, for a while, and see where it goes."

I made some food and we ate, then just talked. I learned a lot about him and what he likes and doesn't like. The entire time I just kept thinking of ways to compare Luke and Lucas how they were alike not a like at the same time. I was also comparing him to Joel. He reminded me of him sometimes. The way he talked. He was interested in the same things. I debated most of the day whether or not I really wanted to be in a relationship with someone so much like Joel. I finally got him to put his shirt on after I beat him in a blinking contest. We watched a movie, but I felt as if he were watching me, not the flick. When I looked at him, he would be grinning at me.

"I have a question for you." He said, interrupting the movie.

"And what is that?"

"If I was a vampire, would you allow me to make you into my vampire bride?" He said as he shifted so his upper torso was facing me.

"Well, technically you would be a vampire Prince." He seemed to enjoy this.

"Well, if I was a vampire Prince with this super hot body, would you let me make you into vampire Princess?"

"Hmm... I don't know, what do I get out of it?" I cracked,. He laughed at me.

"First, you would be able to check out this super hot body whenever you wanted." I smacked his arm hard. Twice.

"I am doing that anyway," I said. He nodded.

"But seriously, would you?"

"Yes, I would let you make me your vampire Princess!" I said, drenched in sarcasm, going back to the movie.

"Thank you," he murmured.

I had time to wonder why he was thanking me as I felt his hand on one side of my neck as a sharp pain sank into the others side of my neck, quickly replaced by pleasure. I tried to move my head to see what was happening. I couldn't because I was being held down so I couldn't move. This lovely sensation reminded me of when Luke bit me and the realization hit me about a second before I blacked out.

I AM GOING TO KILL YOU!

I heard voices in the distance. They seemed very far away. I just wanted to stay asleep as long as possible, but the voices were making it impossible. As I slowly began to open my eyes, I looked to the massive open windows allowing a breeze to come into the room. I sat up quickly, and I looked around the palace room that I was held in for a week. A sharp, shooting pain throbbed in my head as the memory of what happened in my house came flooding back to me. I stood up quicker then I thought possible and was surprised I was not dizzy from the fast movements. I hurried into the bathroom and looked in the mirror, to see the damage that bastard had done to my neck. But when I looked, there was no marks. I placed my hand on the area I know he had bitten me. I felt tingles of pleasure run through the site.

The sharp pain in my head came back. It made my vision become blurry and I had hold onto the sink to stable myself. I heard people talking as if they were standing next to me, but there was nobody in the room except me. I did not realize until it was too late that the counter was breaking under the pressure of my hand. How was there was a piece of the sink in my hand? I squeezed the chunk and it crumbled into smaller pieces as if it were made of dried mud.

The voices came back as the pain throbbed in my head and I tried to cover my ears from the noise. That is when something in my mind clicked. I remembered the words I spoke and my entire body started to shake. All I could manage to do was scream, which caused a few windows and mirrors to break. Oh, there were some vases in the room that shattered, too.

"Annie are you okay?" within seconds of me screaming, Luke came rushing into the room. I stood in the doorway of the bathroom. I could not even respond. My body was shaking and doing things I didn't even understand. "Annie, please calm down." I instantly, without thinking, through myself at him with the intention of ripping him to pieces.

Out of nowhere I had two sets of hands on my wrist and shoulders as I was pressed forcefully against a wall. Josh and Bobby pinned me forcefully as I struggled to get away from them. Luke came closer with his hands up, with a contrite expression.

"Annie, listen to me. You are not in control right now. Breathe deep, and try to relax and they will be able to let you go." I just struggled harder. I heard animal like growls coming out of me. This isn't real, I thought. "Annie, the more you struggle, the worse off you will be."

"I will never forgive you. I am going to kill you."

I felt fire course through my veins. All I wanted to do was to break out of Josh's hold and fling him across the room into the opposite wall. Bobby had his hand around my throat. He picked me up, slamming me to the ground, pinning my arms above my head. I felt a second pair of hands grip my ankles.

"Annie, you are going to wind up hurting yourself or hurting someone else." I tried struggling even more, but the pain I felt in my head was starting to take over.

"Let me go! After I kill you, then I will calm down!" I heard Bobby laugh. I glared up at him, renewing my attempt to regain my freedom.

"Annie, there will be no killing. I know you are probably upset about what happened. But you also gave me your permission to change you," he said, coming closer, but not close enough, unfortunately!

"I did no such thing, you asked me as if it were a hypothetical situation, and I was being sarcastic." I snarled this at him, continuing to fight. I really wanted to get my hands around his neck and strangle him to death.

"I was not being hypothetical, you just presumed I was. I asked a legitimate question. You answered it positively, regardless of being sarcastic." I growled at him, trying to bite Bobby on his wrist.

He hissed as one of my arms came free and I elbowed him in the stomach. I was about attack his hand with my nails, when I felt if my entire body lifted into the air, then slammed back down to the ground on my stomach as both hand held behind my back. Next, I heard a people running into the room. I turned my head to see Max looking down at me. He looked tired and concerned. I continued to thrash around trying to get free.

"I told you she was going to be like this!" Max said, coming close and kneeling down next to me. I tried to bite the hand he had placed on my shoulder trying to comfort me.

"Annie! Did you just try to bite me?" He looked at me horrified. I heard Bobby's chuckle.

"That is why I'm standing over here." I saw Luke leaning against the wall, appearing bored.

"You could have warned me," Max complained, scooting a few feet away from me.

"I could have but what fun would that have been?" Wow, Luke had picked up some pointers from me, it seemed. As everyone laughed, I was growling louder. Bobby and Josh's grip became tighter.

"Annie, can you please try to calm down?" Max asked. I looked him dead in the eye, and he could not look back at me.

"Never! I want him dead!" I said, not recognizing the icy cold sound of my voice. The room fell silent.

Luke's face was a mask of emotionless stone.

"Give her an injection and knock her out for a few hours," he said, breaking eye contact with me.

"Luke! That will only going to knock her out. She will be even angrier when she wakes up!" Max said, standing up and walking closer to him. I was kicking my legs trying to make it difficult to stick the needle in me.

"I know Max, but she is refusing to calm down or try to be rational." he said, going for the doors. "Josh, please just give her the shot now."

I felt someone press down on my leg and stick the needle in. I immediately felt the adrenaline start rushing through my body. I moved to see where Josh and his needles were. I really hated needles, just the idea that something could go into a vein so tiny and inject a liquid into you and the weird sensation when the cold liquid flows into your warm vein. I was struggling to get away from Josh and Bobby, as Josh picked up a small bottle filled with a clear liquid from a nearby table. He stuck the needle into the top and started to fill the syringe. I screamed as loud as I could non-stop.

"Annie just relax. It will help you calm down," Bobby said, sounding truly concerned, as Josh came closer. I started to cry and thrash even more, but it was to no avail.

"Dammit, Josh, get away from her with that!" I heard Max come back into the room as he started to walk over to me fast.

"Max, Luke gave me orders to give it to her to calm her down." he said pausing for a moment.

"I am asking you to ignore that order!" I felt Bobby's grip loosen, but not enough for me to get away from him. I almost thought I saw sympathy in Josh's face.

"You know I do not have the rank that you do. I cannot defy the prince." Max cursed and walked out of the room quickly. I heard loud banging, then it stopped.

"Josh. stop please! Look, I'm calm, there is no need for that. please get it away from me!"

I could feel the room grow silent. Everyone was listening.

"Annie, you are not calm," he said. "I have to do it Annie, I'm sorry." I screamed as he kneeled down next. I could see the glint of the needle in his right hand as he disinfected the skin with the other. I was so desperate. Somehow I heard myself screaming the word "Luke!" over and over.

"Stop!" Luke was back. I felt the pressure on my body holding me down lifted. I instantly curled up into the fetal position to protect myself from the needle.

I was shaking violently and felt like I was going to pass out. I really just wanted to go to sleep. I felt a someone beside me as, then felt a distinct burning sensation. The ringing sound in my head faded and the constricted feeling in my lungs started to decrease. Someone lifted me into the air and I was carried against a hard chest and arms wrapped around me. There I was clinging to Luke as if my life depended on it. All I cared about was that I was safe from the needle, and had been moved into a another room. I looked around and saw we were alone. I was almost comfortable, and started to almost relax. I was so totally overwhelmed.

"I'm sorry I did not know about you and needles. I would have never asked him to do that if I known," he whispered into my hair, as he rubbed my back, trying to soothe me like a baby.

"I still hate you," I said, as calmly as possible.

"I know," he sighed. "But for now, just relax and take a nap." He was brushing the hair off my face. It was all wet and sticking. "Mary will bring some food soon, and you will feel much better." I nodded as I slowly drifting off to sleep in Luke's arms.

I'm not sure how long I was asleep, but I felt like I had not slept in days now that I finally was. I smiled to myself. I felt so warm and comfortable in this bed. I never wanted to leave. Then I remembered what happened before I went to sleep, and I was suddenly wide awake and pissed, again.

I do not think I over-reacted. How did they think I was going to react? Luke had tricked me. He made me doubt my own sanity over the last four weeks. A strange thought crossed my mind, causing me to laugh silently. Alexis lost Luke, and I had won him. I know it is mean and Luke's using her was wrong, but she is such a brat and so of deserved it.

Stretching in my bed, I realized I wasn't able to get up. I was tied down by something around my waist. I opened my eyes to see an arm draped over me. I winced at the fact that Luke was sleeping in the bed with me. Right on cue, his arm pulled away. I looked, and I saw him sitting on the edge of the bed, his back to me.

"I know your angry, but if you could just try to talk normally we won't have another incident like yesterday." I jumped off the bed and walked into the bathroom ignoring him as I took a long shower and got dressed. I felt like I had not gotten dressed for days.

When I came out, Luke was sitting on the couch

with food all over the table in front of him, eating. I couldn't take my eyes away from the food. I was starving.

"Come sit down and eat something, Annie. We have a lot to talk about." I walked over and grabbed some fruit and started inhaling it like it was nobody's business. I only stopped when I heard him laugh. I looked up to see his grinning face.

"Annie, I know you are not very happy that I changed you."

"Happy, in what universe would you think that I would be happy?" Luke looked down.

"It does not really work that way. I asked if I could. You granted me the right. I understand why you feel that you were tricked. I'm sorry for that, but there is nothing we can do about it now," he said.

"How did you do it?" I asked, wanting answers.

"Do what? Not sure what you are asking."

I was done eating. I got up, not really wanting to be to close to him. I was just itching to rip his head off. They know I have an ultra fear needles, so they would use it against me if I attacked him or tried to escape. I tried to let go of my desire to kill him, but it was so difficult to control my emotions now that I was a vampire. I shied away from the thought. The room spun when I thought about it.

"How did you get the entire town, my parents, hell, even Macy to go along with your ridiculous plan to make me feel like I was a crazy person? What did you do with Joel and his family? I went by their house, and they were just gone. What did you do to them?

"Everyone has a price, Annie. I just figured out what they wanted or needed, and everyone cooperated when I gave it to them. He sighed, as if explaining himself were tiresome. "As for Joel?" He said his name in a weird way, as if he were having some kind of inner war. "He and his family are fine. We just relocated them to a new area that is actually closer to us." His eyes did not meet mine.

"Did you make everyone lie to me, even my best friend, about Joel and me breaking up?" He finally looked at me.

"Yes. We thought that maybe, if you believed that Joel did not love you anymore, then you might be able to move on." I watched him as he spoke, like a kid owning up to being guilty.

"We?" I asked. "Who besides my parents and Macy? Who?"

"Annie, it's not important. I will take all the blame for what happened. I forced everyone to take part in this, so you can hate me, leave the others out of it, please." he said softly. How is it possible that he can make me feel sorry for him, after all he has done to me and put me through? Yet I could see he was very conflicted. I could feel he was in pain.

"I have a few meetings to attend, " he said abruptly. "Mary will be up soon. Also, I am sure my mother will stop by eventually. Please try to be nice to her. My mother is a very sensitive person. Just so you know, she was really against this idea from the beginning and truly believed it was wrong."

"It was wrong!" I snapped at him. He nodded and left the room.

A DRESS FITTING

That was probably the worst day of my life. Why, you ask? Because there was officially no way I was ever going to be able to leave this place now. I hated everyone coming to see me, pretending to be all sympathetic. I am sorry, but the last thing a person I want is for people to feel sorry for me. I think every person had said how sorry they are that things happened they way they did, say, at least twenty times in the first week. The first week I was a new vampire. Well except Mary. She flat out told me to stop being a little drama queen and she would not be apologizing because it was her job to do as she was told. I think that was the only time I smiled that first week. At least she was honest. I hated them for what they allowed to happen to me. I all but stopped talking to people and only spoke when I had to. And as little as possible then, too.

Luke finally started to get the point that I was not going to talk to him and was finally leaving me alone. He would come into my room in the morning, ask if I was okay or if I needed anything. When I didn't respond, he just left. During meals, it was worse, because we were forced to eat together. We didn't speak to one another. I tried not to look at him and he reciprocated. It kind of started to bother me in an away. I figured it may be that he was guilty about what he had done and was acting like a coward at this point. After all, I was the one wronged. I still was not really talking to Max, either. He did not visit after the first few days I came back. He finally stopped by again.

"Annie, there is something I need to talk to you about." I looked at him, not responding as he sat on the opiate couch. "You have a dress fitting today with Victor..." I cut him off with a growl. I was getting the growl down!

"Why, what stupid event do I have to go to now?" I asked. Max frowned.

"Well it's not a stupid event, it's my wedding, unless you don't want to come." I had forgotten he said he had a mate.

"Oh, I didn't know," I said quietly. I felt a little ashamed that I called his big day stupid.

"Its fine, but you need to go see Victor for final approval on your dress."

"I have plenty of dresses in the closet. Why can't I wear one of those?" I wondered.

"You have to match the color scheme because you are the bride's maid of honor." That got my attention.

"What? Why?" I yelped. "I don't even know your mate. How can I be in the wedding party? Doesn't she have her own friends to be in it?" Max rubbed the back of his neck, clearly stressed out.

"Annie, Luke is my best man and my only groomsman. Since he is your mate, you must fill the same role in the wedding party." Max was not making eye contact with me. There was something he was not telling me.

"I cannot," I insisted. I made a promise to Macy. We would not be any other girl's maid of honor. I am sure her actual friends would be very happy to do this for her."

"I know Annie, but this is not up for argument. You must do this, whether you like it or not." Max said this in a very authoritative tone. "Be ready to go down to see Victor within the hour."

I thought this is another example of why I hate this place, these people. I do not even know this chick. Do I even get to meet her before I stand next to her, to support her on one of the most important days of her life? I couldn't believe Max's was making her give up her friends for me.

"This is not up for discussion. Just so you know, you were her first choice." He walked out of the room.

Wow, sounds like his mate is a loser. She chose a total stranger to be her maid of honor, nice. I just did not understand how they could do this to me. After everything they have taken away from me, they keep taking more. Why can't they just leave me alone? I guess the time passed even more quickly than I realized. I was sulking around and feeling sorry for myself about how much a hate it here. Luke walked in, wearing a tee shirt and jeans, very unusual for him because he always wore such professional attire.

This casual look made him appear more normal. And kind of hot in a way. Mentally, I was berated myself for thinking stupid vampires are always so hot.

"Come on, we're going to be late. Victor is waiting for us," he said. I groaned at the thought of having to spend the day with him.

"Let's go and get this over with," I said, less than cheerfully.

"Well, that wasn't so hard," he said softly to himself. That was enough to set me off.

"What was so easy?" I demanded.

"Getting you to come with me. Based on what Max told me, you were going to be difficult," he said, walking quickly.

"What's the point of fighting. Everyone makes the decision for me. They don't care what I want or how I feel. I just get order me around like I'm a prisoner. Or I am threatened with needles. Or mental games that last for weeks. Lies and torture."

"That not how it is. We were trying to make things less difficult for you."

"Have you ever thought of maybe asking and explaining things to me, give me a little respect, maybe? Perhaps if I had information I may be more open to some options."

"This is not negotiable. You are going to be her bridesmaid," he sighed.

"I am talking about in general, for future events."

"Fine. There is a ball coming up in about a week."

"What is it for? Why do I have to go?" I was whining. Great.

"It is your second ball, wherein you are to be presented to the people as a vampire and their future Princess."

"Sounds like fun, NOT. I do not want to go," I said, as we came to Victor's doors,

"I am only informing you early, as you suggested. It is not an option, unfortunately." We entered the fitting room.

Victor was running around the room, filled with dresses and fabrics and sewing machines and tables, a mad house. He spotted us, and took off for a few seconds into another room. I heard him talking to himself about where "it" was. I heard crashing things. I personally thought this man was a little on the crazy side. Somehow, I found myself smiling whenever he was around. He came back in with a male mannequin with a very interesting looking mint suite, obviously for Luke.

"Please sit down," he pointed at me. "You, go change," he directed Luke, as he was undressing the dummy. He escorted Luke out of the room. I sat in a creamy colored arm chair. It was way too comfortable. I looked around, noticing all the nice dresses and suites on about 15 different mannequins. However, there was one that was all covered up by a silky looking sheath. I figured it was probably the bride's dress. I was curious, and decided I have to take a peek. Can you blame me? I was going to have to stand next to this. I was just hoping it was not tacky beyond words. Even though I was pretty pissed at my brother, for some reason I wanted him to have a beautiful wedding. I hoped his bride was worthy of him. After a few minutes of debating with myself about whether to look or not, Luke and Victor came back into the room.

"Luke out, I need to work with Annie alone," I heard Victor say in his high pitched voice, as he walked up to me, grabbing my hand and dragging me back into the room they had just came out of. "I will be about twenty minutes. Just wait outside for us." Luke nodded, walking out as I was shoved in. "Get nude and raise your arms," Victor ordered.

I did as I was told. Raising my arms, and instantly a dress was slid over my body. Then, I was dragged back into the main area and was placed next to the covered dress that had captured my curiosity. I glanced in a full length mirror and saw the dress I was wearing. I was flabbergasted. It was beautiful, elegant, and fit me perfectly. It was a painful reminder of Macy. It looked just like the dream dress we talked about so long ago, when I promised to be her bridesmaid at her wedding. How could she have helped Luke with his brainwashing scheme? Helped him with his big lie...so he could trick me and make me a vampire. I felt ugly. I felt like some kind of monster.....Then, as if on cue, Victor uncovered the bride's dress. I tried to hold back tears threatening to spill out of my eyes.

"My dear, what is wrong?" Victor noticed.

"I cannot wear this dress," I said quietly.

"What? Why? I do not understand, what is wrong with the dress?" Victor seemed perplexed.

"This dress is an exact replica of the dress I chose with Macy, back when I had hopes and dreams for what our weddings would be would be like," I said, mourning the death of those dreams. What I did not say was that was her exact bridal gown. I knew it.

"I do not understand what the problem is?" He was genuinely perplexed.

"I cannot wear this dress," I said a little louder, my emotions winning out over my better judgment. "How are these dresses exactly....? I made a promise to Macy. I don't even want to be a bridesmaid for this chick! I do not even know her!

"Annie, the Bride designed this dress specifically for you," Victor said, trying to soothe me. "She was very specific about the precise cut, color, and design."

"How did she know about these dresses? No one besides Macy would know about this dress." I said, looking at the bride's gown. It was an exact replica of what Macy had drawn for her wedding dress, what seemed another lifetime ago. "This is Macy's design," I spoke these words out loud, without realizing it.

"Well of course it is," he looked at me like I was a crazy person. Suddenly, the pieces of the puzzle fell into place.

"Annie, are you okay" I heard him say. It sounded like he was so far away, when in reality, he was right next to me. I felt this white hot fury filling me up like lava, seeping through my body. "Please, please! Let me get the dress off. I see you are upset, but I do not have time to make another one." Instantly, it was off and back on the mannequin. I threw my clothes on.

I wanted to find Max. I needed hear it from the horse's mouth. Luke was sitting on the stairs close to the fitting rooms. He stood up as I stormed out. I moved past him and made my way up the stairs to where I instinctively knew Max's rooms were. I kept my eye out just in case he was out and about. I made it to the second level before Luke stepped in front of me, prevented me from going any further. I growled.

Annie, What's wrong now?" I tried to push him away from me.

"Where is my dear brother Max?" I was shouting.

"Probably in his room, why?" He actually looked like he cared. Uh, huh.

"Tell me something. What happened in the woods that night, on my birthday?" Luke just shrugged.

"Annie, I brought you here, where you belong," he explained, as if I had lost my mind.

"I know that. What I want to know is, what happened with Max and Macy in the woods, while you were busy biting me and kidnapping me?" He was caught off guard. I didn't care, and pushed on.

"Annie, wait," he called after me. Fat chance.

At top of the stairs I started knocking on Max' door. I realized vamps must be a little psychic I just knew. When no one answered, I started to bang on it. The sound echoed throughout the halls. Luke was standing slightly off to the side, hands in his pockets. Still nothing to say? The door opened and Max slipped out like a shadow and closed it quickly behind him.

"Annie, what..." I cut him off.

"What happened to Macy in the woods, Max?" He flinched, looked at Luke, then back at me.

"Annie," he said, trying to console me with a hug.

"Stop it!" I screamed. "What did you do, and where is Macy now?"

Pearson

WHAT HAPPENED TO MACY PART II

"Tell, just tell me!" I shrieked, as he turned away from me. "Max, don't you dare walk away from me!"

"I do not have to take this. You are not a Princess yet." He kept walking

"Max, I swear if you don't talk to me, I am going to make both of your lives a living nightmare!" Max stopped by Luke. They seemed to be ignoring me at this point. "Fine, if you're going to act like I am not here, then I might as well not be." I headed down to the third floor, where my rooms were.

I slammed the door behind me and ran for the closet, finding a largest suitcase I could find, tossed some clothes in and was right back on the stairs. I saw no one. The sun was bright overhead, so I knew Luke could not come after me, but the others probably would. But it didn't seem that they were. I was mentally berating myself for not taking off sooner if it was going to be this easy. But unfortunately, as I rounded a corner to go outside, there they were. Luke, Bobby, John, and two big guys I had never seen before.

"Annie, we cannot allow you to leave," John was saying, as he and Bobby walked towards me.

"Have either of you met Max's mate?" I demanded. They both stopped advancing and looked back at Luke. He was looking at me, his face looking very tired and defeated.

"Annie, let's just go back to your room, things will look better later," John said.

"No! All I want to know is what happened to Macy. I want to meet my brother's mate, right now!" I stomped my foot. Somehow, that action seemed to drain all the strength I had left in my body. Tears welled up in my eyes. Everyone was staring at me in silence.

"Annie, let's go back up to your room," Someone was saying. "I just want my questions answered!" I was crying. I sounded so pathetic, I thought. I was mortified. Suddenly, Luke's father, King Jace, appeared out of nowhere. Everyone looked down, and started acting pretty guilty.

"Why is she screaming her head off in my hallway?" His booming voice echoed. The sound of his voice totally unnerved me. Pure fear, like I had never experienced before, shot through my body. It was like I had just received an electric shock. I heard him come closer and I dared not look. "Is anybody going to answer me? I want answers, and I want them now!"

"Sir, she was trying to leave. We were just trying to persuade her to go back to her room."

"Why is she trying to leave? Luke, you said you were taking care of the problem!" Jace was definitely not pleased.

"I am trying father. We keep having to deal with different issues. We are at a bit of an impasse."

"Impasse? What kind of issues? How is that possible?" I felt his gaze descend on me. I couldn't breathe.

"She is upset about Max and ah, his mate right now." Was Luke in trouble? I felt the fear dissipate.

"How could you two have issues? She is your mate!" Was that a hint of sarcasm I was hearing?

"She wants to meet Max's mate, I guess, and Max is definitely against it." I was glaring at Luke, which I am sure did not go unobserved by Jace.

"Then, let her meet the girl, by all means! You are trying to woo her, not cause more distance between yourselves. Give her what she wants." He took a step closer to me. "Come along, let's get this introduction over with." What had just happened!

"Wait, are you agreeing with me? I get to see Max's mate?" When he turned to look at me, he looked just like Luke. It was so disconcerting.

"Of course," he said as he started walking away. Immediately I ran after him.

"Thank you so much!"

"Annie, you need to understand. You need to be happy, to settle in. I am going to pass the title on to my son and his mate, you." he said, walking very quickly. I was trying to keep up. "To do that, all my my son and his idiotic friends obviously do not understand is just to give you what you want, you are not asking that much."

"I want to leave, can you allow me to do that?" I

pleaded.

"Annie," he sighed. "That is the only thing I cannot allow. You must take my wife's title so she and I can '*retire*' and live out the remainder of our years twilight years together." I smiled. He spoke with such tenderness when he mentioned Krista. How in love he must be with her. I was surprised at how much this seemed to affect me.

We walked in silence up to the top floor. I had not seen him and Krista together very often, but they seemed beyond happy together. When we arrived at our destination, Jace knocked. All I could think of was: I won! But noticed no one was answering. Luke looked pretty worried from across the hall.

"Sir? How can I help you?" I heard Max saying through the door.

"Max, Annie is here to meet your mate now."

"Sir, I beg your pardon," he replied opening the door and stepping out into the hallway. "But I do not think it would be in either of their best interests to meet at this time.." Right. Like my best interests have been first and foremost around here.

"I said I would not involve myself in this situation. However, I am tiring of the severely confrontational atmosphere around here. I feel I must interject. You and Luke are going about this in the wrong way!"

"I understand that it is taking a while for her to come around, but..." Jace raised his hand.

"I do not care to hear any more. Step aside. You may go wait in Luke's room until this introduction is over. That is NOT a request." Max moved away from the door, looking worried and defeated. I felt so powerful. I was getting my way! I giggled. Jace looked at me. "Annie, you may go in there and meet your brother's mate, but there are not to be anymore attempts to leave, is that understood?" I nodded.

As he moved out of the way, I came face-to-face with a big white door that was directly across from me. I reached for the door handle. I was suddenly afraid to see what lie behind the door. What if it was not Macy? What if it is somebody I do not know? Would that be worse than what thinking, what I thought I knew? I took a long, deep breath as I twisted the door handle and pushed the door open. I took a step in and looked around the room. It was decorated similar to my bedroom, just with different colors. There was no one in the room. The bathroom was empty as well. I was so confused. I turned to look back into the room. I felt like I was being watched, but saw no one.

"Is this some kind of trick," I mumbled. I heard a muffled giggle from behind me. Spinning around, I came face to face with Max's mate. "MACY!" I screamed, full of joy and anger at the same time. How is that possible? I big, dumb grin was plastered across her face.

I ran at her tackling her to the ground, at the same time flinging my arms around her to hug the living daylights out of her. Once on the ground, I sat up and punched her in the arm. "Ow," she whined, rubbing her arm. "What was that for?"

"That was for lying to me! Did you know I actually thought I was crazy for a month?" She stopped grinning and looked guilty, like she should. .

"I was just trying to help Luke, Annie, don't be mad," she said, and smiled her winning smile. That was Macy, always tried to help people.

"But why would you help him, I don't understand!" I wondered. "He basically kidnapped me and you wanted to help him? Have they brainwashed you, too?"

"Annie," she said, seemingly weighing her words carefully. "He did not technically kidnap you. You were 'sold'". I decided right then and there that I was having a nightmare and would never wake up.

"Like that makes it better." I said out loud. I am sure it came out as sarcastically as I was feeling. I looked at her, and burst out laughing hysterically. She began to laugh with me.

"Okay, your right. There is no way I can spin it to make that look good." She finally stopped laughing. "I just think Luke is a really great guy, Annie, once you get to know him."

"You think he is a good guy?" I repeated. I could not be hearing her right. But then, she nodded.

"Annie, I know your upset about Joel, I, I would be too. Joel was a wonderful boyfriend. But, Annie, you have to face the fact that Luke is your soul mate and..."

"What! Are you kidding me?" I couldn't take any more. "Macy! Luke has ruined my life. And you think he is a is a good guy?" I emphasized this using air quotes.

"Annie, I know both Max and Luke didn't bring you hear in a very civil way, believe you me, I a have already let them know how dumb they both were for that. Believe you me, they are truly sorry for their behavior. But he really does care about you, Annie! It makes me want to cry, seeing him after you fight," she was shaking her head, as if she were trying to shake the vision of him out of her head. "He just looks so sad all the time Annie. I you could find it in your heart to at least give him a chance."

"Macy," I said, not able to trust what she was saying. "I cannot give him a chance. I am in love with Joel. I can't just turn it off, even if he abandoned me, too." I was shocked how bitter I sounded! "If Luke cares about me as much as you say, then he would leave me be and let me be with Joel." Wow, did she look disappointed!

"Annie, it doesn't work that way. Luke is your soul-mate, and he is yours. Once you finally accept that, you will not be upset about Joel anymore. Luke will make you unimaginably happy, if you let him." We were both silent after she said this. I really had nothing more to say.

"So, you and my brother." I remembered, the silence becoming more and more uncomfortable. She giggled, nodding her head. She was actually blushing! Macy was my brother's mate? Wow.

Pearson

ROOFTOP

"Macy and Max." I continued.

"Yeah, I know, huh! She grew redder. "Are you mad?" She looked a little scared of how I might answer.

"What? Macy, I'm not mad, why would I be?" They didn't seem to be holding her against her will.

"I don't know,.since you were so unhappy here, I thought you might lash out at me because I was basically, um, sleeping with the enemy. Maybe, you would be angry that Max brought you here, too," she said, avoiding eye contact with me.

"Does he make you happy?" I really wanted to know. She smiled angelically and nodded.

"Then that's all that matters. If my brother can do that for you, I'm all for it. We hugged.

"Thank you, Annie!" She smiled, and wiped away a tear of happiness.

"So, what actually happened on my birthday, then?" I asked. Macy looked shy, guilty and happy all at once.

"Well, basically, after you took off into the woods,

I followed a second or so after you, in the same direction. I was hoping I would catch up to you. I tripped, and Max caught me. I screamed my head off because he virtually "appeared" in front of me. Like Houdini, or something. Anyway, he covered my mouth to stop the screaming. Max told me he was going to bite me and it was going to hurt, at first. But he promised he would not kill me. He told me that he just needed me to sleep and he would explain everything to me in the morning. He did bite me, and I woke up in his room to loud music blasting." She smacked my arm. I had to smile at the memory of jacking up the music on that first morning I spent here. Max was sitting there, watching me sleep. He told me we were mates, and you and Lukie were mates. I honestly didn't believe him at first, but I felt this strange need to be around him. And when he touched me it, it was as if I was touching something burning hot." She looked at her hands questioningly, "But it didn't hurt. I didn't understand, because I was afraid he wanted to hurt me. After a short time, I started craving this feeling of the heat siring into my body, I liked it. I needed it. When he would hug me, I just wanted it to never end." She was blushing again. She looked the prettiest I had ever seen her look. "I guess I don't really need to tell you about that kind of stuff, you already know, right?"

"Yeah," I said, grudgingly.

What she said had me thinking about when Luke would touch me, and the burning sensation I always felt. I don't believe I thought it felt good. Well, when I was drinking that one night, it sort of did. I tried to block the memory. Every time he would touch me, I would be angry, and I thought the burning sensation was my anger expressing itself physically.

What Macy said had me wondering if I had misinterpreted what I was feeling. I thought about the other night, when Luke held me after the needle incident. I felt the warmth and safety she mentioned. I thought I would feel even better if it had been Joel who saved me. I thought I would be grateful to anybody who saved me from a needle. Macy was still chattering about Max and how amazing he was to her. I was in the presence of the most pure and simple kind of love.

It reminded me of the way John and Susan, Bobby and Mickey, and especially the King and Queen all acted toward each other. I actually felt a little empty in my heart. I had never experienced that kind of love, and was sad that I didn't think I ever would now. I knew I loved Joel, but I realize we never had that "glowing" quality to our relationship. Trust was important to me, I don't think we had what I needed.

We talked about her wedding, about everyone she had met since she came here. She mentioned her position with the vampires, which I guess is like, right under mine. If something were to happen to me or Luke, Macy and Max would eventually become the King and Queen. It was like a great weight was taken off my shoulders to find out Macy was safe and happy.

I was finally ushered out of her room by Mary Bell and Macy's maid, because we had to get ready for this party on the roof. Basically, it was a conjoined bachelor/bachelorette party. Personally, I thought it was a really dumb idea. However, it is not my wedding so I kept my mouth shut. I wondered who was going to be there. Obviously, Macy, Max, Luke and I.

I hoped the others would be there, and I hoped it wasn't going to be an all night party. After all, the wedding was tomorrow. It can't get to crazy. Maybe it would be like that poker party I went to, not that long ago, really, although it seemed like forever! I would not try that method of escaping again. Seducing Luke failed miserably, to say the least.

I heard a knock on my door, letting me know they were waiting for me. It infuriated me that they didn't tell me Macy was alive. They thought I would be upset. I was only upset she was a vampire. Obviously, they did not know anything about me. It hurt that Macy was my best friend and Max was my brother, and yes, they both betrayed me, but I still loved them. I opened the door. I was a little surprised Luke didn't just strut in like usual. Instead, he just stood there, looking at me questioningly.

"Are you okay?" he questioned.

I had been staring at the door, lost in my own thoughts. He jolted me out of it.

"Yeah, why wouldn't I be?" I said, trying to play it cool.

"Are you sure? You seemed somewhere else just now," Luke said hesitantly. I ignored him.

"I'm fine, just leave it alone!" I snapped at him.

"Fine," he shrugged. "We should go, they are probably already waiting for us." He started off down the hall so fast, I had to run to catch up.

I followed him through the doorway at the end of the hall that led to a stairwell. I realized this was how they body guards usually get in front of me whenever I tried to run. I mentally stored that knowledge for future reference, WHEN I try to escape again. I quickly went up the stairs after I realized I had stopped dead in my tracks. Luke stood at the top of the steps watching me.

"What were you doing?" He asked, pretending not to care.

"Nothing," I said, walking toward the door. Luke took my arm and held me back.

"I want to talk to you before we go outside," he said.

"Okay. Make it quick," I replied.

"Never mind, it's not important, let's just go to the party." He walked out the door.

Outside the rooftop was set up with four comfy overstuffed couches surrounding a fire pit,. There was a small bar set up where I could see Macy, Mickey, and Susan all standing around chatting, fresh drinks in hand. To the side I could see a table where Max, Bobby, and John sat playing cards. At least there was not going to be a lot of people here I would have to pretend for. I headed to where the girls were, but Luke grabbed my wrist.

"Don't drink too much. I do not need a repeat of the last time," he said, and released me. He went to where they boys were playing cards, and sat down.

"Annie, what took you so long?" I heard an already tipsy Macy shout as I walked over.

"Oh you know I had to be late," I said sarcastically. "I need a drink!"

We all started drinking again and laughing in our world as soon we were together everything just faded into the background. I was happily chatting away when I got the distinct feeling that I was being watched. I was brought out of my drunken haze and looked over at the boys and Luke was sitting there giving me a disappointed look. I mouthed 'What' to him, but he looked away, and went back to playing his card game.

I just did not understand why he always had to put me in a bad mood when I was having fun. We sat around the fire talking about girly things when the door to the stairwell opened and Leah walked out, striking a ridiculous pose. It was ludicrous, and I am sure she thought she was being sexy, while staring openly at Luke. A scoff came from Mickey. I had to stop myself from doing the same.

"Macy, why did you invite her?" Mickey looked really annoyed.

"I didn't want to, Max said I had to. Something to do with protocol, blah, blah, blah." They growled as she walked over to the card table and sat on Luke's lap. I watched as nothing happened. He didn't even push her off when she wrapped her arm around him. I looked away, not wanting to watch anymore. I tried to listen to the conversation, but could not get the image of them out of my head.

"I can't wait tell she finds her mate. Hopefully, she will stop acting like a hooker," Macy said. The girls all laughed loudly.

"I just don't get it. Why does she keep trying? Her mother failed, her mother's mother failed. They all failed to get the crown back," Susan said, as she downed another glass of champagne. My heart twisted a little bit in my chest.

I kind of zoned out of the conversation. My brain kept going back to the picture in my head of Luke and Leah. My eyes drifted in their direction a hundred times. I watched them talk, laugh and touch one another. My own words kept replaying in my head. 'I don't want him, you can have him...' I had said to Leah at that not so long ago poker party. . I could not focus on anything but what Luke and Leah were doing. It was driving me crazy.

Pearson

NO

I have no idea what was going on around me as I sat there. Everyone laughed and drank, but it was like they were on mute. It was all I could do was attempt to pry my eyes away from the poker table and pretend to be a part of what was going on at our table. I could barely control myself, I was having a hard time staying in my seat.

"I must not make a scene," I chanted to myself. I am sure Macy would be pretty ticked off with me if I ruined her party.

So I glanced back to Luke's table, and my eyes met Bobby's. He was smirking at me. I tried to turn away from him, but then I noticed Leah whispering into Luke's ear. I felt my eyes narrow at the site. A thunderous laugh snapped me out of my obsessive thoughts. The laughter caught everyone's attention as well. Everyone stopped and stared at Bobby, trying to figure out what his sudden outburst was about. I knew he had been watching me and was laughing at me. I was mortified.

I watched as I saw Bobby stood up and walked

over to where we were sitting. I became defensive at the thought he was going to point out that I appeared jealous. I wasn't sure if I was jealous in a romantic way, or just pissed off at the fact Luke had ruined my life, and was now going to go off and be with another girl. He came closer, the smirk plastered on his smug looking face.

He ended up sitting on the opposite couch with Mickey as he slid his arm around her. I also noticed the others at the table slowly begin to walk over. I shifted uncomfortably, and noticed Macy get up and moved to the only open couch. Josh sat down in her former spot. Max, Luke and Leah were now at the bar getting drinks. I noticed there were only two spots left to sit at our table, and there were three people on their way over. I knew Max would sit with Macy. The real question was, who would sit with me. I didn't really care if Luke sat with me. But, if Leah sat next to me, or if Luke sat down and Leah sat on his lap again, I was going to let them all have it. I was pulled from my thoughts as Bobby spoke to me.

"So, Annie, how are you?" I knew he was goading me and I was not going to play.

"Awesome," I smiled my sweetest smile at him. "I am so excited for Macy! She is getting married after all." I looked over to Macy who was grinning from ear to ear as Max sat next to her and wrapped his arms around her.

"Well that's good, because I thought you might be upset about something. I guess I was wrong," he said, still grinning.

"Guess so," I said in my most innocent voice.

As everyone discussed the card game, I zoned out and watched out of the corner of my eye as Luke left the bar followed by Leah. He walked into the circle of couches and came over and sat by me. He handed me a glass of champagne like I had seen Max do with Macy a few seconds earlier. I also noticed Leah stop about two feet away and I inwardly laughed. She had nowhere to sit. Maybe she would leave, I hoped.

"Annie." I heard her say. I ignored her, listening to Macy talk about the honeymoon trip that they were going to go on.

"Annie!" She said, much louder this time, getting everyone's attention. Everyone became very quiet. Wow, she was irritating me, standing there with her hands on her hips.

"What do you want?" I said trying to hold in my anger and not launch her off the roof.

"Can you move please?" Everything around me became still. All I heard was the sound of wood popping from the fire.

"What?" I said, shocked at her stupidity. And her audacity.

"I asked if you would move so I can sit with Luke," she said slowly, as if I hadn't heard her right the first time. I felt my lungs begin to burn. All I could think about was strangling her.

"Excuse me?" I felt my hands tighten into fists, ready to punch the living daylights out of her.

"I want you to move Annie, so I can sit with Luke." She was glaring at me, as I was quickly losing what little control I had left. I stood up and shoved her, sending her flailing over the end table between the couches. She was up instantly growling at me, "You little bitch!" S he lunged and I froze.

I am not really a fighter. I've never really been in a real physical fight. I remember wrestling with Max, but that didn't really count because Max tried not to hurt me. Leah probably wanted me dead. In the blur of what was happening I heard a crash. I wondered if I had been hit, hurt or worse, but I wasn't. Luke was standing in front of me. Leah was crawling out from a pile of wood that was once a table. She stood up, looking just as shocked as she was furious.

"Luke!" She screamed. It was deafening. "Why are you protecting that bitch? She doesn't even want you, she told me herself!" The room was still a little blurry, but it was also turning red. I was enraged in a way I never had been.

"Leah, I think it's time for you to take your leave," Luke said. His voice was so cold. It sent shivers down my spine. Somehow, that excited me!

"No, you make her leave," she said pointing at me. "She isn't good enough for you, and she definitely doesn't deserve the crown. I do, and you need to figure that out, for your own good."

"Leah, I don't want you. You are nothing to me but a clingy little leach. So, move on!" I giggled. I was just tipsy enough to associate how close Leah's name was to leach, and she was one too. She snarled, storming off toward the door. I was feeling a bit smug. I had somehow wanted this, but did that mean I wanted Luke? Before she was out the door,

Luke called out to her. My heart dropped.

"Leah!" she turned, glaring at him. "If you ever attempt to hurt Annie again, I will take it as an act against the Kingdom, and kill you." She closed the door behind her, disappearing into the stairwell.

I felt myself smiling. Then I saw Luke's face, and froze again. I could tell he was angry because his eyes were black. A bit of the color in his iris was still there so I knew he had some control. But I knew not to push him anymore tonight, or I might end up dead, or well, more dead. I instinctively stepped back from him, feeling more than a little intimidated, as he stood there towering over me. He took my hand, preventing me from moving away. It didn't hurt, but it probably would've broken my arm if I were still a human. He moved, breaking the intense look he was giving me. He looked at Max and Macy, who were ignoring us, cuddling and cooing on the couch.

"Max, Macy, I am so sorry for causing a scene at your party. I think it's time we take our leave." I was more than slightly annoyed.

"But I am not ready to-" He turned his attention back to me, and from the look in his eyes, I knew better than to say anything else.

"We will see you both tomorrow." Max nodded in our direction as Macy waved. Luke pulled me into the stairwell, moving very quickly.

He pulled me down the stairs, through the hallways. He pushed me through the doorway of my room. I looked back at him. He was standing with both hands pressed on the door jam, facing away from me. The lights were off, but I could see he was breathing heavily. I didn't know what to expect.

I was becoming increasingly nervous the longer he stood there, just breathing. He turned instantly and had me pinned across the room onto a wall. His eyes had not changed and were still mostly black. His hands were pressing on both of my shoulders as his body pressed against mine. I couldn't breath!. My body felt like I had some kind of fever, I was burning up! I couldn't think!

"Annie," he said, his voice sounding haggard. He was looking directly into my eyes. He exhaled loudly, resting his head against my shoulder. His breath tickled my collarbone, and I gasped.

"Do you have any idea what you did?" He said softly into the crevice of my neck. I could not respond with words, so I shook my head no.

"She could have killed you very easily and I snapped," he paused, then sighed. "I couldn't let her harm you! I have never wanted to kill anyone, until tonight." He placed a light kiss on my neck where he had bitten me. I no longer had control over my body or mind.

Everything happened so fast after the second he kissed my bite mark, my entire body arched and a moan escaped my mouth. I felt his hand grab my hips and lift me off the ground as my legs wrapped around him as I heard a small gasp come from Luke as he pressed his hips into mine. He bit into my neck, leaving me even more breathless. I didn't want to stop him. I was on fire, and it is unexplainable. The longer I burned, the better it felt. I was somehow now on the bed as Luke hovered above me. He was out of breath and I realized I was too. His eyes were so captivating, especially now that they were back to normal. He started to lower himself onto me. I felt how excited he really was and gasped in shock. He froze, looking confused for a moment. My eyes glanced down south, then I looked back at his face. He was grinning. I thought that he was going to kiss me as he leaned closer to me, but he didn't. Instead, he whispered into my ear.

"Any time you want me, Annie, all you have to do is ask." I exhaled, which came out a small moan. He started to kiss my neck again and pressed his friend into me for a second time.

I felt his hand start to travel up my outer thigh and slide under my dress as his other hand moved slowly down my neck. I felt like I was melting into him, and closed my eyes, thinking I could gain some control back if I didn't look at him. I reopened them received a horrific shock. I had the vision of Joel standing in front of me, asking me to marry him. I was delusional. I knew this was not real because I could still feel Luke touching me and kissing me and the pleasure I was feeling from it. It was like I was stuck in my memories and all I wanted to do was to escape them, and begin again with Luke. Moments later it felt as if I was electrically shocked to the heart as I heard Joel's voice in my head saying:

"Annie, will you marry me?" I screamed.

"No!" I screamed again. I opened my eyes to see Luke hovering over me. The look in his eyes was not what I had expected.

"N...No?" Was all he said, pulling away from me. I didn't understand. My heart fell. I was so confused, was he rejecting me after all this time, after everything he had done to me?

All I could do was look in his eyes as he slowly pulled himself away from me. I couldn't move. His jaw tightly clenched, and his face turned to stone, with no human emotion whatsoever. His eyes told me something that caused all the heat in my body to run cold. It felt as if I was punched in the stomach and I was not able to breathe and tears started to form as he pulled away completely and sat on the edge of my bed facing away from me. All he did was look at his hands and stay silent before he spoke; though he was not talking to me he was talking to himself out loud.

"I cannot believe I fell for that again. I am so stupid for actually believing you could want me." He lowered his head into his hands, and then he got up and walked to the door.

"Luke!" I didn't understand what just happened and why he was acting this way. He turned around and looked at me. He looked like he was on the verge of tears.

"What? Did you not get your fill of making a fool of me?" I shrank away from the harsh tone of his voice and his icy cold eyes. "Well, you will have to wait till tomorrow. I can't take any more pain tonight."

With that, he walked out, slamming the door behind him. My body lost the all consuming burning sensation, and was replaced by an empty coldness, the coldness from his eyes! You might call it a burning coldness. I crawled under my covers trying to make it go away. They smelled faintly like him. I began to cry silently as the cold in my body starting to become a piercing pain. I didn't understand what had happened.

I had actually wanted Luke, very much. But then he freaked out and left me here all alone and confused in the dark. Maybe this was a sign that it was not suppose to happen. Perhaps the universe was telling me that it was a mistake making Leah leave and going off to be alone with Luke. I eventually drifted off to sleep, my body still laden with the cold pain.

Pearson

WEDDING DAY

I awoke being violently shaken. My eyes shot open to see Mary standing above me, a completely stressed look in her eyes. The second she saw my eyes open she pulled me out of the bed and practically dragged me across the room to the bathroom. I heard lots of people shouting and running around out in the hallway. That was when I remembered today was Macy and Max's wedding day. It was probably late, and I would be late, as usual. Which explained why Mary looked so freaked out. Weddings are extremely stressful, especially the day of. She shoved me into the bathroom, closing the door behind me.

"Annie, shower and make it a quick. We will all be ready to go when you get done," she said. I started stripping off my clothes and turned the water on.

I stepped into the soothing warm water. The memories from last night came rushing back to me, racing through my mind at the speed of light. I kept coming back to the way I felt last night with Luke. I really didn't know what to do, or how I should behave when I see Luke later today. I mean, I was feeling something for him. I'm not sure if it's love or not. But I definitely didn't want him to leave last night, it was something...Should I tell him, or not, about these feelings? If I did, will he believe me or think I was lying and/or trying to trick him again? Luke's face kept popping up in my mind and the heart breaking look he gave me before he left made me cringe as I washed my hair. All these things and more just kept repeating in my mind, until I heard loud banging and Mary yelling at me to hurry my butt up.

I jumped out quickly and decided this was not the time to obsess over my personal problems. My main focus needed to be on Macy. I walked out in my towel and was instantly dragged to a chair in front of the vanity. About five different people's hands started working on my face, hair, hands, my feet. Somehow, someone was shoving toast into my mouth and I was chewing. I glanced at the clock in the reflection of the mirror and was shocked to see it was after 11 am. Wow, how could I have slept so late. Why didn't anyone wake me up before this? Was Mary too busy?

After being yanked, prodded, pulled, stuff slapped on all over my face, and feeling like I had basically been beaten up, Mary ran in with the bride's maid dress and started to help me into it, so as to not ruin the perfect hair and makeup job done by the rest of the staff. I slipped my shoes on and was pulled out of the room and up the stairs into Max's room. Macy and the Queen were sitting on the couch talking and laughing and both looked up as I walked in. They both smiled and instructed me to sit on the opposite couch as they continued to talk about wedding details and married life. I really wasn't listening to them. I wondered where Luke was, what he was doing, what he was thinking. Every time a door opened, my heart jumped, in hopes that it was him. But he didn't come.

When it was time, the three of us went down to the main floor. I could smell the flowers. The smell was so strong they that it made my head spin as the first wave hit my nose. We were being instructed on what to do, but I noticed Macy looking down at the ground, looking pretty frustrated. I could hear her sighing heavily, and she was crossing and uncrossing her arms.

"Macy, are you okay." She looked up, looking slightly scared.

"Yeah, I'm just getting really nervous." Macy tried to smile, but it looked more like a grimace.

"Macy, it will be all right," I said lamely, and she giggled.

"Are you sure, I mean, what if he says no or something?" she said, fanning herself with her hands. "I don't think I could handle that." I puncher her arm, to show her I thought she was crazy, but she looked at me as if I were.

"First of all, you are talking about my brother. I know for a fact he is probably more nervous than you are that you will reject him." She smiled and looked a bit more calm. "You've got Max wrapped tightly around your little finger, believe me, I should know! It's like nothing I have ever seen! What's more, I think he wants to be!" Macy finally laughed and hugged me tight.

"Thanks Annie, I needed that. I am so glad you're here!"

Suddenly, we were separated as a bouquet of flowers was shoved into my hands and Macy was pulled in the other direction as I was pushed through a white curtain. I was stunned. The ballroom looked amazing, and almost unrecognizable with the exception of the chandelier. I heard someone behind me whisper an order to "walk". I stopped gawking and started to move my feet.

The aisle was impossibly long, and there were so many people there. I was positive Macy didn't know half of them, and was curious as to who they all were and why they were invited. When I reached the end of the aisle, I was at the bottom of the stairs. I looked up, and saw the King and Queen beaming down at me from the top. That was when I saw Luke walk up and join me from the right. He linked our arms together and formally escorted me up the stairs. I could now see Mickey and Susan to the left of me, and Bobby and Josh on the right.

"We bow to my parents, then turn and bow to the audience," I heard Luke whisper, when we were almost to the landing. I nodded.

We bowed, then he turned and faced me, gently taking my hand. I finally got a good look at him. He was dressed in a some kind of a uniform. It was black with a golden sash starting at his left shoulder going across his chest. His hair was, for lack of a better term, very professional looking I felt his hand guide my hand up to his lips, where he pressed a small kiss on it. What was happening to me? I wanted to kiss him, and was bewildered by my desire. It took everything in me not to throw myself at him. What was I thinking! This was Macy & Max's wedding. I was losing it! I forced myself to behave.

I looked away from him, and saw Macy step out from behind the curtain. Next, Max joined her, offering his arm to her. Max looked unbelievably happy as they both looked into each others eyes. It was such an amazing moment. I had never seen anything like it, and one I will never forget it!

"Annie, you need to go stand in front of Mickey." I felt Luke's breath against my ear and his hand pressed against my lower back.

I watched him walk away, and I had to do the same. Max and Macy continued to walk down the aisle, and rarely looked away from each other. They had these big, goofy smiles. At the top, they bowed to the King and Queen, then the audience, then back to the King and Queen. The King was officiating, saying the normal things that one says at regular, non-vampire weddings. I always found this part of weddings beyond boring. I really just liked the receptions.

So, I kind of zoned out, stealing glances at Luke. He seemed to be paying attention to what his father saying. But I wanted him to look at me. Unfortunately, he never did. And then it was over. I heard the King say Max could kiss his bride. I looked at the bride and groom again. They were kissing with all the passion I was feeling inside of me. The way I wanted to kiss Luke, the way I wanted him to kiss me!

The entire room burst into cheers and applause as they walked back down the stairs. I felt Luke take my arm again, and we followed them down the stairs and through a doorway. We were immediately surrounded by chaos. Servants were helping Macy change for the reception party. Mary appeared slipping me into another dress. We were quickly ushered back into the ballroom, and the festivities began. Actually, the reception turned out to be really fun. I met so many people, and the food and drinks were delicious. The only thing that bothered me was Luke. The only time he had talked to me today was during the wedding. After that, he seemed to always be moving away from me. He had a drink in his hand every time I saw him, which I thought was unusual. I never really saw him drink before.

I was shocked to see Leah here. I saw him talking to her. She was behaving, by at least not sitting on his lap. There was at least one seat between them. But I was really not happy. I think she was flirting with him, but I couldn't get close enough to tell.

"Annie, come with me, we need a little girl talk," said Macy, who was a little past drunk.

"Okay." I helped her not fall as we made our way to the bathroom.

"Annie, I need you to promise not to start a fight

with Leah, at least for tonight." She stumbled into the stall.

"I wasn't going to start anything," I said, more than a little irritated.

"Okay, but you have been glaring at her all night, and I wasn't sure."

"I have not been glaring," I mumbled. She came out and was washing her hands.

"Annie, you kind of have. I don't understand what you're upset about." I checked my makeup in the mirror.

"I am just so confused, " I said, and she just looked loopy.

"What do you mean Annie? We all saw what happened last night. I don't understand how you could be even a little jealous.

"Macy, I am not jealous!" I said. "I don't know what I am feeling. I am just so confused!"

"Annie, when you and Luke left," she said while intently trying not to fall over, "I heard you got pretty intimate with him, then did a 180 an flipped out and were screaming at him, everyone could hear you screaming. She looked at me like she was at a loss.

"That's not what happened." I said, pretty much at a loss myself.

"Yes it is Annie. Everyone heard you scream 'No'," she said slowly. My heart felt like it was being stepped on. "Max and I ran down to your floor and Luke coming out of your room in tears again. He broke down and told us everything." She put a hand on my shoulder.

"But..." I said, starting to shake.

"Annie, do you not remember telling him no?"

"I did, I just didn't know I was saying out loud let alone screaming it, I...I-I was not saying it to him." I looked down, embarrassed to admit I actually wanted Luke, even to myself, let alone out loud too another person.

"If you weren't saying it to him, then who? He was the only one in the room with you!" She looked confused, and I just kept trying not to cry.

"Macy...I...I...I said no to..." I couldn't believe that I had said it out loud. I didn't realize Luke thought I was talking to him. Oh, I get it now, he thought I was rejecting him again!

"Annie, who did you say no to?" She looked almost anxious.

"To Joel." She just stared at me, as tears ran down my cheek.

"Annie, Joel was not here last night." I tried wiping away my tears.

"I know that Macy, we were doing stuff and it felt too good and I don't know what happened," I ran my hand through my hair, "I closed my eyes for a second and I thought I saw Joel standing there asking me to marry him and-"

"And you said-screamed, no." She was looking back at me, horrified as I nodded my head trying to hold back my tears.

"Annie!" She pulled me into a hug, trying to comfort me, but it just made me sob more. "Annie, you need to tell Luke what you told me!"

"I tried to talk to him, but he keeps avoiding me."

She grabbed a cloth napkin from the counter and handed it to me.

"Well you can't blame him, he thinks you were messing with him again. He is really hurt!"

"What should I do, Macy?" She looked like she was thinking really hard. A grin spread across her face.

"Go, ask him to dance," she stated simply.

"What?"

"Trust me. He loves dancing with you, he told me so. Just go ask him to dance with you."

"Okay," I said, trying to wipe my face and make myself look presentable.

Pearson

YOU WANT TO DANCE WITH ME

Macy patted me on the back for support. I took a deep breath and followed her out of the bathroom. I was going to ask Luke to dance with me, then somehow work in that I think I might actually have feelings for him. Without making him think I was toying with him again.

This was going to be harder than I thought. I could feel waves of anxiety swirling around me. I tried to think of how I was going to do this. I was biting my lip so hard it hurt. I mean, how could I even approach him if he was already dancing with Leah? Or, what if he just flat out said no? I felt Macy grab my hand and pull me along with her because my pace was slowing and I knew she wanted to get back to Max.

As we walked further back into the room, it was apparent that the light had been dimmed more, and the music being played was louder than before we left. The majority of the people were dancing and only a few were sitting at the bar, where Luke and Leah sitting. I felt a growl escape my lips and heard Macy giggling next to me. I glared at her as she raised her hands in surrender and started walking off toward Max, who was doing some weird dance with Bobby. Yeah, that really needed to stop.

I started walking over toward the bar while my courage started to grow as I gave myself a pep talk in my head. Except, when I was half way there, Leah stood up, a triumphant smirk on her face, grabbed Luke's hand and dragged him to the dance floor.

I instantly stopped walking and looked away from them as they were coming in my direction and I didn't want them to see me. I did the first thing I could think of and grabbed two glasses of champagne off the table I was standing in front of and downed them as fast as I could. I really didn't even care whose glasses they were I just really needed something at that moment. But as I finished the second glass, bitch had the nerve to bump into me on purpose. No way it was an accident, and it made me stumble. It definitely had a bit of force to it. I ended up dropping both glass and they crashed to the floor. We were the only ones that knew what happened because the music covered the noise.

"Leah, why did you do that? Apologize to Annie," Luke said, looking irritated. He also let go of her hand. Score points for me!

"Why? It's really not my fault she was taking up the entire walkway." She was on crack. I was leaning over a table. They could have avoided me altogether. Leah needed smacked. Twice.

"Annie, are you okay?" Luke asked me, touching my arm. The way he was looking at me, I just wanted to kiss him. Leah interrupted my thoughts.

"Luke, the song is going to be over soon and it's my favorite, you promised to dance with me," she whined, sounding like a spoiled child. How pathetic. I turned back to the table and downed another glass of something that really burned going down.

"Leah, relax. Are you okay, Annie? Uh, those drinks aren't yours...?" I refused to look at him. I didn't want him it hurt that he was going to dance with her.

"I'm fine," I said quietly, side stepping him and moving toward the bar.

"Annie.   Please talk to me." He sounded concerned as I he touched my arm. 'Talk to me."

"It's not important Luke," I said, looking anywhere but at him. You already have a dance partner." Leah couldn't hear me, as I whispered this last part close to his ear.

"You...y-you wanted to dance with me?" I glanced up to see his face and he looked happy, but really surprised. "Why didn't you just ask?"

"I was going to, but you were already headed to the dance floor with her," I said, in a nasty tone. She interrupted us by clearing her throat.

"Luke, I am still here, and we're missing our song," she whined, that's it, I thought, I am going to slap her! Luke read my mind, and blocked my access to her.

"Leah, surely you realize, I can't dance with you right now," he said slowly. "It's inappropriate for me to dance with anyone before Annie. She is the future Princess. I need to dance with her first, then I will dance with you later this evening." She scoffed.

"It's not like anybody would care, nobody likes her or wants her as the Princess," she said, flipping her hair. "The people want me as the Princess. It would be better for everyone if we danced first." All I could hear was the music and my heart stop beating for what felt forever when Luke didn't respond to her immediately. Finally, I pulled my wrist from Luke's grasp and started walking away. I had to get away from them!

"Annie, stop." I did my best to not look upset when I turned to see what he had to say.

"What?" I said. Damn, I sounded irritated.

"Dance with me please," Luke pleaded.

"Luke, what about our dance?" Leah demanded, stomping her foot.

"I'll dance with you after Annie." He said, and my heart sank.

We walked past a furious Leah hand-in-hand toward the dance floor. I could see people dancing to a slow song. I should be happy. I was getting to dance with Luke, but I wasn't. He only chose me over Leah because of what people might think if he danced with her first. We stopped moving and I felt Luke wrap his arms and I wanted to feel happy but I didn't. I wanted to dance with Luke because he wanted to, not because he had to because of social protocol. I never should have taken Macy up on her suggestion of him to dance. It was stupid and now I felt like crap and I just wanted to leave.

I heard the song come to an end only about a minute after we had started to dance, and I knew that leach was slinking around somewhere nearby waiting for it to end so she could take my place. I tried to disengage from his embrace, but his grip became tighter and he pulled me tighter against him. I was confused. I couldn't help but smile and quite naturally, I nestling my head into his chest. It felt so nice, so safe, so right.

I liked the way he was holding me. But I had this voice in my head that kept saying over and over again that this was not right. He was only doing this for his reputation.

"I didn't want to dance with her. I was just pretending, to be polite, you know." He said quietly into my hair as I bit my lip to try not to yelp for joy at his words. "She's been bugging me for the last week about dancing with her, and I kept avoiding it until she cornered me and I had no choice but to agree," he sighed. "Then you came in and saved me." He kissed the top of my head. "Thank you. You have no idea how much I like dancing with you." His words boosted my ego, and it was a moment until I was able to speak.

"Is what she said true?"

"About what?"

"About the people not wanting me to become their Princess?" I said, worried.

"No, the people don't care who becomes what as long everything is taken care of and everyone takes their position seriously." He said, somewhat sarcastically. "If they truly didn't like anyone, it would be Leah. She is the last of the old family that once ruled before my family. They were overthrown because they were not good leaders, to say the least."

He sighed. "I almost attacked her for saying such nasty things about you. It took everything in me not to cause a scene, like last night." I smiled to myself, feeling lots better about what happened.

I don't even know how many songs we danced to, but can't ever remember a time when I was this happy. I didn't just dance with him. I got to dance with my brother, too, and that was nice. I had never imagined being able to dance with him before. I had thought he was dead for so long...

I also danced with Macy. Well mostly we were laughing while trying to hold up each other because we were watching both Max and Luke waltz with each other. That was just a great moment. At the end I was tired, and all but forgotten about the leach that wouldn't go away. When another slow song started to play I was once again wrapped in Luke arms, where I felt warm and loved. Like how Macy had described she felt when Max held her. When the song ended, it was quiet for a few moments. I heard someone clear their throat behind me. I looked to see a very annoyed Leah standing there with her hands on her hips.

"Luke you promised to dance with me," she said a little louder then necessary. I could feel all eyes in the room were on us.

"Leah, now is not the time." He said, holding me even tighter.

"But Luke," she whined. "You have been dancing with her all night. You said you were only going to dance to one song. I want her to leave now, it's my turn."

"Screw off Leah I'm not dancing with you!" His words came out in a low growl. She took a step back and looked shocked. I know it was childish, but I stuck my tongue out at her. She sort of hissed at me and stormed off. I heard some applause, but mostly ignored them, nestling my head into Luke's chest. I felt his thumb and forefinger stroking the back of my neck and I felt slightly weak. It just felt so nice. I wanted to stay still like this forever. When Luke moved, I forgot my thoughts as I felt his lips close to my ear. I became increasingly nervous.

"Are you tired?" He asked, and I nodded because I was. "Let's retire for the night then, there is something important I need to discuss with you." I nodded because there were some things I wanted to say as well, and I preferred to do it in private.

We said our good nights to the happy couple. Most everyone were was still there. Macy grinned at me and raised her eyebrows at me in an exaggerated manner. Luke was waiting by the door, and he offered me his arm which I gladly linked with mine. We walked in silence up all the flights of stairs. I remembered when I was human I got so tired of doing this.

I began trying to formulate how I was going to tell him I was suddenly having feelings for him. I was so nervous about how he was going to react. I stole a glance at him. The look on his face was the stone cold face I had come to know so well. I began to panic. His signature stone mask was unreadable. I was desperate to know what he was thinking.

I thought about the evening and wondered if I had

done anything more to disappoint him or anger him in any way. When we reached the level of our rooms, I became increasingly worried that I had done so. I wanted him, I realized, but he was silent, and we were almost to my door. I had to let him know how I felt before anything else happened and things got confused again. We stopped. He turned to me and as I was about to begin telling him how I felt, he began speaking

"Annie, I want you to know that I'm not a bad guy." I was so shocked at his statement. I just looked at him like a deer caught in the headlights. "I truly just want you to be happy, and I love you more than you can ever imagine. I understand you don't love me, so that's why I have done this." My heart fell as he took both my hands.

"What have you done?" I asked worried and scared.

"You need to understand there are rules I have to follow, so you still must pretend to be with me," he said. He was staring intently at my hands, deep in thought. He seemed to be struggling with his emotions, but all I could think about were his words..

"Luke I don't really want to pretend anymore, I-" He cut me off before I could finish telling him that I cared for him. "Annie, please, I'm just trying to make you happy." Luke turned, opened my door and gestured for me to go in.

"Luke I-" I froze when I entered my room and became utterly speechless.

There, sitting on my bed, was Joel. He was smiling at me sheepishly. I was frozen. I loved Joel.

He was my best friend, my boyfriend, and even an older brother figure to me at one point. I ran to him and threw my arms around him as I burst into tears of joy, of relief that he was alright. He hugged me back. I pulled back to look at him as he smiled his wonderful smile, how I had missed that smile! He looked a little tired and had a small scruff that was growing that made him look older. He hugged me back, and I remembered how much I missed him and the feelings that I had for him not so long ago came rushing back. Then, I heard Luke sigh.

I turned back to the doorway. I had completely forgot that Luke was there and it was awful when I looked back at him. Although he was wearing his stoney face, I could see in his eyes how he crushed he was. I wanted to throw my arms around him! I felt as if I were being being ripped in half.

"These are the rules," he was saying stoically. You can see him, but only in your room, and his room. You are not allowed to spend the night with each other. You must not tell anyone. Especially my parents, that he's here. And you still must to be seen in public with me." I looked at him in pure confusion.

"Luke..." Was all I managed to say.

"Annie, I know you love him and I just want you to be happy. If that means you need to see him, then I will give you him." I just stood there. He didn't even look at me, just stood leaning against the door staring at the floor.

"Thanks man." Joel said.

"I'll leave you to talk. Just remember, he can't

stay the night." Luke turned quickly and walked out, closing the door behind him. A small voice inside told me to go after him. But it was silenced the moment Joel pulled me into his arms.

WHAT TO DO

Joel stood hugging me. What had just happened? I was in shock. I thought I would never see Joel again. Then suddenly, like a light flickering on, he was here in my room. I was being told told I was allowed to see and be with him. The door clicked shut and I remembered Luke. I wanted to chase after him, but I was incapable of movement.

"Luke, what is that boy doing here?" I could hear Max outside the door, almost snarling.

"I brought him here," Luke said softy.

"Why would you do that, are you crazy?" Max sounded really ticked off.

"Because Annie loves him. All I want is for Annie to be happy." His voice was so soft...

"Luke, didn't Annie talk to you tonight?" I overheard Macy say. I bit my lip.

"It doesn't matter. Annie is with Joel. She is happy now. That's all that matters."

"What about you? Are you happy?" Max demanded.

"No, but there is nothing I can do about it." I heard a door open and close. I was devastated.

I was brought back to my present situation when Joel broke free of our embrace. I realized he could not hear the conversation. His hearing was not enhanced like mine. His smile pulled at the corners of his mouth reaching up to his eyes. I had developed feelings for Luke, but Joel was my first love and he will always have a special place in my heart, cliché as that sounds. He took my hand and we sat beside each other on the bed.

"Annie," I looked at him, and melted the way I us used to. "I have something I need to ask you."

"What is it?" I asked, my voice cracking with emotion. I was almost afraid to hear what he had to say.

"Do you still love me?" He asked. He looked sad, although he tried to hide it. I wasn't sure how to respond to this. "It's been two months since I've seen you. I understand if you don't feel the same as you used to." The happiness faded from his eyes with every word. He was not only asking if I still loved him, but if I loved Luke. "Annie, I need to know. I will understand if your feelings have changed. After all, Luke is your mate." He smiled weakly.

"Joel," my voice was quivering. He looked at me, his eyes wide and questioning. It made me want to wrap my arms around him and comfort him. "You were my first love, my first everything. I don't think I could ever not love you!" I said, not knowing how to explain to him my feelings for Luke. He smiled, hugged me, then kissed the top of my head.

He didn't realize I never actually answered either

one of his questions. The truth was, I really didn't know the answers myself. I had merely bought myself some time to think about what I really wanted. I had to make an impossible decision between my first love and my mate. I had a dull throbbing pain in my head. Time passed, and I was lying on the bed and Joel was holding me. I could hear the thump-thump of Joel's heart. I guess I was hungry, and I couldn't focus.

"Joel?" I asked a small 'hmm' was all I got for an answer.

"Were you ever going to tell me about my brother?" I felt him sit up and I did the same. He looked guilty, as I guess he should..

"Annie, I wanted to tell you, I truly did. The look in your eyes when you talked about him, or saw your friends with their brothers...or looked at pictures of him...," he ran his hand through his hair. But I was not allowed to. My entire family works for the royals. I had no choice, my family had no choice. It could have meant my life, or worse, my families' lives....

"I kind of understand," It came out as a soft whisper.

"It sucked being caught in the middle, but once I married you I could have told you, which would have made me feel less guilty." I playfully smacked his arm.

"Is that the only reason you wanted to marry me, so you wouldn't feel guilty?" I giggled.

"No, of course not, it just came out wrong." He kind of giggled back.

"I know.", I said, thinking of another question. "Did you know?"

"That Luke was your mate? No. I knew he had found his mate. But I didn't have a clue it was you," he looked sad again. "If I had known, I probably wouldn't have gotten involved with you."

"What?" That was a little harsh.

"When you were brought here, I was hurt so bad I felt like I was going to lose my mind. My own father wouldn't even tell me how you were, or if you were okay. Nothing. Plus, Macy vanished too. I was left alone. It was so awful!" The sound of his voice was rising as he spoke. "If I would have known, I would have stayed your friend and not have had to go through this horrible pain." Tears welled in the corners of his eyes.

My body moved on its own accord but to be honest I didn't really want to stop myself. My lips touched his softly. His lips automatically moved as mine followed. It felt good to be in his arms again. But I couldn't help but feel like I was doing something wrong. There was a tiny voice in the back of my head that I couldn't ignore.

'But do you love him?'

It was saying. To be honest, of course I did, but it was not the same. Love, but not in love? I felt off, like, when I kissed him, I felt like I was definitely cheating. Really confused. Joel finally left, and I was left alone with my thoughts and no resolutions.

The next morning, after a mostly sleepless night, I awoke to the same question spinning around in my head. I had no idea what to do or say. No idea what

I was really thinking or how I felt.

I went to talk to Luke, I wanted to see him. I reminded myself to not act cowardly Mary told me Luke was in his office. I never knew he had an office. There was so much I didn't know. I didn't know about how this Country within a Country was run, or even what went on in this house. By the time I found myself facing the dark ebony door of his office, with its woodsy smell, I hadn't thought of what I was going to say to him. I was just asking myself more questions.

I stood there outside his door like an idiot chewing my lip off as I debated what I was going to do. I took a deep breath to calm my nerves and raised a shaky hand to the door and knocked. Maybe I wasn't supposed to knock, maybe it was better for me to walk in. I realized I was way over thinking this and acting like a crazy person arguing with myself for knocking on a door. I heard him say 'enter' and I sighed, opened the door and walked in. He sat behind a large desk with papers strewn here and there, a few were even tacked to the wall. He held two particularly large pieces in his hand and was looking at them very intently. I mentally smacked myself for bothering him since he looked busy.

"Annie," he said glancing over the papers then returning to his work, "what can I do for you?"

"Uh-um-I was..." I said nervously, sounding stupid. He glanced at me again. "I...," I took a big breath and tried to speak. ", I, I...was...I was wondering..." I felt heat rush to my cheeks as I stammered .

"Yes? You were you wondering?" Taking a deep breath and trying to compose my thoughts so I could tell him what I was thinking and how I was feeling. But I seemed to be having a panic attack or something.

"I was wondering..." was all I got before I noticed that I seemed to be annoying him. He looked like he was putting up with a saleswoman that wouldn't leave.

"Yes, I know, you were wondering." He said impatiently. "I'm very busy today. I don't really have time to chit-chat." His words were like a cold hard slap. My fears were replaced by anger and hurt.

"Never mind, it was stupid of me to even come here and waste your precious time," I spat at him. I turned on my heel to walk out.

The door opened before I could open it, startling me. I took a step back. My anger flared to fury when I saw Leah come strutting in like she owned the place. She had a giant smile plastered on her face, which got even bigger when she saw me standing there. I wanted to scream every profanity I ever knew. I really hated her at that moment.

"Luke, are you ready to go?" She said, as if I wasn't there. But that wasn't what ticked me off. Luke stood, put his paperwork down and walked toward Leah, who was standing a few feet in front of me,

"Is this why you are 'busy'?" I said to Luke. He stopped by Leah. She grabbed his arm.

"We have plans to get fitted for our matching outfits for my birthday party," Leah said smugly, flipping her hair over his shoulder. "Oh, and you are not invited." I started laughing.

"Why would I want to go to a ho's birthday party?" I said, still laughing.

"You won't be able to talk to me like that anymore after our Petition goes through." She viciously.

"Like I care about any Petition of yours." I just couldn't stop laughing.

"So, Luke hasn't told you." That got my attention. I tried to stifle my giggles, noticing she looked even more smug than before.

"Leah stop. Annie, I think you should go back upstairs," Luke said, not looking at me.

"Don't tell me what to do." I was tired of being the last one to know anything about my life.

"My Petition to the Court is to allow Luke to marry me instead of his mate. You are not worthy of becoming Queen." Leah sounded overly pleased with herself. I wanted to attack her, but I couldn't move.

"Is that true?" I looked over at Luke, who was standing silently beside her with his hands stuffed into his pockets. He nodded.

"Annie, it's just better this way. Leah wants to be with me and to become Queen. She has already accepted the position as the Princess. This way, you and Joel can be together and I won't bother you anymore." He said, walked out of the room leaving me and Leah alone in the room.

"So, when the Court approves, which they will,

Luke promised he will propose to me and I will become a Princes, as it always should have been," she said, striding towards the door.

I wanted to scream, but no sound would come out. Everything around me turned fuzzy except what was right in front of me, and I wanted to go Tasmanian devil in Luke's office. I just barely controlled myself and ran out of the room to the stairwell that led up to the roof so nobody would see me in this state. I don't think I had ever run that fast before as I climbed each flight without even touching half the steps. I realized I must have looked like a fool back there. I was about to spill my guts about how I cared for him when he was planning to propose to the biggest bitch I ever met.

I got to the door of my room and opened it, but instead of opening, it came off the hinge and slammed into the wall then fell to the floor. I didn't think I was that strong, but I guess my anger amplified everything. I had no control right now. Macy's door came flying open and she came out looking concerned, until she saw me and her face turned into confusion.

"Annie, are you okay? What happened?" I couldn't even talk to her. I blamed her for encouraging me to care about Luke. It was her fault that I just went through all that. She said to tell him how I felt and when I tried to, this is what I got. I walked past her, but she grabbed my arm.

"Annie, you need to calm down. I'll get Luke, he will help straighten out whatever is wrong!" She said slowly.

"No!" I hissed, and then I heard another door open. I looked over to see Joel without a shirt on and my mouth started to water with thirst and passion. All I wanted to do was bite him, and be with him, really with him.

"Joel, go back in your room! Annie, control yourself. I need to get Luke up here to help calm you down before you hurt someone."

"Don't you dare call that bastard, I don't want him anywhere near me or I will rip him to pieces." I snarled at her, pulling away. I walked back to my room. Someone had already replaced the door. I turned to see a very angry Macy stomping toward me.

"What the hell was that, Annie? You told me last night that you had feelings for him and then less than twenty-four hours you want him dead. What the hell is going on?"

"I thought I had feelings for him, but I don't. Plus, he's already planning his engagement to that fucking bitch Leah, did you know that? They petitioned the Court to have me legally removed as Princess." Macy looked horrified.

"Where did you hear that?" She took a step toward me. "That cannot be true. Luke would never marry Leah. He despises her!"

"It's true. I went down to talk to Luke this morning, and that bitch walked in and told me everything. All Luke said was "It's for the best." I mocked his voice, starting to pace around the room. I felt like I had just drank an entire box of sugar and washed it down with a bottle of hate.

"What did you say?" She said quietly.

"It really doesn't matter now, because all the feelings I thought I had for him are all gone, replaced by pure hatred!" I scoffed. Macy flinched. I heard a small knock on my door and I heard Joel's delicious sounding heart in the doorway.

"Annie, are you okay?" I walked over to the doorway as Macy stood watching me with a bewildered look on her face.

I pulled open the door, yanked him into the room by the shirt and smashed my lips on his. He didn't respond right away but eventually he started to kiss me back. We we landed on my bed and I started to rip his shirt off. I heard a sigh and a door slamming, so Macy left. Finally. Good, I though, as I had my way with Joel. It was not about love, I did it to spite Luke and release my anger.

A PRIVATE MEETING

Yes, I was angry, hurt, and upset about what Luke and Leah were planning. Yes, I slept with Joel just mostly for revenge on Luke and whoever else that wanted to hurt me. I was beyond upset and I thought by being with Joel I would feel better. But I didn't No, I almost felt worse than before and what was worse, I felt dirty in a way. Being with Joel just wasn't the same anymore. I had basically lied to Joel, and I was feeling pretty awful for doing that. I was more than leading him on and eventually I was going to hurt him. Especially if I ever forgave Luke for humiliating me in front of that leech named Leah.

I splashed some water over my face, feeling uneasy about sleeping with Joel. I practically ran and hid in the bathroom. My life felt like it was spinning out of control and everything I did just seemed to make it ten times worse. I could hear Joel snoring lightly on my bed. At least he didn't notice my speedy exit to get away from him. I needed to wake him up and send him to his room, so we didn't get into trouble per Luke's stipulation allowing him to be here at all. All my anger at Luke washed over

255

me again. I just wanted to punch him in the stupid face sometimes for making me feel like this. How he could have done this, when I was feeling all these wonderful feelings for him? I had wanted to be with him, and then he goes and pulls this. I should have been overjoyed to have Joel here with me. But Luke has ruined that for me now.

What if Luke had planned all this all along, if he could have petitioned to marry me someone else,why didn't he do this from the beginning when I said I didn't want this? I know he is smart and likes to play games, but could he have been planning this all along? Leah has been around Luke for a long time, maybe he truly wanted to be with Leah and was just waiting for time to pass.

That way, it looked like he tried to make it work, and when it didn't, he and Leah could be together. I felt the bile start to rise at the thought. My stomach twisted and I tried breathing slowly in and attempt to calm down. I was letting my imagination get the better of me. No, I thought. Max would never have allowed Luke to do that to me, would he?

My brother was supposed to protect me, even though he lied to me so many, many times. I'm not sure how long I sat in the bathroom contemplating the events of the last few months, becoming more and more paranoid. Everything was wrong, every single person I trusted and loved has lied and betrayed me, even Joel. I felt totally so alone.

I finally pulled myself together and walked back into my room to see a naked Joel sprawled out on my bed. I took a deep breath and walked over to wake him up. He couldn't stay even though I really didn't want to be alone right now. He woke up and we didn't talk about anything that mattered. He told me about his dad's job and that his mother also worked for the vampires sometimes. My mind was racing and I couldn't really focus on what Joel was talking about. My paranoia was still on overdrive and I was believing everything I had been thinking was probably true. When Joel finally left, I lay curled up in a ball, silently weeping. I didn't want anyone to hear me, lest they come to investigate.

I was awaken in the morning by someone knocking on my door. I could tell my eyes were swollen from last night's pity party.

"Come in," I said with a cracked voice. I couldn't believe I was being so polite. I sat up and looked away from whoever it was, so they couldn't see how bad I looked.

"Annie, the Queen wants to have a private meeting with you as soon as you get dressed." Mary said quietly. She looked sad. Great, now what?

"Okay, I'll be ready soon." I rushed into the bathroom before she could get a good look at me.

I knew better than to lollygag when it came to the Queen, so I rinsed off fast, but still felt slightly dirty. I covered my face with make-up to hide the swollen eyes and dressed in a simple, light yellow summer dress. I walked back into my room and looked at Mary, who stood by the door. She would not even look at me. I knew instinctively this meeting was not going to be a pleasant event. I wondered what it could be about. There were a few things she could be unhappy about. First and foremost, me and Luke were not together. Secondly, there was Luke and Leah's Petition. It may be embarrassing to her. Thirdly, she could have heard me and Macy arguing and possibly heard me and Joel afterward. This was definitely going to be a difficult meeting. I started chewing my lip so hard, I'm surprised I didn't chew a piece off and eat my lip. I walked in silence behind Mary. My anxiety sky-rocketed with every step.

"Go in, she's waiting." She stopped and gestured to a set of doors, still not looking at me. I took a deep breath and entered.

This must have been the Queen's private office, and it was very elegant and classy. She sat in her chair with perfect posture, completing this picturesque scene, behind a highly ornate wood desk.

"Come, sit down." The Queen said, in a monotone voice as her face showed no emotion. She was reading a document, and continued to do so as I sat across from her. I sat there waiting for her to speak as I clutched the arms of the chair, anticipating the worse. I silently prayed I was overreaction b, but my heart was just pleading unheard wishes.

"Do you know why I called you here, Annie?" She said, not taking her eyes away from the paper that seemed to hold her interest, at least more than I did.

"No, I am sorry, I am not really sure." I decided it was best to speak the way she did, with dignity and class. And I decided to play dumb, to find out what she knew before I let her in on things she would think were even worse. She sighed heavily, laying the paperwork down on the desk, and pushing them toward me.

"Annie, playing dumb is not going to work this time. I am very upset over what has been transpiring right under my nose." I was dying inside, and I looked at the paperwork, seeing it was a court Petition.

"I was in the hall last night and overheard you and Macy's argument," she stood up, slamming her hands on the desk, making me jump, "So I ran down to the Council Room and pulled a copy of this Petition that Leah filed. I'm very upset about what my son has done. Even more, I am disappointed in the fact that you allowed this to happen." She sighed, turning away from me, looking out the massive windows. At that moment, I felt so bad for her. I hate disappointing people.

"I'm sorry, I didn't know about it myself till last night. I had no idea he was going to do this." I was trying to hold back the tears I felt threatening.

"Annie, you have no idea what you have done," she said, finally turning back to look at me. "There is a good reason why Leah's family is not in power anymore. They were horrible to the human race and kept the world from advancing for centuries." She sat down, looking very tired. "Luke's great grandfather was the one who overthrew Leah's family, for crimes against the world, especially the ill treatment of humans. They enslaved the humans, killed them left and right. In the process, almost put us into extinction. My family lived in the shadows. Humans suffered from a lot of animosity toward vampires until recently, the past 150 years or so. Mostly, humans have forgotten about the horror of the past. They believe us to be folk lore at best.." She paused and was rubbing her temples to relieve some of the stress I had obviously caused her. "That petition is ludicrous and the majority of it won't be passed, but most likely, the court will grant the separation between you and Luke, unless you fight it." I glanced down at the paper again.

"What do you mean, fight it?" I asked, a more than a little confused. And a little suspicious.

"Well, when you get called in front of the council, and you will," she said, because I probably rolled my eyes. "They will discuss what they will allow and what they won't allow. Then, they will ask both party's if they agree to the terms of the Agreement. If you do, then you sign it. If you or the other party doesn't agree, then one or the other will have to file another petition with different stipulations, until both agree, or no more petitions are filed." My head started to spin.

"What are the terms that I have to agree to?" I asked, my heart sinking, she picked up the papers and shook her head with a scowl.

"Well a lot will be cut out because it is ridiculous, but I will read them all to give you a little glimpse of what Leah and her family are like." She looked at me in a way that made me feel bad and more nervous.

"First: Annie Erickson is to relinquish all present and future right to the crown and royal family; Second: Annie Erickson is to publicly announce to the vampire community in this country that Leah

Mohan is and will be the better Queen; Third: Annie Erickson will be punished for anything Leah Mohan deems punishable during her stay in the royal house; Fourth: Annie Erickson is still to produce the crowned prince Luke with a child, being Luke's actual mate, and the only one who can give him an heir to the throne; Fifth: Annie Erickson is to be executed after delivering an heir to the throne." I gasped as she continued to read.

"Sixth: The heir is to never know of Annie's existence and the replacement Princess chosen by prince Luke will be his official mother; Seventh: Anyone contradicting this will be punished by death; Eighth: Prince Luke's choice for replacing Annie Erickson will be Leah Mohan; Ninth: All history will be wiped clean of Annie Erickson's existence in vampire and human form."

Queen tossed the papers on her desk and started to rub her temples some more. I'm not sure when the tears started to fall. I couldn't breathe, the room was kind of shimmering. All I could think was how could Luke do this and agree that I should be punished by Leah, and forced to have his baby, and then be killed off. He truly hated me this whole time. He ruined my life and was just using me. I started to sob at the realization.

"Annie, calm down. The court will never allow half of this. I revised a version with Leah being your replacement. You, must produce a child since you are the only one that can have Luke's progeny But you won't be killed off because that would kill Luke. Mostly likely, you will just be sent away from here."

Really? How could she really expect me to calm down after that? How could Luke do this to me? I understand I hurt him, but did he really want me dead because I would not be with him? I couldn't wrap my mind around this. The only reason I can see that he brought me here was to get a kid out of me and kill me off.

I stood and ran from the room not wanting to hear any more of what my future had in store for me. I reached my room and locked the door. I was grateful nobody had seen me in tears and running from her office like a crazy person. I rushed into the bathroom and turned the shower on as hot as possible. I got in with all my clothes on. I didn't care about anything at this point. I just wanted to feel the burning heat on my body and the water to muffle my tears and then so nobody could hear my pain, and then wash them away. The Queen's words as I ran out of her office still rang in my head.

"This could have been different. You could have just loved him!"

TURN THAT LIGHT OFF

I sat on the tile of the shower floor as the water continued to fall down on me. The water started to feel like ice hitting my skin, now that I used all the hot water. My head was buried in my arms. I'm not even sure how long I had been in this position. Every time I tried to move, a ripple of pain went through my body. It felt as if there were nails inside my body and they were trying to break the surface of my skin and get out. But I didn't want them to leave my body because it was so painful, everything was so painful. I could tell it was getting dark outside, based on the light that was getting dim in the bathroom. I just didn't care. I didn't want to move. The water that covered my body was filling my ears so I could hear nothing but my own thoughts.

What I didn't understand was that if Luke never wanted me, then why not lie and say he never found me? I could have just been oblivious to this entire world and not be sitting here. I knew Max and Macy would not be together and so happy, if he hadn't. He must have known what his best friend was up to.

Max is my brother, and he always said he would protect me and never let anyone hurt me. Where was he now and why wasn't he protecting me from this? Why was he always pushing me toward Luke? Nothing made any sense to me. I was so tired. I somehow ended up sleeping in the shower because I just didn't have the strength to pull myself together and get into my bed.

I was awakened with a severe shock of pain that ripped through my body; it felt as if a searing hot knife had been stabbed right into my heart. I could barely breathe and all I could do was gasp and plead that the pain would stop. It was very dark in the bathroom. The tile was hard and uncomfortable, but it was bliss compared to the pain in my heart. I couldn't do anything against the freezing drops of glass like water. What was going on, I kept thinking, why was this happening to me? After the pain stayed for what felt like hours, it finally just disappeared and I was left with what felt like a hollow hole in my chest. That's when the tears began to fall uncontrollably again.

I didn't sleep the rest of the night, fearing the pain would come back and be even worse than it was before. I endured the pain and moved so that I was lying down away from the water but facing it, watching it flow down the drain, wishing that I could do the same. Flow carelessly down the drain without a care in the world. The bathroom light started to change again and things became lighter as a new day had already started. I drifted into the dark abyss of sleep.

My eyes opened to see that the water was turned off. It was dark in the room and the only light I could see was coming from the doorway to my bedroom. Then I felt a soft warmth drape over my body and a hand pulling me out of the shower, I wanted to fight but I couldn't. I could already feel the pain coming from moving my body. I sat against the shower door as the light flashed on. I moaned and tried to crawl back into the shower and hide.

"Turn that light off!" I heard someone yell behind me, and then embracing me, stopping me from crawling back into the shower and hiding away from the world. "Annie, its me, Macy," I relaxed when I heard her voice and let her hold me where I was sitting.

Tears began to fall again as the pain started to seep into my bones. I felt another set of warm hands touch my body. The hands on tilted my face and head back, as a glass was pressed to my lips and pure blood started to drip into my mouth. I jerked away, not wanting it. I felt it drip onto my face as I pulled away. I couldn't see who was touching me. I couldn't open my eyes enough to even see, then realized I didn't want to.

"Please Annie, you have to drink." I heard Macy beg me, as the glass touched my lips and the warm liquid filled my mouth. She sounded frustrated, so I swallowed it, but when it was pressed to my mouth again and I put a hand up and pushed it away. I heard the crashing of the glass as it hit the floor.

"Annie, what is wrong with you?" She yelled at

me. I growled back at her.

She had the nerve to ask what was wrong with me. Like she didn't know what was going on or why I would be upset. About my life being ruined by Prince Luke, who tricked me into loving him, all so he could make me have his spawn and then kill me to be with that whore. All I could do was shake my head. I did not want to listen to her. I felt the second pair of hands taking off the soaking wet dress that I had put on to meet with the Queen. I heard a loud scoffing laugh, and instantly wanted to kill everyone around me.

"Can't you all see that she is just doing this for attention," the voice said, dripping with sarcasm. "She's just throwing a fit because she's not going to be Queen anymore, and can't walk around acting like she's better than everyone else." I wish my body was not in so much pain or I would have ripped her head off and kicked it across the country, but all I could do was growl my frustration at her. I was not able to deal with this!

"Leah get your nasty ass out of this room right now!" Macy screamed from where she sat next to me. I finally opened my eyes wide enough to see Macy holding me up as Mary was taking the wet clothing off my body that was covered in towels.

"You can't speak to me like that. I am the future Queen, you must treat me with respect, don't you understand? I am above you and can have you killed," I heard a slamming against the bathroom wall.

"You're not a Queen yet bitch! Don't you ever

threaten my sister again, do you understand me?" I flinched at the sound of Max's voice. It hurt my ears, it was so loud!

I just looked at the ground where the little glass that had been filled with blood lay shattered on the floor. I could smell the blood and I wanted to crawl over and lick it off the ground. I realized I hadn't eaten in such a long time. I actually debated forcing myself to crawl over to it for a tiny drop. I felt my new fangs come out and I realized I was clenching my jaw really hard. I heard something fall and loud coughing coming from somewhere close to me. But I just didn't care.

"How dare you treat me this way," I heard Leah scream, and then gasp for air. "Luke! Are you just going to stand there and let you your hillbilly friends treat me this way? I am your future Queen and you need to punish them for that." I couldn't control myself. and let out a long guttural growl and I heard one come from next to me as we

There was a long silence as everyone sat there waiting for Luke to respond to Leah bitching, with orders to punish my brother and my best friend. I hated being like this, not being able to scream and try to kill her for what she had just said about the people that mean the most to me. Although I was unsure of how loyal they truly were to me, they were here helping me right now. Did I mention how pissed off I was that Luke was here, and that he brought his whore with him to see me me like this. Probably to go off and laugh about it later. I growled even louder as my thoughts kept racing.

"Annie, try to calm down," I heard Macy whisper next to me. "Luke, get Leah out of here now."

"Luke, why are you just standing there, defend me!" Leah screamed and I growled more. I really need her to get away from me before I overcame the pain and ripped her to shreds. "Luke!"

"Leah," I heard him finally speak quietly, which was shocking since everyone else was screaming and yelling at each other. "You need to leave immediately," he said. The room went silent. I could feel myself drifting toward sleep again.

"What!" Leah started to scream again "You're supposed to be on my side, not theirs!"

"Leah, you're causing a scene. Nobody wants you here." I wanted to smile at his words, but I stopped myself. I was never going to forgive him for what he was doing to me.

"What! You are going to allow this attention whore and her moron family and friends to treat me this way?" Leave." I heard Luke's voice echo throughout the room.

"Whatever. Let's go have some fun and get ready for our engagement party tomorrow." I was wide awake now, a growl escaping my lips that almost matched Luke's voice when he yelled at her. All I could see was red and all I wanted to do was shove my hand in her chest and rip out her black heart.

"Leah," he shouted, "I will not tell you again, stop telling people we are engaged. I never gave you that ring, you bought it yourself." I heard Macy giggle next to me.

"But Luke, we will be so why put off what's

already going to happen?" Leah said, in her whinny voice.

"Leah, leave the room before I throw you out the window." He growled."You're working my last nerve."

"Fine, let's go," she said, I could hear the clicking of her heels retreat. "Let's go, Luke" I heard the sound of her heels coming from near the doorway.

"No, Leah." Luke said. "Go." I heard her huff and stomp loudly out of the room.

I was somewhat aware that Mary had been changing me like a rag doll this entire time, putting fresh, dry clothing on me. To tell you the truth, I did feel much better, but didn't really want to admit it. My anger dissipated now that the bitch from hell was gone. I could feel myself drifting off as I laid my head on Macy's shoulder while she held me rocked me like a baby. I just want to sleep, to forget everything. I must have dozed off for a few seconds because when I opened my eyes I saw that Max was holding me. He laid me down and stood up abruptly.

"Give her to me." I had actually forgotten that Luke had been in the room. I heard a growling sound I didn't realize was me at first, sending Max a warning that he had better not hand me over to him.

"Luke, I don't think it is what she wants right now," Max said hesitatingly. "She's weak. She needs rest. I don't think upsetting her more is the answer."

"She may not want me, but I'm her mate. Being with me will help her recover faster." Luke insisted through clenched teeth. I growled again when I felt a Max shift in a way that told me he was unsure of what to do.

"Luke, please. Don't do this."

"I order you to give her to me," Luke ordered. I flinched and tried to bury in Max's protective arms.

I could feel anger radiate off both Max and Luke who stood in front of each other. I really felt the stand off, but I knew max was going to give me over to him because of Luke being who he was. But I could fight against Luke. He was the last person I wanted touching me and so when I felt Max shift me and extend his arms out I held on to him for dear life. Unfortunately I was no match for him pushing me away and Luke pulling me into him. I growled once again when I was no longer in Max's care. I instantly felt warm and safe, and a lot of the pain in my body seemed to melt away. I drifted into a in and out of consciousness as Luke started to walk into what I hoped was my bedroom. All of the pain disappeared the second he laid me down. I involuntary growled when he let go of me. But within seconds I was wrapped up in Luke's arms again and he was laying beside me, holding me tightly.

"Luke, she's going to be so angry in the morning." I heard Macy say quietly. She must have figured that I was asleep.

"I am sure she will be. But she needs me," He whispered. I could feel his eyes on me. "I need to do this." Macy sighed.

"Okay, just let me know if you leave before she wakes up and I'll-"

"I'm not leaving."

I lay still with my eyes closed and listening silently to see what they would say, but nothing else was said. I just heard two sets of foots steps, one lighter than the other,, leaving the room, the door closing gently behind them. The room became perfectly still and silent as I lay in Luke's arms soaking up all the warmth he was willing to offer. I felt the blanket being pulled over us and he pulled me against him tighter. I drifted off to blessed sleep, wishing him to be gone by the time I woke up.

Pearson

YOU WANT THE TRUTH?

It felt wonderful sleeping in a bed that was soft and warm. How different it was from last night when I had slept on the shower floor. Throughout the night I awoke from what felt like I was being choked and my throat burned. I could smell something in the room that caused my body to ache. My vision was like a blurred tunnel, everything was fuzzy except for the glass that sat on the bedside table. I knew that was what I smelled, but my body was in such pain I couldn't move to grasp what I needed. All the warmth and comfort of my bed disappeared as pins and needles felt like they were stabbing every part of my body. The weight on the bed shifted as the glass was brought to my lips.

The upper part of my body lifted and I gasped at the pain it caused, it felt like every bone was ice and shattered. The beverage in the glass pressed to my lips was the most irresistible I could imagine, and it was right under my nose. The warmth of the blood dripped into my mouth, and I greedily swallowed, opening my mouth wider in anticipation of more. The pain in my throat started to subside, and my vision focused more. I could hear another person breathing close beside me. I was able to drink normally though I found it hard to hold the glass. It felt as if it weighed as much as a freight train. I also was aware that I was being cradled, which upset me but all I was able to do was focus on drinking the precious liquid.

The glass taken out of my hands when I finished, and I moaned. I looked up to see Luke holding me and setting it back on the table. Why was he still in my room and why was he treating me like a child? He laid me back down and wrapped his arms around me in which I fell back to sleep almost immediately. This happened many times throughout the night. Every every time I awoke I felt better. My vision increasingly became clearer. I was able to move around and get my glass that seemed to be refilled every time I awoke. Yes, Luke seemed to have never left my side always trying to help me in some way that seemed overbearing. He didn't say much except one time when I choked from drinking too fast, and it was just a question if I was okay.

After about the fifth time I woke up, the the glass of blood no longer sat on the nightstand. The sun was finally up, and the clock read 7:49 am It felt like I couldn't have gotten any sleep last night, due to the countless times I woke up, but somehow I felt rejuvenated. Luke's arms were still tightly wrapped around me and I silently removed them. Moving to get off the bed, I noticed that my body was oddly sore in a way I had never felt before, I decided from the shower floor. Then my vision blurred and I became light headed, and lost my balance. Of course, Luke caught me.

"Annie, baby, you are still really weak. I don't think standing and walking around is the best idea right now," he said quietly, as I tried to take a step away from him and almost collapsed again. My head was exploding, I was so frustrated.

"I have to use the restroom," my voice was very weak.

"Mary Bell, come here, quickly." He said, his voice loud enough to cause my head to pulse with pain.

Mary came rushing in and stopped in front of us. He stood and said something into her ear. She nodded, and he walked away. Mary began to help me stand and walk over to the bathroom. I felt useless and hated needing help just to get to the bathroom. I splashed water on my face and it felt wonderful. I stole a glance in the mirror and became horrified. How sick I looked, paler than I have ever seen myself. There were dark circles under my eyes. My lips looked dried and cracked as I ran my tongue over them. They hurt, too. I gathered up every bit of strength I had and stepped out of the bathroom. Mary waited outside the door, looking worried. I let her support a lot of my weight because to be honest I was just too tired to make it back to my bed without help.

"Here Annie, drink this." She pushed another glass of blood in my hands. I wasn't really thirsty but I was just too tired to argue with her. "The more you drink the better you will feel," she said.   I chugged the glass and handed it back to her empty. "You still need to rest. You deprived your body of food for two days and it will take the rest of the morning until you feel somewhat normal." I nodded while she pulled the blanket over me and walked away.

I felt weak, but not like before. I knew I needed more sleep, but I just felt restless. I lay in my bed and just looked out of the window. I wasn't really paying attention to noise in the house or the small pain that remained in parts of my body. I just watched the clouds gracefully roll by my window. I didn't even notice when another person entered the room and climbed into the bed with me. It caused me to jump when I felt an arm wrap around me and pull me toward the center of the bed. I turned my head to see that Luke had come back. His eyes were closed and he looked as tired as I felt. My eyes became heavy when I looked at the sleeping Luke, and wondered why he had come back into my room. I guessed he was trying to be a nice guy and make up for everything he had done. It was hard to stay mad when you're so tired. I gave up and drifted off to sleep.

When I awoke, the clock finally came in to view when my eyes adjusted to the lights. 11:27 am I rolled from my side to my stomach and stretched, which felt so good. I looked next to me where Luke sat up against the headboard tapping away on his phone and stopped as soon as I sat up to take the other drink off the table and drank it all.

I stood up and didn't fall over. I was still a little

stiff and some joints were sore, but nothing too extreme. The fresh air did wonders to my aching body when I walked outside. I had not been in direct sunlight since I changed. It was a weird feeling, and hard to describe how the sun felt against my skin. My thoughts overwhelmed me until I heard someone clear their throat behind me. I had forgotten that I wasn't alone in the room and that the other person couldn't come out here in the sun. I knew I was going to have to talk about what had happened the last couple of days. I just wish they would put it off until I could think of something better than the truth.

"Annie, can you please come inside? We need to talk." I sighed. I am not going to get my wish. I hesitated, not wanting to leave the odd but rich sensation of the sun on the balcony. I slowly gave in and made my way back into the room. I could feel his gaze burning holes in my back. I turned and saw Luke standing there, leaning against the bedpost wearing nothing but black pajama bottoms.

I have said it before and I will say it again, damn these vampires and their sexy bodies. I felt my fangs extend and I looked away as fast as I could. I noticed the bedside table where another glass of fresh blood had been placed. Thank god for Mary, I thought. I rushed over and grabbed the glass pretending to be absorbed by it so I would not be distracted by the half-naked Luke standing at the end of the bed.

"Annie, do you have any idea how badly you frightened everyone?" I finished off the glass of blood, and immediately regretted not savoring it more. "Annie! Answer me, and stop pretending I don't exist." I flinched at the coldness of his voice.

"What do you want me to say?" I replied, trying to mimic his tone. Was he trying to make me feel guilty? Really? I hate being interrogated, and I will not tolerate it.

"Don't get smart with me, Annie." Luke said, in a much less arrogant way, although through clenched teeth. He came toward me.

"Then don't question me like that!" I said loudly. I walked away from him.

"Stop avoiding the question and just answer it!" He bellowed, grabbing my wrists and yanking me around to face him.

"I didn't mean to 'scare' anyone," I said, using bunny finger air quotes. "I didn't know taking a shower was a crime even in this screwed up vampire country. I didn't know it would cause the world to panic. I just wanted to be clean." I pulled away from him, trying to get to the bathroom again.

Everything happened so fast and I was disoriented, and somehow, my head hit the wall with a huge bang. If I was still human, I am sure I would be dead. As a vampire, it only felt like someone had slapped me upside the head. Suddenly, Luke gripping my shoulders and holding me trapped up against the wall. He was angry, but he was in control. I know because there was no black in his eyes. I wondering if I was going to probably piss him off even more in the next few minutes, and I would see them turn.

"Why can't you ever just give me a straight

answer? Please, just stop these games and tell me the truth," he screamed, sounding angry and defeated.

"You want the truth?" I screamed, a rush of adrenaline shot through me, and was able to shove him with such force that he slammed up against the wall opposite me. He opened his eyes, the whites of his eyes were gone and there it was, the solid black eyes I expected to see. But I was not done, and I was beyond being afraid, so his being all pissed off was not going to stop what I was going to say. He walked toward me with his fists clenched. I stood against the wall, ready to attack him.

"I hate you! I hate what you have done to Joel, Macy and Max! I hate what you have done to me. I hate everything about you, and I wish I had never laid eyes on you!" I screamed at him, with everything I had inside me. He stopped. His eyes were no longer black. He just stood there listening to me rant. "I will always hate you! I wish your family never got the crown from that bitch's family! Then I wouldn't be stuck here with you! I have never hated anyone or anything as much as you!

Luke was in front of me, putting his hand over my mouth so tight that I couldn't even move my jaw to bite him so he would release me. I could feel his body shaking violently against mine. His head was beside mine resting against the wall that I was pinned against. His ragged breathing was hissing in my ear. He sounded like he was out of breath. I tried to move, but his grip on my mouth tightened and I started crying when I felt the pain sharpen in my wrist. Tears fell down my cheek. Gradually,l I noticed the grip he had on me started to loosen as his breathing slowed.

"What is it you want from me?" He said in a low whisper. I wasn't even sure if he was talking to me or himself, so I stayed silent. His grasp was not as tight, but I knew I would not be able to get away from him.

"Annie?" He said softly as he pulled away from me and took a few steps back. He stared at the ground shoving his hands in his pockets.

"I'm sorry. I just..." Luke stopped and just lowered his head. "I don't know what to do anymore." I wiped away the tears from my eyes and stood up a little straighter.

"I think what you should do is leave my room." I tried saying in a strong voice, but it came out sounding scared and frightened. He shook his head, and he walked out the door without another word. As he was about to shut the door behind him, I remembered there was something I needed to tell him.

"Luke, wait." He stopped in the open doorway, but didn't turn to look at me.

"What do you want, Annie?"

"There is something I need to tell you before you leave." Somehow, I had won.

"What is it?" He did sound vanquished.

IN WHAT UNIVERSE

"What is it?"A big smirk appeared across my face and I saw a slight gleam in his eyes.

"I'm not signing that petition," I said, letting him know that getting rid of me was not going to be so easy. He just stared.

"What?" He said as he closed my bedroom door and took a step toward me while I took a step away from him.

"I said that I'm not going to sign that petition that you and that whore made." I said a little louder this time.

"Why? Why won't you sign it?" Luke demanded. I stood my ground; he was not going to intimidate me to.

"In what universe would you ever think that I would sign that pile of trash?" I spat at him.

"I don't understand why you won't sign it. You don't want me, you have made that perfectly clear over and over again. Didn't you just tell me how much you hated me in no uncertain terms?" Luke was ferocious. "You don't want to be my Princess or the Queen. I don't understand why you can't just

give me a little peace and a chance to be happy?"
He shook his head. "I know Leah doesn't love me,
but at least she wants me, even if it's just to get to be
Queen. It's the best I'm ever going to get since you
hate me so much." This last sentence came out
much quieter, his voice cracking

"Did you think I wasn't going to read it before
signing it?" I said.

"What are you talking about. You always read
everything before you sign it." Luke countered.

"Actually, your mother read me the Petition. She
wasn't very happy." I walked back over to my bed
and sat down. "I will never sign that Petition or
agree to anything that you or that bitch wants."

"So, this stunt is about giving your having to give
me a child!" Luke scoffed, shaking his head again.
"I'm sorry but you're the only person that can
produce my heir. Like it or not, you are my mate."

"Actually it has nothing to do with that!" I was
seething. This was true. "I understand that I'm the
only one that can provide you with your heir. But
you are not getting away with the rest of it!"

I decided I didn't want to be in the room with him,
and just had to get away, anywhere he wasn't. I
pushed past him while walking toward the door. I
started to wonder what had happened to Joel. I felt
his hands wrap around my shoulders as I was forced
to stop and spin around to face him. I could feel his
breath, the hotness of his touch.

"Okay, Annie. I'll bite. What are you talking
about?" He seemed a touch confused.

"The only stipulation there is for you to provide

me with an heir." Again, I pushed him away.

"I don't believe a single word that comes out of your mouth," I said, almost laughing. "I read the Petition, Luke! I know exactly what the stipulations are." I stopped and took a deep breath to calm myself. "What a liar you are. You used me, and you want to kill me, and I'm not going to stand here and listen to you lie about *your Petition*," I put the emphasis on 'your' by poking him in the chest. I actually reached the door, and was hoping to slam it shut, when I felt Luke's breath on my neck.

"I didn't write the Petition," he said whispering into my ear from behind me. "I couldn't even stand to read the damn thing, let alone write it." He sighed, putting his hand over his eyes. "It took me hours to work up enough strength to sign my name, followed by the hours of crying alone in my office because even though you hate me, I'm still in love with you." Luke walked out of the room, making sure to slam the door. I listened to his footsteps echoing down the hall.

What had he just said? It felt as if my heart were racing, but I was frozen in the entry way. He slammed my door, I thought, becoming hysterical. My mind was racing trying to process what Luke had said to me, and what it all really meant. Was he telling me the truth or was he lying to save himself? Which did I want to believe? It felt like my heartbeat was echoing in my ears to the point I couldn't discern from them and the footsteps retreating in the hall. I couldn't calm down. A sick headache started to form and I felt the room start to spin. It all stopped when I heard a knock on the door. I took a deep breath. Opening the door, I found a very distressed looking Mary.

"The Queen wants to speak with you, immediately," she said, looking around nervously.

"Okay, I'll change and go with you." I went toward my closet.

"No, the Queen said now, she doesn't care what you're wearing."

She grabbed my wrist and started pulling me toward the back stairwell. She never let go until we were inside the Queen's office. The Queen, Macy, Mickey, Susan, and three other women that I had seen around but didn't know were all standing around the Queen's desk. When they saw me come in, they stopped what they were doing. They stared at me for a moment, then looked down. Except for the Queen, of course. Krista started walking toward me. She wasn't any happier than the last time I saw her. She raised her hand and slapped me across the face. I just looked at her in shock as the stinging and burning sensation grew.

"Don't you ever do that again!" She said in a loud but controlled voice. "I put up with a lot of things that you do, but that little stunt just crossed the line." Krista went back to her desk. She turned to face me, and pointed at me. "You will not endanger my son again, do you understand?" I just nodded my head. I could not speak. I was still in shock that she had actually hit me, and hit me that hard.

"Good, now get over here, we all need to discuss what our plan for tomorrow is," she said, returning to her desk. I followed slowly, still holding my cheek.

"What's happening tomorrow?" I said quietly, as I felt Macy wrap her arm around me.

"Well tomorrow, my dear Annie, there is a Court Council Meeting, where they will discuss the Petition, " her voice was dripping with sarcasm. "We need to know Annie, what are you going to do?"

"I don't know, is there anything I can do?" I answered meekly.

"Yes Annie, there is! You need to fight this!" Krista was yelling at me. I flinched, the slap was still fresh in my memory.

"I thought the Council wouldn't agree to any of this. so why do I need to fight?" I said, somewhat confused.

"No, that's not quite how it works, Annie." Krista said picking up the papers off of her desk. "It's somewhat like a Court Hearing. They will ask if both parties have fully read and understand the Petition at hand. Then, they will ask you if you want to sign as is, sign with revision, or refuse to sign."

"What happens if I choose any of these options?" Krista sat, and everyone else followed suit.

"Well, the first option is simple, the stipulation that I told you about will be enforced, the second they will read and discuss things openly with you, Luke, and Leah. There will be compromises made until you agree to a document both parties will sign. The third option is you refuse to sign it and the Petition will be thrown out and can't be submitted for approval again." She was looking at me with a questioning look as the options rolled around in my mind.

"What are you going to choose to do?" She asked. I felt every persons' eyes in the room on me.

"Well, I would never take the first option unless I am forced to. So, I just need to decide if I want to take the second or third option." I heard a few deep breaths being released.

"That is a start, I guess. You need to think over the options very carefully before tomorrow." I felt Macy and Mickey's hands pat my shoulder for reassurance. "Now on to the second issue. The engagement party that Miss Mohan is throwing tonight," Macy spoke up this time.

"We believe, based on Luke's reaction and statements, that it is not really an engagement party as she calls it." She smiled oddly, almost mischievously as she said this.

"I already know that. My son has told me all about her buying her own ring. What I want to know is whether you three will be going to the party." I looked down, remembering Leah had said that I was not invited.

"No," Macy said firmly, "I will not be in attendance, but Max feels the need to go and stand beside Luke, as he is required." Krista nodded at her response and looked over to Mickey.

"I will not be attending either." She said with a slightly sad undertone. Krista nodded. Susan began speaking

"Josh and I have decided that we will not attend the *party*, and have informed Luke already of our decision and our loyalty to Annie." I was shocked, Susan was loyal to me. I knew that they were my friends, but hearing them say they were loyal made me feel an unexplainable but empty sadness.

"Very good. That makes me feel much better about the situation." Krista said looking to the women surrounding her. Then it hit me, those ladies were her friends, too.

"Okay, that is all the work we have to do. Oh, and, Annie." I looked up at my name.

"Yes?" I asked, coming out of my self indulgent thoughts.

"Please, make sure to have your decision ready by tomorrow morning when I send for you." She waved her hand in a brushing motion, signaling for us to leave the room.

Pearson

I HAVE A THEORY

As we walked out of the Queen's office I felt Macy wrap her arm around me and pulled me into a tight hug then gave me a sympathetic look.

"Are you okay? That slap looked like it hurt," Macy said, as we all started walking up the back stairway.

"It did. Why did she slap me anyway?" I said, rubbing my slightly swollen face.

"Because you came close to starving to death." Mickey piped in, holding the door to the top floor open.

"And why does she my starving to death would be endangering Luke?" They all followed me into my room.

"Well, Annie, you and Luke are mates. If one of you dies, the other dies soon after," Macy said simply.

"Oh," was all I could say. I truly didn't know that, understand it or even believe it. The Queen could have done a lot worse to me than just a slap for inadvertently almost killing her only son.

The girls started talking to me, but I wasn't really able to focus on what they were saying. I kept thinking about almost being responsible for killing Luke. I may not like Luke, but I didn't want him dead. After a while of mindless chattering, food appeared and everyone drifted off to dine with their mates or go get ready for Leah's party. Susan didn't leave and we sat quietly on the bed for a few seconds before she spoke.

"Annie, have you thought about what you're going to do tomorrow at the Council Meeting?"

"Not really," I said quietly. I knew she could hear me. I just wanted to make sure people that might be listening in to our conversation couldn't.

"Are you considering the first option?" Susan asked in a quieter voice.

"No," I almost laughed. "I would never allow Luke or Leah to get away with that." I giggled.

"That's good. So, it's really just a decision between editing the Petition or simply refusing to so sign it."

"Yeah, and that's where I'm stuck." I said, resting my chin on my hands and chewing my lip.

"I see," she said thoughtfully. "Do you want to talk about what you're stuck about?"

I stayed silent for some time. I wasn't sure how to answer this. My thoughts were all over the place. If I choose option 2, Leah still wins and gets to be Queen. I didn't want her to be Queen! I fear she would become an even bigger monster and just start destroying everything like her family before her. It felt like there was an elephant sitting on my chest thinking of all the horrible things she was capable of. On the positive side, I would finally be free of Luke. His words from this morning echoed in my head.

'I couldn't even stand to read the damn thing let alone write it. It took me hours to work up enough strength to sign my name followed by hours of crying alone in my office because even though you hate me, I'm still in love with you.'

Did I believe him? Not really. He has done nothing but tell me lies and trick me in the short time I have known of his existence. How could I believe him now? I could still feel Susan's eyes on me, and she was saying something.

"Susan, to be honest, I don't want Leah to be Queen," I said, interrupting her. "Something inside me just hates the idea. I can never allow that leech to be Queen!" I could hear Susan let out long, deep breath of relief.

"Okay. Why do you suppose that is?"

"I just hate her. Plus, something that Luke said makes me wonder what she would do if she did become the Queen." I said. I felt the bed move, Susan shifted next to me.

"What did Luke say?" She looked worried.

"Have you read the Petition?" I asked. She shook her head no. "I don't have the authority to read council documents." I did a quick run through of the Petition's stipulations as her eyes grew wide with shock. "Annie, I'm so sorry, when did you find this out?" I shrugged my shoulders.

"A few days ago. I just wanted to take a hot shower because I felt so cold and my body hurt so badly," I said, sitting up and leaning against the headboard, "I fell asleep and I couldn't get up and just kept going back to sleep and..." She pulled me into a hug.

"That explains so much, everyone was freaking trying to figure out why you acted that way. Everything makes sense now." I wasn't really sure if she was talking to herself or me.

"Well," I said after a long awkward silent moment, "that's not even all of it." She looked at me wide-eyed.

"What else could there be?"

"Well, I told Luke this morning before I went to meet with the Queen that I was not going to sign petition, and he got really angry." Susan's forehead creased up and looked really confused.

"Wait, he was angry, are you sure?" I nodded.

"I'm pretty sure he yelled at me, when I told him, and he sounded pretty angry." She shook her head.

"I don't understand, I figured he would have been happy." I could see that she was trying to figure things out.

"I have a theory about it all," I said. "I think he had this planned all along. He has always wanted to be with Leah and I ended up as his mate. So he did everything that would make me hate him and it worked," I said almost giggling. "He finally got what he wanted, me out of the picture. He literally wants me dead. Then he gets to have his life with Leah." I felt the sharp shooting pain again in my heart. It was weird. It was like a fire poker that's burning hot point was shoved straight into my heart.

I almost giggled at the thought that it could be heartburn but Susan started talking and I was pulled out of my thoughts.

"No, I distinctly remember the day he came back with Max after he found you." she said solemnly. "He wouldn't do that. He would never want you dead, Annie. He would die too."

"But if our bond was broken he and that bitch could just kill me off and it wouldn't matter." She shook her head again.

"No, a broken bond doesn't work like that. As a matter of fact, there has only been one other vampire whose bond was broken, and it almost killed him. Really, it would have been better if it had."

"Why is that?" I wondered. "What happened?"

"Josh told me about it, so I'm not really sure if I can remember it all, but this vampire, he was older than us when he was turned. I think he was in his mid-30's or so, but when you find your mate, they are usually younger than you are or about the same age. So, when he found his mate, she was already married with two children and another on the way." She looked sad. "The way Josh told the story, this vampire couldn't bring himself to take her from her children just because he wanted her. So, after some time he just tried to avoid seeing her and get over her but he couldn't. Finally, he decided to go to the Council and beg them for help. They suggested they break the bond for him. So, he agreed to do the ritual. Josh explained that it's like experiencing the thing you love the most just being ripped away but in the end you still love them and want them more than anything. You just can't see them," she said as I watched her eyes glaze over as she tried to hold back the tears.

"What do you mean you can't see them? What happened to this vampire?

"Exactly what I said, you can't see them, they are invisible. It's like they don't exist anymore, but you remember them. You're still left with all your feelings, the wants, the needing....," she looked down. "He lives down in the basement of the palace now. He lost his mind and killed a lot of vampires and humans trying to find her. But of course, he couldn't. He is in a room down there. He's allowed to leave, although he never does. He was even forgiven for what he did. His mind is just gone.

I couldn't bear to hear any more about this sad vampire. I felt so bad for him and what he had gone through, all because he loved his mate so much. As soon as I thought of this man sitting alone in the basement I wanted to see him. I don't know why, but I just wanted to talk to him. I could feel my heart accelerating as I imagined what the bond being broken would feel like. My door swung open, and Max and Macy came walking in all arm and arm. I looked away. I was happy for them, but I was kind of jealous, and I hated feeling that way. Josh was right behind him with well as Bobby and Mickey.

"So we were thinking we would hang out at the pool tonight and basically get drunk," Susan said, all chipper. It shocked me how happy she compared to a few seconds ago.

"Oh yes," Macy and Mickey said at the same

time, which made me laugh.

Everyone started chatting about mindless things, I could tell they were all basically avoiding the topic on the part which I wish they weren't, and it just made me feel more uncomfortable when it had an awkward silence. Josh was talking about the work he was doing for the King and was not going to drink with us girls all night at the pool. This made me think of something.

"Hey Macy, where is Joel? I haven't seen him in a few days."

"Oh he went on a business trip with his father. Joel is training to take his father's place soon. I forgot to tell you. He will be back in a week or so."

"Oh, sounds fun." I shrugged.

To be honest, I wasn't even very interested in seeing Joel. I was more concerned that he was okay. I was about to respond to Macy, but there was a knock on my door. Luke came in and stood in the doorway dressed in dark pants and a black button down shirt and had rolled up the sleeves. I quickly looked away from him, thinking he was all dressed up for Leah and his engagement party. I resisted the urge to growl at him and make a scene by insisting he leave my room. I resented him just coming in like that.

"We need to go, or we'll be late." Luke said as I just looked out the window and realized how dark it was. The moon was so big.... I heard Max getting up; I also heard kissing noises. I shut my eyes.

"So is there any chance that we can leave early if we arrive early?" Bobby said, chuckling.

"Let's hope so," Max said, the door closing behind them. The room was silent for a bit.

"Can we go drink now?" I said, staring at the moon again.

"Yes!" Everyone said, simultaneously.

They all left to go change into swimsuits. I found a beautiful, pure white swimsuit. It reminded me of the moon in a way, and I felt it was very fitting. I looked good in it. There was a knock on the door, and I hurried to open it. Mary stood there, looking more than a little confused.

"Annie, I was just coming by to remind you about your meeting with the Queen first thing in the morning. She said to have your answer for her by then."

"Thank you Mary," I nodded and she started to walk away. "Oh wait, can I ask you something?"

"Of course you can, Annie."

"The man who lives in the basement, what's his-"

"You mean Egon Morris?" She interrupted

"Is he the man that broke his bond with his mate?

"Yes. Normally, only prisoners are held in the basement. He chose to live there."

"Oh, I see. Thank you Mary." I said. She did not look happy. In fact, she looked a bit ticked off.

"Annie, you cannot go down there. He cannot not help you with the situation you are in." Her tone was cold and flat. "I don't know who told you about him, but please trust me when I say this."

"Okay, I just wanted to know his name. Thank you." She nodded and quickly walked away.

Mary's words freaked me out slightly, but all was

forgotten when I finally reached the pool. They were all there waiting for me. We had a few drinks and I was laughing my ass off. They were sharing largely embarrassing stories, which just got funnier and funnier. Yes, somehow Egon Morris' name would pop up in my brain, but I quickly shoved all thoughts of him away. I couldn't shake the feeling that I really needed to talk to him. I realized at some point I was wasted. We were all just lying around on the deck chairs. It was all too funny for no clear reason. I remember hearing a weird clicking noise, and then it was gone. Then I heard it again, it seemed to be getting louder by the second. I was frightened out of my mind when I heard a high pitch scream a few feet away from me.

"How dare you not come to your Prince and Princess's engagement party!" I opened my eyes. I guess I didn't realize I had started to drift off. As I looked around trying to figure out what was happening,, I could see that Macy, Mickey, and Susan were disoriented, too. I started laughing again, and they did too.

"You think this is some type of joke?" Leah was there. Why was she there?

"No, but I think your make-up is." Macy said. We all started to high five each other. This was great. I failed and almost did a face plant, but I caught myself just in time.

"When I become Queen, you are really going to regret saying that to me, bitch," she said, pointing her finger at Macy.

"What have I told you about threatening my

mate?" Max was was somehow in front of Leah. I could feel the white hot anger radiating off of him.

"Luke!" She screamed. Great, I thought. Everyone is going to come join our girl's night out. I looked over and saw Josh and Luke talking to each other. I glanced over to Mickey, who was already cuddling into Bobby's lap like a cat. That made me laugh.

"You Bitch, stop laughing!" That's it, I thought, getting up. I was going to wipe the ground up with her..

"Sit down Annie," I heard Bobby say. "Don't even think about it." He winked at me. I was taken aback. I looked back at Leah. Max still stood there, blocking her view of Macy.

"Leah, we had this discussion earlier today. You cannot threaten my friends. You also need to stop telling people we are engaged and that you are a Princess. You also have been informed that if my bond is broken, you only get the title and nothing more. You will not have any of the privileges or power that goes with the title besides the name." Luke said this walking up and standing next to Max.

"But it's not fair!" Leah shrieked. Those three just publicly humiliated me by not showing up to our party. Why are you not upset about this? Plus, are you really going to let Annie get away with undermining you? She is turning your so called 'friends' against you." She was wagging her finger at all of us, and I started laughing again.

"First, nobody is getting punished," Luke said patiently. "Annie had nothing to do with who came and who didn't. Secondly, your party was not an official royal party so they had no obligation to come." She stared at him a moment, then stormed away, amid a rash of stifled and not so stifled laughter.

"I have some business to deal with and I will see you all tomorrow." Luke said.

"Why don't you stay and relax with us?" I heard Max say, sitting down next to me.

"Thank you, but no. I know when I'm not wanted." Having said that, Luke walked quickly back to the house. It was pretty quiet then. I had nothing to say and everyone was having mate make out happy hour. I'm not really sure how much later, but I quickly drifted off to sleep.

Pearson

EGON

I shivered; a cold breeze washing over me woke me up. I sat up and became confused as to how I had gotten to my bed in my room. It was early morning and the sun had not even rose completely. The sky was a swirl of light pastel colors. The palace was silent. I sat on the edge of my bed. It felt odd to wake up at this time in this way. I showered and changed, and still the sun had barley risen, although I could hear people moving quietly around now.

My stomach was queasy and I felt the need to keep moving because sitting still was driving me insane. The Council Meeting was today, and I had no idea when it was going to start. I just had to sit here and wait until the Queen called for me and my answer. The answer that I still didn't have. The the idea came to me. I must go speak to the vampire in the basement, Egon. I got up, ran to my door and to the back stairwell as fast and quietly as I could. I ran down all the flights of stairs, stopping only at the door. I had never been in the basement before. I wondered how much trouble I would be in for being here.

I decided it didn't really matter, because I didn't have any time to waste deciding. I needed to talk to Egon. I opened the door and was met by an empty hallway with many doors lining the walls. Walking forward, many of the doors had black title plates on them. I eventually found Egon's door and froze before it, staring at the metal door. What was the real reason I came down here? This man could be very dangerous. I stood there, biting on my finger nails and debating what I should do, when I heard a man start yelling from the other side of the door.

"Will you stop biting on your nails!"

I was too scared to do anything besides stand there and look at the door, like a complete moron. My heart rate finally slowed down, after standing there for what seemed like a long time. I have no idea what I was doing and I really should have run away the moment he yelled at me. Suddenly, the door opened, and I felt my stomach drop and I wanted to scream for my life. Egon's hand gripped the door and pulled it open enough to see only half of his dark silhouette.

"You need to leave." Was all he said, and he closed the door, which just pissed me off. So, I did something that I can't seem to stop doing. I provoked him.

"Well you really need a bath! We all don't get what we want now do we?" I said as nastily as I could, crossing my arms over my chest. I was feeling quite pleased with myself.

There was silence for a long time as I felt that he was never going to speak to me again, until I heard a sigh and the door opened again. Egon stepped back away further and further as the door slowly moved open showing me a darkened room. It was actually a cell. I stood motionless. I was unsure of what he was doing or what he wanted from me. Was this his way of letting me into his room? Or was he just setting up some kind of trap? Would he kill me as soon as I entered the room?

"If you're not going to leave, then come in," he said. I heard a match being struck, and saw through the open door that he had lit a candle.

His back was to me and I could tell he was a very tall, lanky man with untamed hair that hung past his shoulders. I stepped in, glancing around the dimly lit room. There was a small bed, a desk and chair. There was also a window that had no light coming through it because it was covered. Egon moved and sat on his bed and just looked down at the ground. I closed the door, and went over and sat on the chair opposite him. He was shifting his feet back and forth around in the dirt which made up the ground.

"Why are you here?" His voice was soft. I couldn't help but wonder what type of person he was before his bond had been broken.

"I wanted to talk to you about what happened to you when your bond was broken," I said. Never known for being subtle, I even shocked myself.

"Like I told the prince, I cannot help you." Egon said. He lay down, facing away from me.

"Luke came down here?" I was shocked.

"He's been coming every day for the past week." Egon said. His voice was a singsong.

"What does he want?"

"The same thing as you. Your bond's is about to be broken, and you're both scared." He started laughing manically. "Well, maybe you're not scared, because you want this. You must be elated that you are going to get your way." Egon said his last statement in a way that shook me up pretty badly.

"Do you know what I would have given to have what you're just throwing away, like its nothing?"

Egon stood up very quickly, towering over me. I saw his eyes were fully black. I was unable to move, looking up at him from the chair. As fast as he jumped up, he sat back down on his bed. I was afraid to move after his sudden mood swing. I was wishing I had never closed that door and I could have made a clean run for it. But I had shut the door and I mentally slapped myself for that one.

"I'm sorry for the outburst. Sometimes its hard to control my emotions." Egon's voice softened. "I think it's best if you go now." I stood up to go, and he stood also. Suddenly, he was blocking my path.

"I just want to know, how can you not feel anything for your mate?" he demanded. It was heartbreaking to see the sadness in his face, in his eyes.

"Egon," I said gently. "I did feel something for Luke. But then I realized he didn't care for me, and that he was just trying to manipulate me."

He just looked completely confused. "Dear child, what happened to make you not care for him?"

I started telling him my story. Everything, from the beginning, starting when Max had disappeared. My birthday, Joel. How I really loved him and was going to marry him. I told him about Max and Luke showing up and everything that had happened since my arrival at the palace. I told him about what happened at Macy and Max's wedding and what happened the next day. I told him about the Petition and how devastated I was after reading it. I slowly told him everything it said. He looked away, staring at something that wasn't there, it seemed.

"Interesting tales that come to my door," he said thoughtfully. "You tell one story, the Prince tells another. Ultimately, I don't want to be involved in your problems." Egon lay down on his bed again.

"What story has Luke been telling you?" I demanded.

"A story like yours, but with major differences. I told you before, I can't help either one of you. Its best you take your leave before anyone notices you are gone, and figure out that you are down here." I was furious at this point and stomped over to the door, thinking what a waste of time this was.

"Don't break your bond. You would survive, but he is not as strong as you. He won't make it through the pain." Egon said this, before rolling over and blowing out the candle. I was in the dark. Only it seemed I could see things I hadn't seen before.

As I slowly closed the door behind me, his words echoed over and over again in my mind. I walked back down the empty hallway. What did he mean Luke was not strong enough to survive our bond breaking, he seemed pretty strong to me! I pushed the door open to the stairwell and ran smack into Luke.

"What are you doing down here?" He looked very tired. He had gray circles under his eyes.

"I..." I froze, and he just kept staring at me. I looked away from him, not wanting to see him like this.

"I was lost." I lied. He stepped out of my way.

"Don't come down here again," he said, trying to close the door behind him and on me.

"What? Why am I not allowed down here and you are?" I called after him, holding the door open.

"I don't want to fight with you Annie, especially today. I have enough to deal with as it is," Luke said softly, almost to himself, and kept walking until he went into Egon's room.

I walked all the way back up to my floor and when I came out of the stairwell, I saw Macy was coming out of my room, looking pretty upset. She ran over to me and dragged me back to the stairwell and back down I went.

"Where were you, everyone has been looking for you?" Macy said, pulling me forcefully.

"I was in the basement." Macy came to a stop and I almost slammed into her.

"Why were you down there?"

"I wanted to talk to Egon." I said, looking away from her."

"Oh, no! Why? That man is crazy, and he could have killed you!"

"It's not important Macy. Where are we going?"

I attempted to change the subject. I did not want to talk about Egon.

"Oh, right," she started pulling me harder. "It's almost time to meet with the Queen.

The Council will meet shortly thereafter. "I stayed quiet as we came to the floor of the Queen's office. When we entered the hallway, all the women that were in the Queen's office yesterday were there waiting. They were just chatting and stopped when we approached. I really hate it when people do that. It always makes me feel uncomfortable. The door opened a moment later and Krista was standing there, looking irritated.

"Annie I want to speak to you alone first," she said. I walked in and she closed the door quickly behind me, going right to her desk. "Sit, we haven't much time." I sat in front of her. "So, have you thought about our conversation yesterday?" I nodded, and she just looked back at me with anticipation.

"I am not going to sign the Petition," I said softly. Her face lit up so much. She was glowing.

"That's wonderful news. They're going to ask you why at the Council Meeting. You need to be prepared." She began shuffling with the papers on her desk. "You're going to need to give them a reason, and I'll warn you, they can override your refusal to sign if your answer is not acceptable enough for them. So don't go off and say it is because you hate Leah or have a personal grudge against her." Krista stopped fussing with the things on her desk, and looked at me. I felt my stomach drop at the thought of what the Council could to me if I don't have a good reason for them.

"I understand." I said, while trying to think of a better reason besides that I hate her with every fiber of my being.

"Good. You have about twenty minutes to get presentable. Wear something very formal and classy. Mary will help you, if you need her."

"I only have twenty minutes?" My heart was racing inside my chest. How could it all be happening so fast?

"Yes. I wanted this meeting done and over with by now, but you were missing. By the way, may I ask where you were this morning?" She looked stared at me, demanding an answer with her eyes. All I could do was look down in shame.

"I was down in the basement," I explained, apologetically. I felt like a child caught with their hand in the cookie jar.

"You should not go down there, Annie. I could have told you Egon has nothing he can offer to assist you in your situation." Krista was already back to working on some paperwork on her desk.

"Yes, he told me as much."

"Very well then. You should really go and get ready. I will see you there." I got up to leave.

"You're coming then?" I asked.

"Of course," she nodded. "Luke is my son, Annie. You might not have noticed, but he is in a very dangerous state of mind at the moment, and I need to be there for him as a parent." She gave me a look that I didn't quite understand, but it felt as if she was blaming me for whatever was wrong with him, and that pissed me off.

I walked out without answering her, not really wanting to get in a fight when I had such little time to get ready and mentally prepare myself. I raced up to my room, and Mary. When I got to my room, Mary was there waiting and ushered me quickly in. I stripped and she had a dress ready to slip on the second I was ready. It was a full length gown that was a deep red color. It was a very simple, modest dress, not revealing at all with a very classic cut and fit. I knew this was perfect, and I looked perfect. They did a rush job on my hair up, putting it up in a high slicked-back bun. It was elegant and was a perfect fit with the dress. When she was done with me, we had only five minutes to get there, and we were out the door and headed down the stairs to the council hall. Before they opened the doors to the council hall for me, I took a big long deep breath to try to check my nerves, but I don't think it really helped much. Macy stepped in front of me, pulling me into a tight hug.

"Are you ready to go in?" Macy asked, in a way that didn't help me control my emotions at all.

"Yeah, as ready as I can be." I said, looking around. "Macy, where is Max?" I was going to a Council Meeting that could mean my death. Max had know idea I wasn't going to sign it, so why wasn't he here for me?

"He's with Luke." Was all she said, looking away. My head was spinning, thinking about how Max and would rather be with Luke then his own sister, at a time like this. I stepped closer to the door, and Mickey and Susan came running up. They hugged me and I started laughing. I am sure everyone was starting to think I was crazy.

"I seem to be getting a lot of hugs today." I observed.

"Well, Annie, it is a big day," Mickey responded, and I nodded.

"I know, everyone just needs to relax, so I can calm down." The doors were open, and we could see in, but the room was empty still. I could tell they didn't want to go in, either.

"Okay, we were thinking, we should get drunk after this, no matter what happens." Susan said.

"Agreed," Every one said in unison.

The tension was broken for a moment, but then people started arriving and filling the empty room.. I could feel everyone's eyes on me. I could hear them whispering, which was even worse, because I knew it was about me and I hated it. I looked around the room. It looked just like a T.V. courtroom, except the judge's desk was shaped in a long half circle, and there was no jury box, just two tables and a railing separating it from the audience.

"Well, this would be a good time to go to the restroom." Macy said a bit sarcastically. I was a bit confused by her tone, and then, I heard the voice.

"What are you all laughing about? How inappropriate. I can't wait until you are thrown out of the palace." Leah was standing a few feet behind us, glaring. Now I understood Macy's sentiment.

Leah was wearing a halter dress that was cut

lower than her belly button, and I could tell that there was no back to the dress. Her dress was wildly improper for an official meeting. But what really ticked me off was that standing next to her was Luke. He wearing the same suit he had at Macy's wedding. Luke had his arm around her and I just wanted to look away, but I wasn't going to give them the satisfaction to see how hurt I was. So, I focused on Max, Bobby, and Josh, who were all standing behind them. I was being betrayed by all of them. Well, not so much Bobby, as it was his job to protect the prince.

"Leah, do you realize that we're going to a Council Meeting, and you're wearing your stripper costume?" Macy said. It almost went over my head, I was so distracted by my own thoughts. Everyone started laughing, and it occurred to me everyone was wearing very formal and classy outfits except, of course, for Leah.

"I'm about to become Queen," she said. "Soon, it won't matter what you think at all."

"You won't become Queen unless I sign the document." I said, seething.

"You will sign the petition or else," she said, approaching me. Mickey and Susan closed ranks, and she stopped. I could see that everyone was walking into to the courtroom with their mate, except me. Luke was standing behind Leah.

"Or else what?" I said, giggling. I figured I had lost my mind, so I was just going to go with it.

"That little brother of yours, do you remember him?" Leah hissed at me. It would be such a tragedy if anything happened to him, wouldn't it?" I realized no one could hear her but me. I totally lost control and made a move to rip her face off when I felt a burning sensation grasp around my wrist. Luke was preventing me from giving her what she deserved. He was protecting Leah, which infuriated me further.

"Leah go inside, now!" Luke said, in his angry voice. She looked a bit freaked out and quickly walked into the room.

"Collect yourself before coming in," Luke was saying, as I pulled away from him. He started to walk away, but stopped. "I would never let her touch Benny."

COUNCIL MEETING

What he said should have calmed me down, but really didn't. I took a deep breath, looked around and saw I was standing in an empty hallway. I braced myself and walked through the doors, which the guards promptly closed shut behind me. The room was full with no place to sit, except for a table beside the one where Luke and Leah were seated. I walked over and sat down quietly, not looking at them. I noticed Macy and everyone else was sitting directly behind me, which made me feel slightly better. Almost immediately, a door on my left opened and seven people walked in. I was shocked to see Joel's father was one of the Councilmen. I felt so ashamed and nervous that all this was going to be dragged out in front of a man I had considered my second father. It crossed my mind that this was in my best interest because I believed he would look out for me. At least, I hoped he would. The Council was made up of five men and two women of varying ages. I noticed both the women were older and very stern looking

Everyone stood as they entered except for Luke,

Leah and me. I felt embarrassed that I hadn't stood immediately and moved my chair back to stand. My eyes connected with Luke. He looked shocked and shaking his head no at me. I was confused about what I should do. Was Luke just trying to make me look bad, or was I supposed to stay seated? I saw Max out of the corner of my eye, and he looked worried, and was also shaking his head no at me.

David, Joel's father, was motioning me to stay seated, too. I really needed to figure out what the standing thing was all about because it happened a few times before when the Queen would enter a room. Everyone sat down, and a man who looked about my age picked up a stack of papers and stood at the podium.

"Welcome, everyone," he said, pausing to turn a page. He scowled at it, and his face looked like he had a bad taste in his mouth. I mentally hoped that was a good sign. But his expression only lasted a moment, then became unreadable. I suddenly felt nauseous.

"Well after reading the Petition filed by the Crown Prince and Miss Mohan, I am disturbed in regards to the future of our Kingdom." He stated this, barely looking up from the Petition. "I have served has head of this Council for longer than I can remember. I have served this Monarchy and its Government for the same amount of time. I was also instrumental in overthrowing Miss Mohan's grandparents." Leah's eyes were black and she was baring her teeth. I could also hear a low growl coming from her. All rightly, I was sure that was inappropriate.

"May I remind you, Miss Mohan, that your threats do not frighten me, and if you don't control yourself I will have you and this Petition thrown out in the streets where you both belong!" His voice was deep and authoritative. It frightened me, although I cannot explain why. "As I was saying, this Petition is disgraceful. It makes a mockery of everything that I have worked toward my entire life." I saw Luke stand up very quickly from the corner of my eye.

"May I remind you, Councilman Tenion, that what you speak of is an official document that bares my signature." he said, in a very controlled but angry voice.

"Prince Luke. I am fully aware that your name is on this Petition. Please recall, sir, I helped put your family in power. If it weren't for me and the other members of this Council, your lady friend there and her family would be the reigning monarchy." About now, I was trying to stifle my laughter. Instantly, councilman Tenion looked at me, and I and froze. "Miss. Erickson do you find something funny?" I quickly shook my head no and looked away.

"Let us start with Miss. Erickson, then, if there are no further objections." He looked at Luke again, then back to me. "Miss Erickson, you have not signed this Petition. We need to know what your decision is in regards to this. Are you aware of the options you have? Please address the Council." His eyes were burning into me.

"Annie, you have to speak at the podium," I

heard Bobby whisper from behind me. Councilman Tenion was stepping down and taking his seat. He was whispering something to Joel's father.

"Yes, I am fully aware of what my options are, Sir. I have considered each one and have reached a decision." I'm not even sure where my voice came from. It seemed it was powerful and strong, even though I was scared out of my mind. Tenion and the Council seemed to be smirking at me.

"Good, I won't have to explain it all to you." Tenion sat back with a look of satisfaction on his face. "What is your decision, then?" I felt myself get very hot. I could barely breathe.

My eyes met Joel's father's, and the look in his eyes caused the tears to spill over, but I quickly wiped them away. There was a pleading look behind the sadness in his eyes. In that very second, I understood what he was trying to tell me. But I didn't want to see the truth.

"Well, we are waiting?" Tenion said, almost bemused.

"I...I..." I froze again when heard the Council room door open, and saw Joel step through it. I was shocked. Everyone was shocked and we were all just stared at him. He was looking at me, the same pleading look in his eyes as his father. It made me want to run to him and hold him.

"Miss. Erickson. We require an answer please!" I nodded, taking a breath, and looked back at Tenion.

"I am not signing the Petition." I said. I saw something in Joel's eyes change, and although his face went neutral, I could tell he was pleased with my response, as was David.

"You Bitch!" Leah stood screaming, and started walking toward me. I really didn't feel threatened by her. I found her actions almost funny. "You will sign it, Annie!" With that she lunged, but Luke appeared out of nowhere grabbing her by the neck and slamming her down to the ground. She most definitely had the wind knocked out of her. She was gasping for air. Luke stood over her, his back to me.

"Miss. Mohan! I will not have fighting in this Council Room! You have been warned twice now. Do not get out of line again. Leah that was standing up, looking very pissed off, but she nodded to the Councilman and went back to her seat followed by Luke..

"Miss. Erickson. You have decided not to sign the Petition. Please tell the Council Members what reason or reasons you have to support your decision." Tenion sat back, looking very satisfied with himself.

"Thank you," I said. "My first reason for not signing said Petition is: Lea...Miss Mohan does not present herself in a manner befitting for the title of Queen." I said this, looking at Tenion. He motioned for me to address all the Council members. "Her desire to be Queen has warped her. She cares nothing for Prince Luke, and wants to be with him only to get back the title of Queen, which was taken away from her family and for good reason. She wants the Prince, but she doesn't care for him or his well-being." I saw Tenion nod his head slightly, but the rest of the Council remained stone faced, almost uninterested in what I had to say. "My second reason for not signing the petition," I took a deep breath. "This Petition is a vindictive, vile, nasty expression of who Miss Mohan really is. She plans to murder me, but that is not the worst of what she will do, if she becomes Queen. I would never willingly subject innocent people in her service or the good vampires under her rule to her evil ways. She scares me and I am frightened for this Vampire Country for what she may be capable of, if any part of this Petition is allowed." One of the older women rolled her eyes at me, and that just pissed me off. I was about to ask her what her problem was, when she spoke.

"We already are aware of all of this Miss. Erickson. Is there anything new or factual information you can present to us, or are you just going to restate everything Tenion has already said?" I saw from her icy demeanor she was not my biggest fan, to say the least.

I froze. She looked back at me with a sarcastic smile. She knew I didn't have anything. I lowered my head in defeat. Then I heard the most evil giggle come from behind me. I looked, seeing Leah with the an awful smile on that stupid face of hers. I heard the women say something to Tenion, but I didn't want to listen. I was wracking my brain for anything I could say to help me. I was sure what I had said hadn't won the council over. Then as if by chance, Tenion was speaking to David as all the Council members spoke in hushed tones. I heard him whispering a question about how he could not understand how Luke could even sign something so cruel and evil. A light bulb went off in my head.

"I have another reason!" I almost shouted as everyone stopped and looked at me.

"Fine. Let's have it, what is this new reason?" the woman demanded, annoyed.

"Luke never read the Petition!" I said in the overly excited voice. Both women looked shocked, and I heard people whispering and murmuring throughout the courtroom.

"Miss Erickson, are you suggesting that the Prince never read this Petition, yet he signed and agreed to it, sight unseen?" I just nodded my head, unable to speak. "Prince Luke, please step forward. We have some questions that you must answer." I heard Luke walking up, taking his place next to me. I just hoped he had not been lying to me when he told me that.

"Is Miss Erickson's statement true?" Tenion demanded. "Did you sign your name to this document without reading it?" I glanced out the corner of my eye to look at Luke. I figured he would be angry but he looked almost relieved.

"Yes," was said simply. The murmuring seemed out of control, and I felt lightheaded. I held onto the podium so I wouldn't lose my balance and fall.

"Why did you not read the Petition before you signed it, Prince Luke? You could have sentenced yourself to death!" Tenion smiled sadly. "Basically, that is what you did, in essence." The courtroom was silent.

"I told Miss Mohan that she could write it, with

the one stipulation that Miss Erickson had to produce an heir for me, because she is the only one that can," Luke responded, confused as to what they were alluding to. Did he really think that was all the Petition stated?

"A Petition must be read to be signed and agreed to." An older man at the end of the Council table said, clearing his throat. Everyone looked to him. "He may have the chance to read the Petition now if he chooses to. The Councilman was very wise looking. He also seemed to be the oldest member of the Council. He reminded me of a wizard with his white beard and all. All he would need was a big pointy hat. I tried to hold back my laughter at the thought. "Then Miss Erickson's claim will be invalid." I instantly disliked the man. Tenion nodded his head in agreement.

"Prince Luke, the choice is yours. You can read the Petition or let Miss Erickson's claim stand."

"I will read the Petition now," Luke answered. Tenion almost looked disappointed. I felt as if my brain were being stabbed by a white hot burning knife.

"Luke, you don't really need to read it. She will lose, whether you do or not, so there is no need," I heard Leah saying, in an obnoxious, flirtatious sort of way.

"Leah, shut up now, or I will throw you across the country!" Luke growled at her, and I kind of wished he had listened to her as the room was filled with chatter from the spectators. I wished the floor would just swallow me up. I couldn't take anymore.

"Miss Erickson, since the Prince is now reading the Petition, your claim will be void." Tenion said softly, and the rest of the Council Members nodded in agreement. "Is there anything else you wish to say at this time?" I shook my head in response. There was nothing else. They had won.

I stared at the ground and waited with the rest of the room in complete silence while Luke read the Petition in its entirety. I kept hearing Egon's voice in my head, mocking me. 'You're the one that caused all of this...you threw away your bond like it was nothing...nobody is going to feel sorry for you, you did this to yourself.' I wanted to run but I had no strength. I felt a tear finally spill over and onto my cheek as I tried wiping it away as fast as I could but I knew Tenion and David had saw. I could tell from their expression I was going to lose, and there was nothing I could do about it. I just couldn't look at their faces anymore. The realization of what was about to happen to me was having its full impact on me.

"I withdraw my signature!" A very loud and angry voice echoed throughout the small room. The air was gone out of me, like someone punched me in the stomach. I was gasping for air.

"Luke you can't do that, we are meant to be together!" I heard Leah's high-pitched, whiny voice saying. I just started laughing which earned me a growl, but I just didn't care enough.

"Leah! I told you that there was to be one stipulation, and you wrote this? We are not meant for each other! Annie is my mate! We were meant for each other!" Leah began howling as if she were in pain as he speaking. "You have just caused her to hate me even more. I feel sorry for whoever the pathetic soul is that got you as their mate. I pray that he will reject you. I will help him break the bond so he can be free of you." The room was silent as everyone watched Luke berate Leah.

"Since the Prince has withdrawn his signature, the Petition is no longer valid. This Council Meeting is adjourned." I smiled at Tenion. He once again looked satisfied. David looked relieved as I felt.

I turned to see Macy crying, but she also had a big smile on her face. Max looked very relieved. Next to him stood Joel, looking sad. He didn't look up to meet my gaze. Abruptly, he left through the door he had come in from. I was about to follow him when the big double doors opened, and Queen Krista entered with a Petition in her hands. She had a big smile on her face as she strode into the room. Everyone was bowing as she approached the Council Members. I looked at her, confused. She winked at me.

"Queen Krista! What do we owe the wonderful gift of your presence in our humble Council Meeting?" Tenion was saying, showing her genuine respect.

"Mr. Tenion, I am here to file a Petition." She smiled as she handed him the paperwork.

"Well, look what we have here," he said, a giant smile spreading across his face. "We must look over the Petition in private, then we will set a Court date for Public Hearing." Both he and Queen Krista laughed together, like they were sharing a private joke.

"Mother. What Petition are you filing?" Luke asked, looking just as confused as I and everyone else in the Council Room was.

"You're so impatient Luke. But, if you must know, I am filing a Petition against Miss Mohan."

"What!" I heard Leah scream. "You can't do that!"

"Miss Mohan, I am the Queen. I can do whatever I like, and you should remember that before you raise your voice at me again and I have you put to death." Leah ran out of the room like a scared rabbit amid a smattering of laughter.

"Mother, what is the Petition against her about?" Luke still looked confused.

"You're so thick sometimes. Leah knowingly lied, deceived and threatened the safety of the Crown Prince and his mate." Queen Krista said a little slower than necessary. "I am Petitioning the Council to ban her from being Annie's replacement as Queen and forbidding her ever hold the title for crimes against the Royal Family." She kissed Luke's cheek, and walked out of the room in the the most regal manner I have ever seen.

"This Meeting of the Council is Council Members took their leave.

I flew over to Macy and she hugged me tightly. Max was smiling, looking very relieved. I gave him a dirty look. I wasn't going to forgive him that easy. He excused himself, as did all the guys. I was happy that all the girls stayed with me. We kept hugging each other. We, mostly me, were so happy with the outcome! Eventually we left the Council Room. I was really tired and just wanted to take a nap. They all laughed, but understood. I went up to my room alone. I felt so happy and relieved as I climbed the stairs slowly. I felt so free. I could finally relax for the first time in a very long time.

As soon as I reached my room, I ran in and jumped on the bed twisting so I landed on my back on the super soft bed. Have I ever mentioned how much I liked this bed? It was so comfortable. I was rolling around on my bed acting like a complete fool and weirdo, just enjoying myself, with my eyes closed. Suddenly, I felt like I was being watched. My eyes flew open and there was Luke, sitting on the couch with his head in his hands. I lay still, realizing he must have been there when I came in. I was mortified. I got up, fixing my dress, and walked over to him. I was not really sure what to do. He didn't move or even look at me. It was kind of freaking me out.

"Luke?" I said quietly. He moved very quickly, pressing me against the wall with my hands held above my head by one hand, with the other was being cupped over my mouth as I tried to scream bloody murder.

"I need you to just listen to me." He closed his eyes as he rested his forehead against mine. "I didn't know. I didn't know what was in that Petition," he kept saying softly, as his breath fanning over my face and neck. There was that intense burning sensation where his hands held me, causing me to be dizzy and weak. "If I would have known, I would never have signed it."

Finally, he looked me in the eyes and it felt like my heart was breaking and I was burning up at the same time. I can't explain what I was feeling. He released me as quickly as he had accosted me, and walked out without another word. I was so weak, I just slid down the wall. I had glimpsed Luke's eyes before he left. I was so horrified by what I saw. Luke's eyes had changed into haunted empty blue holes and it was all my fault.

Pearson

WHAT'S GOING ON

I sat there on the floor for a very long time. He was damaged, and I felt guilty beyond words. I kept going over and over everything in my head. What had brought Luke and I to this point. I realized both Luke and I were to blame for this mess. He never lets me finish what I'm trying to say. He always storms off or talks over me. He never listened. Luke was always tricking me and deciding things for me. I was to immature to try to negotiate. Or to keep trying.

I kept sitting there, trying to reason with myself about everything. I had not believed him about the Petition, but who would? He has given me no reason to trust him. From somewhere outside, probably in the hall, I heard a loud crash that caused me to jump up from the floor. I noticed my door was slightly open. I guess Luke didn't close it all the way. I peeked out but didn't see anyone, but I could hear people talking close by. They were whispering, and curiosity got the better of me. I started walking toward the main stairs, but stopped when I turned the corner. Luke was standing with his back to me.

Leah stood against the wall looking down, looking almost frightened. Joel was standing in front of Luke, looking freaked out, and then he saw me. They all just stood there in deafening silence.

"What's going on?" I asked nervously. Luke turned his head slightly, and I saw his eyes were pitch-black.

"Nothing," Luke spoke through a clenched jaw. I could see that he was really trying not to lose whatever control he had.

"I-I heard a crash. Is everything okay?" How awkward was I? I saw Joel glance at the ground. What used to be a bottle lay in pieces on the ground beside Leah's feet.

"It's nothing Annie, just go about your business." Luke said, still not really looking at me. Of course, this ticked me off again.

"Stop telling me what to do. I have a right to know what happened." I pretending to be calm.

"It's nothing. Leah's nothing but a clumsy bitch, and your pathetic human isn't any better." I wasn't fazed by his angry words. Leah looked angrily at Luke and Joel just stood there looking defeated.

"Luke, you can't do this, you have no right!" Leah screamed at Luke. I was shocked by how fast he moved. Luke grabbed her by the neck and slammed her against the wall.

"I am the Crown Prince! I can do whatever the hell I want to," he roared, slamming her against the wall for a second time. I slowly started to back away from whatever is going on. "I have given an official order and you both shall comply, or I will personally see you put to your death." Luke continued, slamming her for a third time and final time against the now crumbling wall, finally letting her fall to the ground. He turned away and retreated at quick pace down the stairs. Joel seemed in shock. Leah was gasping for air. He finally came out of his trance moved to help her up. About half way up, she pushed him away and took off after Luke, calling his name. I gagged at how about how desperate she was.

"What happened here?" I asked him. He acted guilty, and forced a smile. Was he hiding something?

"I was talking to Leah and..." He trailed off as he shoved his hands in his pockets.

"Why were you talking to that Leach?" I asked, very suspicious.

"I was talking to her about the Queen's Petition." Joel pulled a bunch of folded up papers from his back pocket.

"Luke came around the corner, overhearing us. He got pretty mad and threw a bottle at her," he continued, looking down at the ground. "They argued, and he slapped her. I tried to stop him. I don't really care if he is a Prince or not. He doesn't have the right to hurt people. She has made mistakes, everybody makes mistakes." I nodded, but it was impossible for me to feel any sympathy for Leah. She wanted me dead and had came pretty close to succeeding. I don't think I care that she was slammed into the wall, slapped or whatever.

"I..." was all I got out.

"The Prince also banned both of us from your level of the palace," he continued. He still wasn't meeting my eyes. I felt like he was lying about something, but didn't feel like fighting with him.

"Well, I give you permission to, so his order means nothing." He smiled at this. "Do you want to hang out?" He looked almost nervous.

"I can't, I have some things to do. A lot of business, and I actually just came up here to talk to Leah. But I'll take a rain check for later today." He started down the stairs.

"Sure that sounds good." I said, not really caring. I didn't really want to hang out with him.

He was acting very weird, but it could be from seeing Luke like that. Hell, I was scared out of my mind the first time Luke went all black-eyed crazy monster on me. I turned and walked back to my room and flopped on my bed, trying to relax. It had been an awful day, and it wasn't even noon. I must have drifted off to sleep because I was awaken by a knock on my door. The clock said 6:23. I couldn't believe that I had slept that long. I rolled out of bed and opened the door to a very freaked out looking Macy. She threw her arms around me, making me take a step back to steady myself.

"Macy, what's wrong?" I said.

"I'm so sorry Annie." Macy said pulling away, a look of sympathy written all over her face.

"What are you sorry for Macy, what's going on? You are freaking me out." My god, now what?

"I can't tell you, pulling me into the hall. "But the King and Queen want to see you in their office, immediately." She was practically pushing me me down the stairs to their offices.

"What? Why? What's going on?"

"Luke is in trouble, and the King and Queen are really angry. With all of us."

"What! What did I do? What did Luke do?" My voice surprised me, it sounded like a crazy lady's voice.

We entered the Queen's office and there they were, the very unhappy couple, standing in front of Joel and Leah. Susan, Josh, and Bobby were there, too, standing on the right side of the room. Max was standing alone to the left side. I could see Luke, his back turned to me, as he leaned against a pillar looking out one of the big windows. Macy let go of my wrist, and went to where Max was standing.

"Luke, would you like to tell Annie what you have done?" said the King, so loud it startled me.

"Not really," he said shrugging his shoulders. The King looked bitterly disappointed.

"Annie, do you know why you're here?" The Queen asked, coldly.

"No." I kind of stuttered nervously. My eyes drifted to Joel. He met my eyes, and turned away from me. Why was he here, how did this trouble Luke was in involve him?

Pearson

IT'S NOT YOUR DECISION

"Annie, we called you here because Luke..." The Queen paused, whatever she was trying to say was difficult for her.

"May I please explain this to her," Joel stepped forward. "I think it would be easier." The Queen nodded. I felt really uneasy. Everyone was avoiding eye contact with me. Everything in me was telling me to run for my life. This was bad. Joel walked over slowly to where I was rooted to the floor. He stood in front of me, and when his eyes finally met mine, I could tell he was riddled with guilt.

"Joel, what's going on?" I asked softly, desperately.

"Annie, do you remember earlier today, when we were in the hall?"

"Yes, of course I do," I said, glancing around. No help from anywhere.

"I lied to you, and I am so sorry for that." Joel dropped eyes to the floor.

"You lied to me about what?" I took a step away from him. He knew how much I hated being lied to.

"Annie, I'm sorry, the Prince ordered me not to

say anything to you. I had no choice." He was pleading with me to understand, but he was still avoiding my question.

"What did you lie to me about, Joel?"

"I lied about why I was in the stairway with Leah," he said, exhaling deeply. "I was speaking to her because I realized at the Council Meeting that...Leah and I are-"

"No!" I shook my head taking another step back. "Anybody but her!" I screamed at him.

"Annie, I am sorry, I didn't know until today."

"Oh, I don't really care when you found out. Why does it have to be her? You deserve someone so much better than that...bitch!" I yelled at him. How could this be happening? He wasn't a vampire. How cold Leah be Joel's mate?

"You think you are so much better than me, don't you? You are such a bitch, Annie. You can't even accept your own mate." Leah yelled back at me. Her words stabbed at my heart. They had a ring of truth.

"Joel, please tell me that this is a sick joke. Is Luke forcing you to do this?" The room became very still and quiet.

"Annie, Luke banned us from being together," Joel spoke up again. "He ordered Leah and I to stay away from each other. We were never to tell you."

I shook my head. Joel couldn't be mates with Leah. She was a horrible person! Joel was so wonderful in every way.. He deserved someone equally as wonderful. Not the leach from hell. Today had been stressful enough, and now this.

When was I going to wake up? Why couldn't I go back to my normal life? I felt Joel's hand brush my against my cheek, and I realized that tears were streaming down my face.

"Annie, I need you to understand," he continued. "What we had was real. I do love you so much and there will always be a special place in my heart for you, and only you." I nodded my head in response.

"The way I feel about you hasn't changed. The feelings I have for Leah are different, eternal.

"But why does it have to be her?" I managed to choke out.

"I don't know Annie," Joel shrugged. "None of us controls fate. But we were not meant to be together. Fate has given us different mates." I looked at him. He believed every word he was saying to me.

"Annie. I am a very patient man," the King began speaking. "I have tried to stay out of Luke's and your business. But there doesn't seem to be any progress in this situation. It seems to be beyond hope at this point. By tomorrow, you and Luke need to come to some kind of agreement, or the Queen and must intervene. We must find him a suitable Queen." Everyone in the room looked stunned. My heart sank again as he said these words. I could feel tears still running down my face.

"This is ridiculous." I said trying to wipe the tears off my face.

"I want to know if you understand." The King said, sounding irritated.

"Yes." I said. I wanted to run, and never stop running away from this horrible place.

"Good, you are all dismissed."

I bolted from the room as fast as I could. I just wanted to be alone. I thought things were going to get better after I survived the Council ordeal this morning. Hah. The Council Meeting left our bond in tact, and the King and Queen were threatening to break it again. They were only giving us a few hours to try to fix the problems between us. We weren't even speaking, how was that going to work? It was basically setting us up to fail. I heard Macy calling after me, but I didn't even want to speak to her. I hated everyone and everything about this place. I needed a break, some peace! I didn't know how much more of this I could take!

When I got to my room, I screamed out of frustration and stomped over to my bed. I grabbed a pillow and sat down on the ground. I buried my face into the green fluffy pillow and screamed into it. I wished that this would all go away. My life is so twisted, and the whole issue with Joel – it was just a sick joke, it had to be. How could his mate be Leah? I couldn't hate that woman more.

"Annie, I'm really sorry about Joel. When I brought him here, it was only to make you happy. I never imagined it would turn out that they would be mates. I only ordered them to stay apart because you loved him and I couldn't let him hurt you. I had already hurt you enough." I lifted my head from the pillow to see Luke standing by the bed post.

"You shouldn't have done that. You have to stop trying to control my life," I was crying, again. "I need to know the truth. Hiding it and lying doesn't change it. It makes it worse."

"I am fully aware of that, Annie. I was just trying to keep you happy. I never seem to be able to do that," his voice was ragged.

"If you didn't want me to get hurt, then why couldn't you have just left me alone? You hurt me the minute you brought me here! And I have been hurt every day since," I sobbed.

"I am sorry, Annie, I can't do this anymore." Luke walked out of my room.

I quickly went after him. I was so sick and tired of him getting angry the minute he doesn't like what he hears or when things don't go his way, he just takes off and refuses to deal with it. I was not done talking and he was going to listen to what I had to say, whether he liked it or not. When I opened my door, I heard a another door slam shut. I saw Max and Macy standing halfway between my room and Luke's. They seemed surprised to see me. I didn't have time to deal with them so I ignored them. I went straight to Luke's door and started banging on it.

"Annie, he wants to be alone, just let him be." Max had come up behind me.

"Max, why don't you mind your own business?" I growled at him.

I decided I was not going to sit and wait for Luke to let me in, since he never knocks or asks to come into my room. I think I have earned the right to enter his room in the same way. I pushed Luke's door open and was shocked at how similar the room was designed and decorated. It was hard to tell the colors of the room because because it was so very dark. The only light that was in the room was the moon light that came through the window and the fire place had a large fire roaring. The door clicked shut only a second after I entered and began to feel fear creeping up my spine. This was the first time I had ever been inside Luke's room. What was even stranger was that I didn't see Luke anywhere. Where was he? I stood there, trying to decided what to do.

"I never gave you permission for you to enter my room." Luke's voice sounded cold and annoyed. I heard what sounded like water sloshing around in a container.

I looked to where his voice had came from, and noticed his feet on the ground. He was sitting in a tall chair that hid most of his body. I walked over to where he sat. I had things I wanted to say and was tired of never getting my chance to talk. I stopped when I could fully see him. He sat pinching the bridge of his noise with one hand and his eyes were closed. In his other hand he held a clear glass bottle of what clearly was a bottle of vodka.

"I don't care if you didn't give me permission. You never ask for mine. So, now you know how it feels. Every time I want to be alone for a few seconds to collect myself from whatever you've done, you barge into my room." He didn't flinch at my words. It was as if I hadn't said them.

"Annie, I really just need to be alone tonight. I just need a little bit of peace in my life." He answered softly. He didn't sound like his usual self. I almost wanted to leave, but then I remembered, we only had tonight to work this out.

"Why do you feel it necessary to always try to control everything about my life? Do my personal feelings not matter? Why couldn't you give me a choice about anything?" Luke just sat there. He only moved his hand to bring the bottle to his mouth.

"Damn it Luke, don't ignore me when I'm talking to you. Will you please give me an answer? Will you please talk to me?" I was pleading.

"Why should I," he said, coldly. "I just don't want to do this anymore. I'm sick and tired of always being the bad guy. I just tried to make you happy." He took another drink and closed his eyes again. "I just don't want to feel this pain anymore," he said, almost whispered. I could feel the sharp stabbing feeling in the pit of my stomach again.

"What don't you want to do anymore?" I asked after a few minutes of silence.

"I don't want to fight with you anymore! I'm tired of trying to get you to love me when it's clear that you never will. I don't want to feel this pain when I see you with another man. I'm so tired of wanting something that I'm never going to get, so I quit. I just don't want to do it anymore," he started laughing as he took another drink. "I have wasted ten years of my life obsessed with you. I stalked him, did you know that?" He said sitting forward looking at me in a way that was not normal, making me feel very uneasy.

"Who were you stalking?" I said in a small voice.

"Your stupid previous human." He sat back and took another drink, closing his eyes. "I had a theory that if I learned about him, what he was like, how he acted, what he wore," he took another drink, and looked back at me. "I thought that if I imitated him you might start to like me." He looked like he were daydreaming. "You didn't notice my efforts." His voice broke. My heart aching. I could tell from the light of the fire he was on the verge of tears. In truth, I think I did notice, at least subconsciously, that he changed the way he dressed and his hair at some point. I just didn't know he did it all that for me. I felt so guilty and the pain in my heart grew. I was feeling nauseous.

"Luke." The second I said his name his eyes shifted to me. He took on the almost evil-like expression, leaning forward in his chair.

"Was there ever a time you wanted me, or even thought of me as a friend?" The intensity of his gaze deepened for a moment, then he sat back in his chair pinching the bridge of his noise with his eyes closed and breathing louder than normal. "Was there ever a time when you didn't hate me, or where you weren't completely repulsed by the idea of me?"

"Yes." I said in a low voice as he took a drink. I noticed the bottle was almost half empty. It was close to being full when I first came in here.

"When?" Luke asked, his voice cracking. I didn't think telling him would help, so I stayed silent. "WHEN!" Luke demanded, his free hand gripping the chair. He was shaking with anger.

"At Max and Macy's party, before the wedding." I gave in.

"You're lying, you didn't even let me kiss you that

night." I could see tears in his eyes now.

"I wasn't saying no to you, I..." I thought about making up something. I was afraid of what his reaction to the truth would be.

"I was the only person in the room, Annie!" He said harshly.

"When you bit me, I had a vision. I thought it was the night of my birthday," I shouted back at him. "I saw Joel in front of his house. He was asking me to marry him again." I said, trying to remain calm. "I said no to him in my vision. I didn't realize that I had said no out loud until I saw your reaction. Then you were gone. I tried to tell you when we left the reception, but you brought Joel into my room. In here. I literally forgot in the excitement of seeing him." I could feel Luke's eyes burning holes though me. I was afraid to look at him.

"The next day when I tried to talk to you again, you wouldn't talk to me. You were going on a date with Leah. You told me about the Petition. I was really upset with you and thought that you were just trying to trick me or use me from the very beginning."

I didn't know what to do. I had just told Luke everything. He was so still. He reminded me of one of those Greek god statues, only he was wearing clothes...I was desperate for him to give me some sign he had heard me, that he understood me,...

Without notice, he threw his bottle into the fireplace, causing the fire to turn blue and flare. I screamed. I looked back to Luke, who was shaking even more violently. All the white had gone out of his eyes. They were the purest form of blackness. Fear washed over me like the day turning to night.

THIS IS NOT A DREAM

The fire calmed down but Luke didn't. I felt a jolt of fear jolting through my entire body like I had stuck my finger in a socket, over and over. I just knew I had really screwed up this time. I couldn't make a run for the door, he would catch me. I guess I could go out the window onto the balcony and make a jump for it, but I had no idea if it was safe or not. But that would never work. If I was okay to jump out the window then so was he and if I knew anything about insane people, running only makes the chase more fun before the killing. I almost screamed when he finally moved, but all he did was run his hand through his hair and lock his fingers together behind his neck as he looked up at the ceiling.

"Luke, I'll stay with you."

"Why would you tell me something like that?" Luke spoke in a soft voice that was strained, almost a whisper. He didn't seem to be in control, although he didn't seem as volatile as before. and not really sure of himself or even in control. I was scared stiff and could not think of a response. I Just kept watching him, so I would know when he actually snapped and lost it.

"Why, Annie? Why couldn't you just lie to me? Why did you have to tell me that?" He screamed, making eye contact. He took a couple of steps toward me, and I retreated away from him. "Answer me!" Luke was yelling. The room was shaking with the sound of his anger or shaking in fear of him, as was I. Luke's eyes were pitch black bottomless pits. I knew I had to respond before I ended up dead.

"I didn't know you wanted me to lie," I said, in a voice that came out sounding as scared as I was. Luke threw his hands in the air and turned and started walking back to the fireplace, but when he was close he stopped and turned, walking quickly toward me.

"Do you have any idea what this feels like? Did you really think I was going to be happy knowing that if I had never brought that pathetic human here, I actually could have had a chance to be with my mate?" That said, he turned away from me to a table that was the only thing between me and my only realistic escape route.

Luke picked up another bottle of wine, popped open the cork and took a long swig from it. When he finished drinking, he turned and threw it at the wall behind me along with every glass object on the table, ending the fit by slumping down to the floor and sitting in all the broken glass in its liquid contents pooling on the ground, resting his elbows on his knees. Luke pressed his face into his hands, his breathing was loud although somewhat muffled.

"If I never brought Joel here after the wedding, would you have let me kiss you?" Luke's voice caused the burning in my heart to erupt like never before as he spoke. "Please answer me." I could tell by the tone in his voice he was crying and I didn't want to cause him more pain.

"I don't know," I said, still unsure about this situation. I heard him scoff and shake his head.

"You don't know," he said sarcastically.. "Typical. Can you please just give me a real answer? I'm sick and tired of having to try and figure out what you mean all the time." His voice cracked at the end. The room became silent and still.

The only sound I could hear was the pops and cracks of the wood burning under the intense heat from the fire. I stood there staring down at the ground, biting my bottom lip raw. I could only stall for a short time before he lost it with me and I was really in need of a good plan to defuse this situation. I could just tell him the truth, but I knew he might react the same way as before. My only other option was to lie and hope he doesn't catch on and become even more furious with me..

I heard a soft sound that made my body feel like it had been pushed into frozen water. Luke's shoulders shook as I realized he was trying to hold back tears.. Luke's breathing was ragged, and his hands moved across his face in a quick whipping motions. I couldn't breath, and my entire soul wanted to run to him and just hold him in my arms.

I took a couple steps closer to him, as the need to comfort him grew more uncontrollable. I was standing by Luke, where he sat on the ground. I was at the edge of the circle that held the red wine and broken glass, I looked at Luke and raised my dress to step over the glass. Luke stood looking at me with a face I had seen many times and it was never good for me when he had an emotionless stone faced mask on. Luke started walking toward me very fast and I instinctively backed up until my back hit the wall. I was trapped as Luke was right in front of me within a second pinning me against the wall and the burning sensation erupted where his body touched mine. I tried to focus on something other than the feeling that this caused me, but it was hard as the more time passed I wanted to feel more of him.

"My entire life I just wanted to be my father, have the love he had with my mother, to have my son that looked at me the way I looked at him." He lowered his head to rest on my shoulder and kissed my collarbone, his warm breath made me shiver. I bit my lip to control myself from moaning at the jolt of pleasure the emanated from the spot his lips touched. "I've worked so hard to be perfect; I never did anything wrong or against the rules just so that when I found my mate I would be perfect for her in every way." Luke's voice was strained and ragged as he lips brushed up the side of my neck to the point below my ear and stopped. I had not control over my body as I wanted to feel more of the effect he had over me.

"In return for all I did, I got to sit in my room alone and listen to my mate have sex with another man!" I felt a small drop of water hit my collarbone and slowly slide down my chest. "Every time you told him that you loved him," Luke said breathing heavily as I felt more tears fall on my shoulder. "I wished I was never born. The pain I felt still hurts, Annie."

Luke stopped talking and took a step back until we were arm's-length apart. "I really didn't want much. I just wanted someone to love only me as I would love only them." A smile appeared on his face as he looked at the ground. "I guess it's a fitting punishment for being so envious of Joel." He walked over to the fireplace.

I stayed frozen for a long time as he stood with his hand in his pockets staring at the fire. I was actually speechless at what he said, and I had to concentrate on remembering to breathe as the feeling of a burning knife stabbed into my heart. Had he really sat in the room and listened to everything me and Joel did? Normally hearing information like this would creep me out, but instead I felt pity and wanted to comfort Luke. I felt so ashamed of myself for what I put him through, when he had done everything I had asked, and I never once said thanks or tried to be nice to him. I looked back to see Luke staring at me with a far away look..

I had a great need to make him understand that I was just thrown into this like a person learning to swim, pushed to the bottom pits of a lake, just to see if I would sink or swim. Yes, I might have handled this wrong, but I'm not the only one to blame here. I decided that I needed to stop standing against the wall, and be near Luke. His eyes told me that he was completely in control of his emotions and I knew it would be safe for me right now.

So, I took a few steps toward the sitting area and stopped when I saw Luke's eyes shift and glance to the doors and quickly move back to me. I looked at the doors trying to figure out what he was thinking, did he want me to leave? Or was he thinking I was trying to leave? I just stared at the door until I realized I had gotten distracted in my mind and when I finally looked back to where Luke was, he was sitting down in his chair again. He sat slouched with his hands hanging over the side of the arms and his legs extended out, and I knew Luke thought that I was leaving. I really didn't want to leave; I think we really need to have a long talk. Something we never really had.

I walked over to where Luke sat, sitting on the ground next to the chair I leaned up against the right side, his hand hung over my shoulder. I decided that I needed to prove to him I wasn't leaving and I wanted to try to work at whatever it is we had going on. But saying it was a lot harder, I am not the type of person that can just go around spilling my every emotion, I over think everything.

My breath caught at my realization, I didn't want to lose Luke, and I got some sick joy out of him chasing me. I liked it when we would fight, I liked the attention he gave me and the second another woman came into view I couldn't deal with losing him. I bit my lip harder as the guilt of what I had done to my mate affected me fully. I wanted the pain to stop, grabbing Luke's hand I pressed his palm to my cheek and he automatically started stroking my cheek with his thumb as the pain disappointed and the feeling that brought a smile to my face crawled over my skin. I only sat this way for a few minutes until Luke's hand was ripped out of my grasp, it felt like I got punched in my stomach and the wind was knocked out of me. But this was replaced quickly when Luke's hand wrapped around my waist and pulled me off of the ground.

Luke's arms wrapped around my waist, my legs hung over the side of the chair, and my face was nuzzled in the crook of his neck. I silently smiled as I nestled into the feelings of happiness and safety that it gave me to have him hold me. His hands rubbed soothing circles on my back in which almost lulled me to sleep.

"What is it you hate about me so much?" Luke whispered.

I just sat there looking at the fire that licked the walls of the fireplace as I tried to pretend that I didn't hear him, or that I was asleep. I didn't hate him, I'm not even sure I ever did, I know I said it but everyone says lots of things that they don't really mean. I was just upset and emotional and he was the best person to take my issues out on.

"Annie, I know you're awake." Luke said as one of his arms loosened and I assumed he was rubbing his temple with one hand. "I just need to know, please, I can change whatever it is." I heard the desperation in Luke's voice.

I moved to get up because I needed to have a clear mind as I spoke and with Luke touching me it would never happen. When I stood up and turned around Luke grabbed my wrist but hung his head.

"Don't leave, please. I'll do whatever you want me to do, just please, please stay with me," I bent down to comfort him, "Please Annie, stay with me for the night. A few hours even? Maybe a few minutes?" I grabbed his face in both of my hands, tears rolled down his face and my hands. "Don't make it seconds, I won't be able to hold on, please."

"Luke, I'll stay." I said softly, he pulled me closer to him and I felt a little nervous.

"How long do I get?" His voice was muffled by the fact that he was pressing his face into the crook of my neck and I could feel his lips moving and lightly brushing against my skin as he spoke. My emotions went haywire at the feeling.

"For..." Forever I wanted to scream at him as his lips lightly pressed against the scar of his bite mark and I let out a soft moan of wanting and needing him to touch or bite me again.

"For how long? I need to know what I can have." Luke pressed his lips against my neck higher this time, making my wish for him grow.

"I will stay." I whispered, but froze when his fingers trailed up my back to cup my neck, leaving a burning path behind it.

"Please, stay the night with me," he whispered back to me, into my ear. I felt his fangs nip the bare skin on my neck. I leaned my head back to look at the ceiling. I wanted him to bite me more than anything and I had a growing desire to mark him as well to feel what it was like to sink my teeth into his neck and taste Luke.

"Luke." I choked out as he nibbled again on my neck lower and closer to his mark. I felt a delicate brush of his fangs against my skin that caused my body to shake as he teased me.

"Stay with me for the night." Luke whispered again, hovering over his bite mark as my body screamed in anticipation, my hands flying to his head and neck trying to pull him into me so I could escape this building energy I felt crashing around in my body. "Say it Annie, I need to hear you say it." Luke murmured, dragging his teeth tauntingly over my skin.

"Luke, please." I said desperately, I could take what he was doing to my body I needed him to give me some sort of escape from this.

"Stay with me." Luke said as he placed his fangs above his mark and stayed still as he waited for my response. I was having such a hard time catching my breath. I couldn't seem to remember how to form words.

"I-" His fangs pressed down a little deeper and I gasped at the burning pleasure. "I'll stay, please Luke." As the words left my mouth his fangs broke my skin and if felt like the entire world had come to a complete stop.

When the feeling stopped, my heart fell as I opened my eyes to see that I was lying on Luke's bed, I was a little confused about how I got here. I could feel Luke's arms around me holding me from behind and I was very tired as I fell into the comfortable warm feeling. I wanted to face Luke, not the windows. I twisted and wiggled until I was finally facing Luke, he was just looking down at me with a small smirk forming on the corner of his lips. I glared at him, but realized nothing but being with him really mattered, as I cuddled up next to him; I was feeling tired and wanted to sleep. I was stopped when I felt his lips on my cheek; I opened my eyes to see Luke just staring down at me with a look of contemplation on his face.

"What are you looking at?" I asked as he just kept staring at me and did nothing else, it made me feel weird.

"You're just so beautiful Annie. I wish I could kiss you." He said as he lay his head down so we were face to face. I cupped his face with my hands.

"Luke." I said as he grabbed my hand and brought it to his lips and genitally kissed the tops of my fingertips.

"I know Annie, it's okay, I understand. It's just hard to get rid of all the hopes and dreams I had." Luke released my hand and laid it on the pillow next to me. A confused look masked my face, I wasn't really sure what this conversation had turned into.

"What is it Annie?" He asked with his eyes closed.

"I want you to kiss me, Luke." His eyes flashed open with a look of shock clearly evident on his face.

"You want me to kiss you, truly kiss you?" I nodded and I felt his arm tighten around me. "Annie, I would give anything to kiss you, but I can't." My heart fell, I don't understand why he wouldn't kiss me, and he said he wanted to.

I lay there confused, rejected and complete taken aback by what he was saying. What was wrong with him? He said he wanted to kiss me, I told him I wanted him to kiss me yet he wouldn't. I felt really unsettled and I knew it was late but I needed to talk to Macy because it just didn't make any sense to me and I didn't want to be around Luke the second after he just shot me down. I sat up brushing Luke's arms from me and sliding to the edge of the bed. I needed to get out of this room. I felt that sharp burning pain pierce my heart again. I needed to run away from here quickly, so I got up and started walking to the door but was stopped by Luke appearing in front of me.

"You said you would stay with me." Luke said, looking tired and hurt as he blocked my way to the door.

"I did stay, I want to leave now." I said dropping my eyes to the floor, not wanting him to see the pain in my eyes.

"Why?" I didn't have the courage to look him in the eyes; I could tell that he was upset.

"What did I do? I was just holding you, I can try not to if it will make you stay," I just shook my head as he took a step toward me. "Annie, please you can't leave yet, I'm not ready to wake up yet." I looked up at him, more confused by his words than ever. I had to look away because the pain in his eyes was unbearable for me to see.

"Luke, you are awake, what's wrong with you?" I felt his hand touch my arm.

"This is my dream Annie, you asked me to kiss

you. That only happens in my dreams; in life you would never let me get close enough to hold your hand." I looked at him confused and bewildered bu his words.

"Luke, this is not a dream." I took his hand, trying to reason with him.

"Yes it is, what other reason could therefore, you want to kiss me?" I shook my head thinking of why I wanted him to kiss me. I didn't know what to say to make him understand.

I stood there wracking my brain of what to say, when I looked back to see him just staring down at me with those broken eyes. I never realized how said he truly was and it was all joyful, he loved me and I treated him so bad, I tricked him and now he would never believe that I would want him. He has every right not to trust me, but I need him to just try and believe me. Then, maybe we can move on. I could just grab him and kiss him but I knew that he was strong enough to resist me. There was a knock at the door.

"What?" Luke growled at whoever was on the other side of the door.

"I have a note that I need to give to Annie." I heard Macy say from the other side of the door, Luke and I looked at each other, very confused.

Why was Macy trying to give me a note and at a time like this? Heck, maybe we were dreaming this. Luke walked over to the door and opened it, closed it, and walked back over to me and handed me the note. I looked at the piece of paper that was folded twice and opened it, and almost laughed when I read the five words written on the paper in all capital letters.

TELL LUKE YOU LOVE HIM

I looked back at it and I took a deep breath and tried to get a grip on what I was about to do. I do love him, he is my mate and I will not let him be with another person. If I didn't do it now, I would lose him and I just couldn't let that happen!

"Luke, I love you." He stood still for a very long time. It seemed like an eternity until he took a step closer to me.

"Do you mean that, do you truly mean that with your whole heart?" Luke stared into my eyes.

"Yes, I love you and I want to be with you." He brought me closer until we were only an inch apart.

"First, you have to promise me something." I whimpered as he spoke, his lips were a breath away and I could almost feel them.

"Anything, just kiss me."

"You have to marry me, and before you agree, you must know that it's a binding contract. There is no backing out of it." Luke said this quietly. I wasn't sure if I had heard him right but the silence that followed was excruciating. All I knew was that I loved the man in front of me more than I ever thought possible.

"Yes." I answered.   It was the most honest, sincerest moment of my life so far. Luke pressed his lips to mine and the thoughts of the future were swept away while the present filled the void with with pure happiness.   Hope coursed through my veins as Luke wound his arms around me, holding my head in place so as not to not break the kiss. everything but him was washed away. The sadness, the guilt, the anger, everything was just gone. He lowered me gently onto his bed.

Luke slowly broke the kiss and I felt something cold slide across my finger. I didn't have to look to know what it was.

"I love you Annie."

THE MORNING AFTER

I awoke the next morning in Luke's bed, his arms were wrapped tightly around me from behind. I glanced at the ring on my finger, finally seeing it for the first time. It was a simple gold band with a elegant single diamond. My perfect and ring made me smile. I closed my eyes and relaxed back into Luke's embrace. Luke's arms tightened around me as I felt his lips press against my shoulder. I turned to look at the now awake Luke.

Luke's normally styled hair was disheveled and his eyes were so blue I was lost looking into them. He smiled back at me as his fingers entwined with mine bringing my hand close to his face. Luke looked at my hand and kissed the ring. I smiled as he released my hand and held me closer, his lips touching mine so quickly and gentle, then he pulled back slightly. My instincts took over and I growled at him as he laughed at my protest and kissed me again. This kiss was what I had originally wanted, it was soft, and sweet. I never wanted anything more than to be kissing him all the time. My stomach turned as the heat of fire burned inside me.

My dominant side was about to take control when I heard a knock at the door. Both Luke and I growled and continued kissing as I slipped my hands under Luke's wrinkled shirt. A second knock came and Luke growled so loud it was frightening, but also slightly exciting Luke turned back to me and our lips was about to touch when I heard the door bust open, as both me and Luke looked over to see the door shattering into large piece's of debris. Max came walking into the room holding what looked like a large water gun and started spraying. I screamed as Luke rolled us so that he was getting the full focused of the cold water being sprayed.

"Max! Stop spraying us now!" Luke growled as Max was laughing hysterically.

"Well I had to do something to stop whatever was going on in here!" he answered, with a big smirk across his face. I could see Macy walking in with an irritated look.

"Max, did you have to break the door, you know it was unlocked," Macy complained.

"I know, I just thought it would be a much cooler entrance." he said proudly, swinging the water gun over his shoulder. Luke released me, and we both sat up in the now wet bed, thanks or course, to Max.

"You are such an idiot. It would have been just as 'cool' to have just opened the door!" Macy stated simply, hands on her hips.

"Do you mind letting me and Annie in on the reason you have the need that would warrant such a dramatic entrance?" Luke asked, obviously irritated with their bantering. Max walked closer to the bed and leaned against the bedpost

"The King wants to see you, Luke, and the Queen wants Annie in her office in two minutes," he said, a big smile plastered across his face. He turned and walked toward Macy, taking her arm. "We have a fitting to attend, and business to attend to for the day, so we will be on our way." Max winked as he and Macy waked out of the room, over the carnage that once was the door.

I just sat there for a few minutes looking around the devastated room. The door was ruined. There was broken glass all over the room, and the carpet was stained from the liquid from the shattered bottles. The sheets where dripping wet. I glanced at Luke, who was also looking around the room, his face reflecting the shock I was feeling..

"The maids are going to hate me after today," Luke said. I had to laugh at that. He looked at me like "What?" Definitely confused.

"Nothing," I said, laying my head on his shoulder I wanted to feel the warm heat my cheek.

"We must go see my parents. I can be late, but my mother won't like your tardiness." He said this, his voice full of regret.

"I don't want too, can vampires get sick?" I whined. Luke laughed, patting my head

"Only by not eating. Come on let's get going," He said, getting off of the bed "I think you should change your clothing, you are still in the dress from yesterday and my mother will definitely notice." I groaned, getting off the bed and walked toward the

359

obliterated door.

"Annie," I heard him say. I turned around to see Luke walking toward me, He grabbed me, wrapping his arms around me in a tight hug, pressing his lips against my forehead. Try to behave today," Luke said looking. down at me.

"Me behave, have you ever known me to behave in the time I have been here?" I asked, sarcastically. Luke laughed.

"No, but it was worth a try." Luke said, winking. He leaned down and kissed my nose and i felt weak in the knees. I could feel my cheek becoming red. I pulled away, gave him my most I don't want to go, I want to stay with you look, and walked out the toward to my room.

I felt this wonderful sense of happiness that I could feel in my stomach, radiating inside me. It was a strange feeling, almost like a small vibration that I could feel in my bones and it was making me grin, I probably looked like an idiot. I changed quickly and was leaving the closet when the door opened and Mary Bell walked in. She smiled and walked over to me quickly wrapping her arms around me hugging me tightly.

"I just heard the news, I'm so happy and excited for you!" She exclaimed, releasing me. I laughed, feeling a little embarrassed.

"I guess the news was bound to spread sooner or later," I was fidgeting with my clothes.

"The Queen sent me to retrieve you. You're late." I nodded.

"Well let's get this over." she grinned, as I

followed her out of the room.

"Don't be so pouty, your supposed to be happy," she said, looking at me questioningly.

"I'm happy about being with Luke. I'm just not happy to be summoned by Krista. She is unhappy about something, I am sure."

"Well, I'm pretty happy", she shrugged. "Luke is like a second son to me. I was with the Queen when she was pregnant and took care of Luke most of his life." Her words were stuck in my mind.. "Like a son to me..."

"Mary, I'm sorry I have been so narrow-minded. I guess I never asked if you had a mate, or anything about you..." she stopped walking and turned to look at me with a gentle smile.

"Its okay Annie, I never offered the information either. But to answer your question, no, I don't have a mate, and never will," she said with a smile, which confused me beyond words.

"But, you said Luke was like a second son, you have children, but no mate?"

"I don't think this is a good time to discuss my life when the queen is waiting for you." Mary sighed.

"She can wait a few minutes. You are my friend, and I have been horribly rude by not knowing anything about you"

"Its okay, Annie. My story is not an interesting one."

"It is to me." I replied, meaning it.

"See, why couldn't you behave this way in the beginning? Okay, in truth yes, I had three children two girls and one boy. They died a very long time ago, during the black death." Mary looked distant. "I almost died with them, but King Jace, who was still a prince at the time, saved me. I was human then, and scared of death. I leaped at the chance to live." Mary turned away from me after this revelation, and started walking again. I followed quickly. "Later, after my change, he apologized and said I would never have a mate like everyone else. I have accepted that fate. I've had a wonderful family looking after his family. I will look after yours as well". She smiled at me as we stopped in front of the Queen's door.

I would think being mate-less would be a sad ordeal to live through. For example, Egon's been driven mad by sadness from losing his mate. Mary seemed happy with the life she had, and didn't seem bothered that she would not have a mate. I just felt this overwhelming sadness for her. I walked into the Queen's office, a bit unsettled by what Mary had said, but I realized that maybe she didn't have a mate because she had a husband that died a long time ago, and he was her mate. Which made me even sadder.

"Annie, you're extremely late!" Krista said crisply, looking over the paperwork on her desk

"Sorry, it was a long night and I overslept." I said as apologetically as I could.

"Yes, I know all about your night, First you need to sign off on some wedding paper work. Next, we need to go over this packet of official documents that aren't too complicated for you to handle.." I tuned out as she started handing me things.

Krista kept handing me samples of fabric item to

approve and images of flowers to choose from for over an hour. Then, she had me reading documents with new rules revised rules that needed approval. On top of that, she also handed me papers about Vampire History to read so I would understand everything that was going on. However, I had no idea what was really going on, I was very confused by the process of things and how fast everything went.

"Okay we are almost done here. I just need to know what you plan on doing about your 'reputation'?" Krista stood looking at me expectantly.

"What do you mean?" I replied, totally confused.

"Well Annie, your behavior has been observed by everyone since your arrival. Many question your ability to be a Queen and whether or not you should be allowed to marry my son." I felt my mouth drop open as she said this.

"I was only reacting to the way I was treated. My whole life was changed in an instant, and it was devastating. I was in shock, and their behavior had a lot to do with what went wrong when I came here." she nodded as if she were agreeing.

"Yes I'm aware of their misguided actions, but that excuse can only go so far," she said sitting back in her chair, scanning a paper she held in her hand.

"What do I have to do then, to make people believe I am good enough to marry Luke?" I said, in panicked squeak.

"I cannot tell you that Annie, it is something you have to do on your own" she replied. "Take a day to think about it, chose something you could do that would help many to even one person, just do what feels right" she said as she nodded to the door. "I'll call on you tomorrow to discuss things again with you." I was dismissed. She went on going through her paperwork and I I stood up and walked out of the Queen's office.

I closed the door behind me, momentarily leaning against the door, just thinking about what she said. What was I going to do, how was I going to be able to do something that helped others? I'm barely able to help myself half the time. I walked up the stairs racking my brain trying to think of something to do that would be construed as helpful. I decided to just sit at the very top of the stairs, looking down at the people going about business and their work, oblivious to problems.

I tried to think about everything the Queen had told me, but there was never really anything I heard about that needed fixed or anyone that wanted or needed help. She said if there was ever a threat the King would deal with it. It was our job, as Queen, to be like a mother figure of the Vampire Country. Those thoughts brought me back to the sadness I felt about learning Mary Bell's situation. I just felt so awful for her, yet she had no problem with never having a mate. I would like to help her, but she seemed content with her life and there really wasn't any need for me to go and mess around with her life.

"Annie, what are you doing?" I jumped at the sound of the voice behind me, as King Jace stood behind me staring down at me.

"Sorry I was just sitting because it is quiet here

and I need to think about things." I said as I jumped up, feeling more than a little embarrassed.

"I am guessing nobody informed you that you have your own office to do those sorts of things in," he said, as he started walking down the stairs, motioning for me to follow him.

"No, I wasn't unaware I had an office." I said, getting up and following him.

"Of course you do, I will show you. May I ask what you were thinking about so intently?" He didn't seem that interested.

"Nothing really," I said thoughtfully. "Just trying to come up with something that would benefit someone, something charitable."

"Ah yes, something that important would take a lot of concentration," he said, looking at me, considering. "Have you come up with anything yet?"

"No." I said, feeling irritated.

"Well, I'm sure you will think of something. You're a clever, resourceful girl Annie. You just need to focus. After all, the answer is usually right under our noses," he said jovially, turning a corner and stopping in front of a set of double doors right across the hall from Luke's office. "Here we are, and I must leave you with your thoughts." I nodded as he left, and I went in.

The office was the same color scheme as my Queen Krista's. As a matter of fact, it looked exactly like the Queen's office, only a little smaller. I went to the big chair and sat behind the big wooden desk. I spun around in the chair, only stopping to look out the window. I could see the basketball court and the pool perfectly from here. I kind of wished I could go swimming. It would have been so much more fun than sitting in an office trying to think of a plan to make myself "acceptable".

I tried focusing like the King suggested, but I just kept coming back to thinking about Mary, and how said I felt that she would never have a mate. I would love to help Mary, but I didn't know if it was possible or if she would even want it if I could. She said she was happy. I started spinning in my chair again, going over and over in my mind what else I could do. I didn't really know many people in this place because the majority of the time I have been locked in my room.

I came to the conclusion I was going to have to choose someone to help I already knew here. I sat and thought about who the most miserable person in the palaces was. Well technically that would have been me a few hours ago. Then, I remembered the sad man sitting alone in the basement, Egon. He would be an amazing vampire to help. I really think I would like to help a few of the others down there as well. I mean it was really scary down there. It was basically the perfect setting for classic horror movie. I bolted up out of my chair and ran to the door as fast as I could. I could feel myself smiling and began running down the stairs. I needed to speak to Egon.

I was excited because I finally had an idea that would show I was capable of being a good queen. I really hated people being locked up and shunned in the basement. I am sure some of them could be rehabilitated and reintroduced back into the world. I was running until I slammed into a maid. I had seen her around, but I didn't know her name or what or who she may be responsible for. I knocked all the folded towels out of her arms.

"Oh Miss Annie, I'm so sorry, I didn't see you!" She started scrambling about for the fallen towels.

"It is not your fault," I explained. "I was the one running around not paying attention. Let me help you." I bent down and helped her pick up the towels. She smiled at me, making me feel good about myself, a feeling I hadn't had in a long time.

"Annie, what are you doing?" I turned and saw Mary coming down the stairs.

"I was running down the stairs and I ran into" I paused looked at her because I didn't know her name.

"Shea, Miss," I nodded, and the maid smiled again..

"I ran into Shea, well, more like colloid. Now, w I'm helping her pick the towels I knocked out of her hands."

"That is very nice of you Annie," Mary was saying, but I could see she disapproved. You cannot be seen helping the help," Mary took the towels from me..

"What do you mean?" was just fixing something I caused..

"Annie, before you accepted Luke's proposal, nobody really minded if did this kind of thing. But things have changed now. You need to act differently, you are now part of the Royal Family. I know you are a gentle person and want to help people. What, if I may ask, were you doing running down the stairs and hallways anyway?

"Well, I am pretty excited because I might actually have a plan to help someone. Queen Krista says I need to do something charitable so everyone will think I am worthy of being the Queen." I answered, flashing Mary my sweetest smile.

"That's wonderful Annie, what is it?" I started descending the stairs, but turned back to tell her my plan.

"Well, if he agrees, I am going to help Egon. I hope to give him back a normal life, after all these years!" I expected Mary to be proud of me, but she was looking at me like I said I was showing her dead baby kittens or something. I stepped back. I couldn't understand her reaction.

"Annie, your intentions are good, but Egon is a very dangerous man. Even if he agreed, he would never be allowed out of his cell. Do you have any idea what that monster has done?" I was shocked, Mary was usually such a happy-go-lucky person. But right now she almost sounded angry. I definitely didn't like this side of her. Nor did like having her tell me what to do! So I told her so.

"Mary, I'm going to talk to Egon and nothing you can say or do can stop me." I am not sure it had ever bothered me before when she told me to do something, but this time it was different.

TO HELP EGON

I turned and stormed down the staircase. I was furious at Mary, but still felt bad for telling her off. She was only looking out for my well being. I was just so happy and excited about my plan, and she more or less tried to shoot down my only hope to prove I was worthy to be with Luke. I turned when I hit the main floor and went to the basement door at the end of the hallway. I opened the door which leads to the back stairwell and I went down the last flight of stairs, and found myself in front of the basement door for the second time.

I stopped in front of the basement door for the second time and pushed it open. The hallway had not changed just a long hall lined with metal doors. The quietness is what really got my nerves and my stomach flip-flopping. I continued walking until I was in front of the metal door that bore the nameplate with Egon's name etched into it. I took a deep breath as I raised my hand to knock. The sound echoed down the hall. I was beyond nervous.

"What?" I heard Egon say from behind the door.

"Egon, its Annie, can we talk?" I said, and in return, there was just silence. I knocked again.

"No, go away" Egon finally answered, mumbling something else inaudible. I suddenly lost my temper. I came all the way down here to help him, and he was refusing to speak to me.

"Open the door!" I demanded, banging on the door. Again, there was silence. Eventually, the door opened with a loud echoing scratch. I smiled at the fact I had accomplished some type of victory as I stepped into Egon cell. He was lighting a candle.

"You are an annoying child!" Egon was sitting on his table, kicking the dirt with his feet.

"I am not a child" I said. He shrugged.

"What is it you want Annie?" Egon was obviously annoyed.

"I came here to help you," I explained.

"Help me, and how would a child who is not able to help herself with her own problems going to help me?" he was glaring at me.

"I do not have problems any more. I am perfectly able to help myself!" I was proud. Egon scoffed.

"So then tell me where is your mate or is he even your mate at this point?" I looked down, forgetting he was probably out of the loop of the everyday gossip around the palace.

"He is meeting with the King. And yes, he still is my mate. I didn't break the bond."

"I should have realized as much, when I didn't get a new crazed neighbor." Egon relaxed slightly, and lay down on his bed.

"What?" I asked, confused.

"I told you Luke was not strong enough to break his bond. He has lived with it for many years. You and I however, only dealt with for a couple of months." Egon laughed bitterly. "People think I was dangerous and crazy. They have no idea what havoc the Prince would have caused if your bond had been broken." Egon seemed to be lost in his thought, almost like he forgot I was there.

"Well, the bonds not broken, and I can't wait to marry him. Now, I haven't been 'informed' I must do something helpful and charitable so the the good vampire folks think I am worthy of Luke, so, I'm choosing you to be my project." I was feeling even more proud.

"No." was all Egon said.

"Excuse me," I said. I was getting really irritated with everyone\'s attitudes today.

I said no, Annie. It's a nice gesture, but I don't want to be helped." He said this with a certain resignation. I didn't believe him.

"Why? I asked, truly perplexed. "Do you honestly like living down here in isolation? Wouldn't you like to have a life, a little social interaction? Egon laughed again, even more bitterly than before.

"Annie, you need to change the way you think about yourself and me. We are not human. I choose to be here. The King and everyone else pardon me for my actions and forgave me for what I had done, but I cannot live among others."

"But, why?" I stuttered out, try to understand why a dark, lonesome cell was preferable to a normal 'vampire' life.

"Why, you ask? Why would I want to be among others finding their mates, others being with their mates, having a life together with their mates." He stood up, getting louder as he did. I could hear all the pain he was feeling as his voice. "To be reminded daily by others' happiness as I sit idly by watching. I know that I will never have that. My mate, the one that I loved so much, is dead, and never even knew I existed." Egon sat down on his bed, looking down at the dirt floor. He was silent.

"Egon I'm sorry," I said, at a loss. "I just thought I could help you, I just..."

"There is no helping me Annie, I think it is best if you leave." Egon abruptly interrupted me, jumping up, opening the door and motioning for me to leave.

I hate it when anyone interrupts me. Not only did he interrupt me, but then tried to tell me what to do, and I wasn't having it. I was going to help him whether he liked it or not. I stood up, grabbing his arm. I started pulling him out of the cell, but he immediately pulled his arm away. We stood there glaring at each other.

"I told you I don't want your help Annie, leave me alone!" he roared, storming back into his cell.

"No!" I shouted running in front of him block his path. "You are going to come with me and at least let me try. I know I can help you! You just need to give me a chance to prove it." Again, we were standing there in a stare off.

"What do you have planned?" Egon finally broke, holding himself up by leaning on the wall.

"Well, I don't have a plan laid out, but I think we should start by getting you socializing and back into a normal routine. I'm sure there is a job that needs done around here we could get for you to do." I said, Egon started laughing, and it echoed all around me in the spooky hallway.

"I already have a job Annie, did you not even read my file before coming down here?" he said as I rolled my eyes.

"No, I was unaware you had a file, but if you already have a job, then why are you not doing it?" he shrugged.

"I was given an extended leave because of my situation." he said sliding down the wall, plopping down on the floor in self pity. I was not having it.

"Okay. so get up. The first step is to get you back into your job. What was it?" I said pulling his arm to make him get up.

"My position was second in command to the King, like your brother is to Luke," he said simply. I am sure I looked shocked. "You don't seem too happy about that, Annie. What, don't want a crazy man so close to being King?" I shook my head.

"No, it's not that, I'm just surprised. I mean nobody told me that." I said feeling embarrassed and at a loss for words.

"So, you still want to help me, or have you changed your mind?" There was a ghost of a sad smile on his face.

I stared at Egon, realizing he looked younger than I thought he had in the dim lighting of his room. ng. If I would have guessed, and he were not a vampire, that he was in his late 20's to early 30's. Originally, I had figured he was a lot older with the crazed hair and the dried up skin. In truth, he was not as bad as I thought. Just in need of a serious bath and haircut. Once groomed, I'm sure he would be decent looking.

"Get up, I need to get you cleaned up and in clothing that is not tattered or disintegrating," I said looking at his clothing which was clearly from a different era.

"And to think I thought you would have given up more easily," he said, more to himself again.

"Nope, I want you looking all shiny and new for your impending return to society. Who knows, you might even attract some girls' interest." I said, just joking of course, than I remembered, cringing. "I am sorry, it slipped out. It is kind of human habit's of not understanding what vampire mates mean...." I was rambling, trying to cover myself.

He didn't say anything, but just followed silently behind me toward the stairwell door. I pushed it open and motioned for him to pass through. Egon stood there for a long time, looking at the door and the stairs a few feet away. After what seemed like a long time, but in reality, probably a minute, he finally took a step out, but acted like a timid animal seeing the light of day for the first time. Followed him closing the door offering him my hand to take him up the stairs, he genitally took it and followed me up to the first floor when I felt hands around me.

"Annie, wait I can't, you have to understand I can't face all those people" I looked up at Egon who looked scared and on the verge of tears "I can't face people whose friends and family I killed, when I went off the deep end" he said shaking my head.

"Egon, people don't blame you for what you did, they understand they don't hate you they're just scared of you" he nodded and I felt his hand off my arms as he looked like a frightened puppy nodding in agreement.

I grabbed his hand to reassure him I would be there for him and smiled, faintly, but it was there. I pushed open the door and started walking to Victor's office to get him so new clothes. What he had on were almost worse than rags, so hopefully Victor could whip something up so he wouldn't look so crazed and smell as bad as he did.

"Annie! There you are. I'm glad I caught you." I heard Mary say, coming down the man stairs. I froze. I knew I was going to get yelled at by the tone of her voice. "The queen informed to tell you that you are not in a position to let Egon out of his cell. It could be dangerous for you." She stopped a few steps above the ground floor. I stood there staring at her. "What is it Annie, are you well?" Mary asked, taking another step toward me. I looked back at Egon, who was giving me a really strange look.

"Don't you think it's a little late for that? I'm fine. I'm more worried about you." I felt Egon's hand on my shoulder. I turned to look at Egon, who appeared frightened. "What's wrong with you, Egon?" I asked. I could also see Mary taking another step closer to me.

"Annie, are you well child?" Egon was asking, as he bent down to look at my face. I smacked at his hand on my shoulder and stepped away from him.

"I'm fine. What is wrong with you, both of you? You are both acting like you are crazy." I noticed Mary had the same look of fear as Egon.

"Annie we are the only people standing here," Mary said looking around. "You are talking to an empty space." I took another step back. Both Mary and Egon stood a few feet away from each other watching me warily.

I didn't understand what was happening. I couldn't understand why they were acting like I had the problem, when it was obvious that it was them. I realized they couldn't see each other.

"Annie!" I heard a loud voice echo down the hallway. I turned to see the King and Tenion walking toward me. "It seems like we were unable to reach you in time to explain the 'situation'." The King was saying as he cam closer, stopping a few feet away.

"Why can't they see each other?" I asked. Tenion took another step forward.

"That what we were coming to tell you, my dear Annie. We are fully aware that Egon and Mary cannot see each other and we believe it is a result of Egon breaking their bond," Tenion said carefully, stepping back slightly,. I stared at him, at everyone really, in shock of what I just heard. Everything started to become clear. I felt very much like an idiot for not realizing this sooner.

"Jace, what is he talking about?" Egon said as I looked back to see a very angry Egon. A very shocked Mary just stood there, looking down at the floor.

"Egon, she became sick shortly after the bond was broken, I kept an eye on her because I knew you could not see her. I just wanted her family taken care of because you couldn't," he said, walking closer to Egon. "She was dying, and I thought if I changed her we could somehow fix the bond, and you both could be happy and live your lives together, but when I changed her you snapped and thought she was dead." King Jace was standing next to him, placing his hand on my shoulder. "But clearly, after her change, there was still not sight between you two."

"Isn't there a way to fix the broken bond, reset it maybe?" I said, looking at Jace and Tenion.

"It's not like a broken bone Annie. we explained to Egon that we didn't even know if it would have worked. We had never done it before. It was only a rumored way, and there is nothing else we know of that can correct this break once it is done. Oh, my god, how did me wanting to help Egon get so messy?

I looked over to see Mary sitting down on the stairs. I walked over and sat next to her. I wrapped an arm around her to help comfort her. She didn't look up. I looked at Egon. He was staring at the spot where Mary sat. I knew they could not see each other, and I had to look away because I felt so bad. I had made him come out here, and now he had to deal with this. I was startled when until I saw Egon walk over closer and sit on the stairs on the opposition side and just stare at the ground as she did.

"Is she still as beautiful, sweet, caring as I

remember?" He said quietly, as I nodded my head smiling at him, but it just made him look more upset

"What did he say?" Mary whispered to me.

"He asked if you were still beautiful, sweet and caring and I said yes." she smiled, but there was a bitter-sweetness to it.

"I don't know anything about him except for what he did, tell me something, anything." she pleaded, taking my hand..

"Well he needs a bath and a good clean set of clothing," I felt a hand slap playfully at my arm. I glared at Egon, who was smiling..

"Annie, be serious please!" Mary said, laughing.

"He loves you more than you will ever know. Egon didn't break his bond with you to hurt you, he did it because you had a family. A very happy one with children you loved. He couldn't take that away from you, or you away from them" I explained.

"And in an ironic twist they all died, I lost everything." Her eyes began to water. At that moment, Egon grabbed my other hand. I screamed and he let go.

The King and Tenion were next to me in a flash, as I shook my hand vigorously. It felt like I had been struck by lightening in both hands. I didn't want to feel that again! Somehow, I knew hat this was a good thing, but didn't know how.

"What is it Annie?" I looked at Tenion as he examined my hands.

"I don't know. I was holding Mary's hand and the second Egon touched my other hand, it was like I was electrocuted." I said, looking over to see both

Egon and Mary looking at their own hands I had been holding. "Did you guess feel it?" I said as Mary's gaze flickered to me.

"It felt like you were on fire Annie, but it didn't hurt." Egon said, looking wonderingly at his hand.

"I don't know what I felt." Mary murmured, totally in shock.

"Hmmm" Tenion said. "Obviously, Annie, you are some kind of catalyst for them. Take their hands again."

"Oh no, whatever that was, not interested in feeling it again. You do it," I was super irritated at the fact he saw my reaction, and wanted a repeat performance!.

"Allow me," Jace took both of their arms and I could see a shudder run down him. He slowly brought there hands to meet.

Watching them touch for the first time made me almost cry. The look of pure joy on three faces was nothing less than perfect. I was smiling, and could see a proud smile on Tenion's lips and a few others who had gathered to watch the excitement. I wanted to dance as Mary started to cry tears of joy, and Egon was laughing. It was not a cynical laughter, but of genuine happiness.

"Can you see or can you just feel each other?" Jace asked, standing a few feet back.

"I can't see her, but I can feel her," he said, lifting his other hand, feeling along her arm untiil his hand rested slightly awkwardly on half of her cheek by her eye. "She really is here!" he cried, happiness radiating from him. I realized I had done this, I had helped them!

"Let us take this to the Council Room and see iwhat we can do to fix this further." Tenion said, motioning for them to follow as most people standing around walked behind them chatting lightly about what was going on.

"Annie, you will be given credit for this, but you're free to go for the rest of the day." The King said, as the hall was emptied. I felt satisfied in a way I had never known before.

I felt like doing a dance in the center of the hall, but decided it was better to cerebrate when I was behind closed doors. I watched the Queen come down the stairs. She nodded when she passed. I guess this was her way of giving me her approval. Anyway, I hoped it was. People passed by as I just stood there, feeling very unsure of myself. I started wondering where Luke was and why had he not come and seen a wonderful thing I had caused to occur. I heard laughter behind me and I turned quickly to see Luke standing against the wall smiling.

"Luke what are you doing?" He smiled and pushed off the wall and walked over to me and I could feel my entire body heat up with anticipation of his touch, but he stopped a few feet away.

"Well, I came to watch, just as everyone else did." I rolled my eyes.

"Obviously, but why did you just stand in the back and not with me?" he smiled.

"Because this was your doing, and you needed to do this on your own. It was like taking the training wheels off, we gave you the push and we had to watch to see if you would sink or swim." I swatted at him and he laughed.

"You could have still stood by me," I said, pouting. He wrapped his arms around me

"I could have, but I think I would have been more of a distraction than helpful." I glared at him as he kissed my forehead. "Didn't I also ask you to behave today?" I rolled my eyes.

"I think I behaved very well, for your information." I said crossing my arms feeling smug.

"Yeah because poking a wild animal is behaving. Annie, you are lucky it turned out good. Please don't do things like that again unless you have bodyguards that could protect you in case things go wrong." I nodded. I realized by the sound in his voice he was worried and anxious.

"I will promise not to go poking wild animals for few days." I smiled at Luke my dazzling smile that heated my entire body. I felt like I was going to melt, until he looked away. I growled at him, as was pulling paper work out of his back pocket.

"Don't worries your pretty little head off. I just need you to sign something first." I rolled my eyes unwrapping my arms from around him. "Don't worry, its good," he was tousling my hair. I smacked his hand away. "Here, please sign, then we can spend the day together."

I snatched the documents away from him, looking them over, and smiling as I read the document title. I looked up at Luke who was watching me intently. "We'll still have a big wedding and a reception. We we just have to sign the documents to make it official." He said in a sheepish smile creeping on his face.

I looked back down at the documents and looked at Luke's signature and smiled. I grabbed the pen from his hand and signed my name on the next line. The second I lifted my hands off the paper, I saw a blur as the paper and Luke were gone. I stood there a little confused on what had just happened and I thought I would at least get a kiss before he ran off, since technically, we were married now, but nope. I started to take a step, but immediately had arms wrapped around me and swing me around. I looked up to see Luke glowing face smiling down at me.

"Now you're official my wife and mine forever" I laughed as he kissed my nose as he literally spewed me off my feet and started walking up the stairs.

I wrapped my arms around his neck and resting my head against his shoulder. I Inhaled Luke very deeply. I was so very happy.   Everything in me shifted as I realized what I had been fighting against so hard was the one thing I truly, finally, wanted. I hugged him tighter. I realized this was now my life and I would never change it. No more fighting against everything, because everything was as it should be..

There is no promise I will never have issues with Luke again. I'm pretty stubborn and have a bad tendency to over react. But, at the end of the day, as long as he is by my side everything will be okay.

I was Sold

EXCERPT FROM
SO I SOLD MY SISTER

It was about a month before my 18th birthday, and I was feeling pretty uneasy about the entire thing. My parents wanted me to go off to college at the end of summer, but I had no idea what I was going to do when I got there if I went. I was a pretty good student and I'm sure I would do fine in college, but it was just I had no idea what I wanted to do with my life.

I was at a park with a few of my friends, just hanging out, messing around, when my friend Alex showed up, with another guy that I did not recognize. She was my best friend Jeff's girl, and I knew this was situation that might turn into some type of argument.

"Hey guys, this is Luke. He is new around here. I met him in line at the store." Alex smiled at us pleading for us to be nice to him.

Of course, Alex and Jeff got in an argument shortly after, leaving me and Luke to hang out on our own. I talked to him for a long time; he seemed really cool. He knew a lot about the music I was in to. You could say we became friends, but it was a strange type of friendship. It was like I had this strange urge to hang out with him and I started to think I was homosexual and Luke made me realize it.

A couple of weeks passed after I had met Luke, and I was becoming completely feeling in captivated by him. I was becoming uncomfortable about the things I was feeling. I made up my mind and decided I was going to tell him and hope maybe after I had admitted what was happening to me since I met him, these feeling would subside. Well, I hoped they would. I wanted to move past this and just be friends with Luke.

I went to meet with the Luke at a coffee shop near my house so I could have this very awkward chat with him. I sat down next to a window and looked outside . It was a really cloudy day, and I knew it would rain soon. I tried breathing slowly and relaxing because I was so nervous. I was going crazy and I felt like vomiting up my lunch. I almost ran away when I saw Luke's car pull into the parking lot. His car was amazing, brand new Maybech Exceler. It was highly out-of-place in our little community.

Luke walked in and sat down at the table with me. I basically froze. How could I tell this guy I was obsessed with him. I couldn't believe I thought this was a remotely good idea.

"So Max, what did you want to speak to me about?" Luke said, as I took a drink of my coffee to clear the giant lump in my throat.

"Luke, I wanted to speak to you about something that is not really easy for me to say, but I want to make a few things clear," I said, looking everywhere but directly at him.

"Very well, speak your peace," he said casually. I took a deep breath.

"I'm not into guys, I like girls, but ever since I met you, I feel like I have been slowly becoming obsessed with you, and it is really freaking me out," I said. Luke sat silently for a moment, then started laughing and I felt like punching him.

"Wow, I was expecting you to say something completely different," he said, as he stood up went to the counter as I sat there dumbfounded. I didn't understand his reaction.

He stood chatting at the counter for a minute. I wondered what he was thinking. What else is there that could have been said? I mean sure, he was kind of quiet type, only really talked when in a one-on-one conversation, and only add a few words in group settings. Luke was clearly not from around here, as he spoke and held himself very differently. You might say his behavior and ma mannerisms were like someone with something to hide. Plus, the way he dressed was very unusual for his age. I mean my friends and I wore mostly inexpensive, casual clothes. He clothes were obviously expensive, especially when compared to the average teenager from around here..

"Let's go, Max." I didn't realize that Luke had come back from ordering and was standing next to me. I stood up and followed behind him quietly. I was confused as to why he wanted me to follow him.

"Call your parents tell them you will be out tonight. I will return you tomorrow."

I nodded and did as he said. I was sitting in the passenger seat of his beautiful car. I felt really uncomfortable, and started thinking that maybe he didn't understand that I was not into guys.

"Where are you taking me?" I said, as we pulled out of the parking lot.

"I'm taking you to my home, to meet my parents," he said, as he drove out of the parking lot very fast. I was feeling fairly uneasy.

"Luke, I'm flattered, but I'm not really into guys. Perhaps you misunderstood." He laughed, almost like he was mocking me..

"I believe you Max. We must talk. Let's start with you meeting my parents. Everything you wish to know will be explained, I promise," he said.

I was confused, yet intrigued.

I was Sold

88183232R00220

Made in the USA
Lexington, KY
08 May 2018